SLENDER

Stormy Souls MC 3

BY

Payton Hunter

Copyright © 2024 Payton Hunter

First print book edition July 2024

Cover design by joetherasakdhi

Editor: Nicola Thorpe

PA: Tammy Carney / Kris Riley

ISBN 978-1-7385414-6-1 (paperback)

ISBN 978-1-7385414-4-7 (e-book)

www.paytonhunterauthor.com

Payton Hunter © 2024

ABOUT THE BOOK

This is the book I always wanted to write but never dared to. It is a pure work of fiction, featuring what I love most. Bad Ass Bikes and the Hot Men to go with them!

All people, places, institutions, and businesses are a work of my imagination, and similarities to real life are coincidental.

TRIGGER WARNING

This book includes scenes of physical- and sexual violence, explicit sexual nature, and strong, explicit language. It is not suitable for people under the age of 18 or people with triggers relating to any of the above.

ACKNOWLEDGEMENTS AND THANKS

Thank you to my editor, Nicola. I would not have been able to do this without you.

Thank you to my family and friends for their continuous support. Thank you to my PA Tammy Carney and Kris Riley, Beta and ARC teams for their patience, Hazel Thorpe and Elizabeth N Harris and the author community for your encouragement.

To my Beta and ARC reading teams: You are the best!

DEDICATION

This book is dedicated to all abuse and sexual violence survivors.

You are the strongest people in the world and awe me every day.

Being Strong
by Douglas Malloch

The tree that never had to fight
for sun and sky and air and light
but stood out in the open plain
and always got its share of rain,
never became a forest king
but lived and died a scrubby thing.
Good timber does not grow with ease.
The stronger wind, the stronger trees.

CHARACTER LIST STORMY SOULS MC

Road Name	Rank	Name	
Raven	President	James Saunders (Jamie)	Old Lady -Chloe
Vegas	Vice President	Vincent Albright (Vince)	Old Lady - Ashley
Slender	Sergeant at Arms	David Brewer (Dave/David)	
Pennywise	Enforcer	Noah Nixom	
Spen	Treasurer	Spencer Dalington	Old Lady Debs
Dawg	Secretary	Pete Cooker	Old Lady - Caroline
Clusseaud	Road Captain / event planner	Robert/Bobby Buck	Old Lady - Theresa/Terrie
Ferret	IT Guy	Zack Owens	
Moggy	Member	Craig Parkers	
Sparks	Member	Jason White	Old Lady - Ally/ Rainbow
Ratchet	Member	Ryder Gleeson	

Zippy   Member   Caden Giles

Dougal   Member   Simon Baker   Old Lady - Sarah

Halfpint   Member   Dave Green

Striker   Member   Eli Waters

Greg   Prospect   Greg Brown

Caleb   Prospect   Caleb Hayes

Mom   Club mother,   Helen Nixom   Mother to Pennywise,

Neil   Bar Manager

Restless Slayers MC

Fury   President Restless Slayers MC   daughter Meghan

Ghoul Vice President Restless Slayers MC

Masher   Sergeant at Arms Restless Slayers MC   daughter Tanya

Ghost   IT Restless Slayers MC

Wild Pixies WMC

Rainbow/Ally   President   Allison White Old Lady to Sparks

Hazel Vice President   Hazel Urquhart   single

Jules   Seargeant at Arms   Jules Ford   single

Former Members and others:

Karen   Bar Manager   sent away

Book 1

Flakey   Member   Carl Staunton   RIP book 1

Rusty   VP, Prospect   Bill Greenwood   RIP book 2

Table of Contents

Payton Hunter © 2024

1 — ELLIE

Present Day

"I'm sorry, but we need to let you go, Miss Greenwood. Here is your last paycheck. We wish you the best for the future." My boss' unemotional, brief speech, and the suddenness of his decision stuns me.

I can only nod, grab the check, shake his outstretched hand, and walk out of his office before the tears fall.

I worked as an editorial assistant in this Publishing House for six years and loved my job. My colleague and friend Andrea watches as I return to my cubicle, tears running down my face.

"Oh no, what happened?" Andrea walks over to me and wraps me in a hug.

"He fired me!" I sob out.

"Oh my God, Ellie, seriously?"

Her shocked voice rings through to me.

"Yes, seriously," I sniff and wave my last check in front of her nose, as if to show proof.

Andrea sighs, walks to the coffee machine, and grabs both of us a cup.

"Here, sit, Ellie. You look as though you need this. We need this. I can't believe I'll lose you." Her sad words fail to stem my tears.

"I'll miss you too, friend. So much." I hiccup, taking the cup she holds out and sipping the hot sweet nectar. I love my coffee black, but sweet.

Dragging my five-foot four-inch short ass to the stationary cupboard, I retrieve some boxes and start packing my meager possessions.

"Stay in touch, Ellie, and don't forget, I'm always here for you." Andrea's eyes are glassy when she tells me goodbye.

Bypassing the lift, I take the stairs to the lobby, trying to avoid others as I go. Not everyone has to see my defeat. It's bad enough, without well-meaning but empty expressions of regret.

After reaching the parking lot, not meeting a soul, I sigh in relief, open my trunk, throw in my boxes, and drive out of the lot for the last time.

What the hell am I gonna do? Yes, I have the check, including a generous severance payment, but the question remains. Finding a new job hasn't exactly been on my agenda.

◊◊◊

Pulling into the drive of my little house, just over the Blatnik Memorial Bridge on the Superior outskirts, my heart pounds when I see the trike parked in my drive.

What the hell is he doing here? Again?

Sighing, I think, *boy, someone has it in for me today. Last thing I need is his grumpy ass now.*

My mouth falls open, and I stare at him in shock. Rusty, my brother and long-term tormentor, looks as if someone has dragged him through a thorny hedge backwards several times over. It's Saturday afternoon. I thought I was safe this weekend as he's supposed to be at a rally!

"Hi," I greet him.

Rusty turns and sneers at me: "What the fuck are you staring at? Get the fuck out of my face!" while standing topless, trying to clean all those scratches off with a wet cloth by the kitchen sink.

"There're dressings in the bathroom. It may be simpler for you with the mirror in there," I reply, ignoring his tone, while my heart hammers like a drum in a heavy metal concert. I remember that tone and fear it.

Rushing out of the kitchen, I enter my bedroom, put my boxes down, and lock the door. Relieved, I flop onto my bed.

How pathetic! Here I am, in my own home, scared of my brother as though still a teenager. I'm thirty years old, for goodness' sake, yet he turns me into a gibbering wreck every time.

◊◊◊

Thirteen Years Earlier

Laying on my bed in my room of the cabin I share with my brother, I flip through my magazine and tap my toes to the beat of the music coming from my CD player. Casting a glance at my watch, I sit up, grab my shoes, and leave my room, walking down to the clubhouse kitchen, where Mom will have dinner ready, so I can grab some before heading back to the cabin.

"Hello, sweetheart." She smiles at me. "How are you doing today?"

I return her smile and reply, "I'm fine, thank you, Mom. What smells so good?"

She slaps Noah's hand as he tries to sneak past his mother to grab some chicken. "You'll wait like everyone else!" she scolds him before returning her attention to me.

"Fried chicken, honey, with mountains of fries, gravy, peas, and biscuits," still smiling at me.

"Help yourself, before the guys come in and clean the bowls out." She winks at me.

Pennywise, or Noah, is Mom's biological son and roughly my age. Allison, aka Ally, and I were classmates with Jason, who gained the nickname Sparks after attempting to assist with welding and accidentally getting sparks in his eyes in the vehicle maintenance class. All of us club brats, and regularly bullied.

Being called biker scum isn't the nicest thing, but I got used to it, being the only girl in my year group from the club. Ashley, slightly older, was a few years ahead of me.

The only one who always stood up for me was David, despite being in the year above me and coming from a *normal* home. He was a chubby kid and bullied relentlessly. Until one summer he snapped. He started going to the gym, took up athletics first, then football. Within a year, he transformed into a tall, well-built, muscular jock. Football made him.

All the girls, including me, had a crazy crush on him. I used to sit on the bleachers and watch him train whenever I had a free period. He'd always smile at me.

If he caught one of the other kids calling me biker hoe, or some shit like that, he'd go after them, scare them, or beat their asses. So, during the last year, I was pretty much free from my bullies, as were Jason and Noah.

Giving a hand with plating up food, I watch as Slender—David to me—walks in with his cut. He started prospecting earlier this year. He turned eighteen last year, hung around for a bit, since he's Noah's best friend, and left his suburban home to join the club. His parents were none too happy, but he came to us anyway. He still smiles at me the same way he did at school.

In a couple of weeks, I'll start at the local college, taking a secretarial course and bookkeeping. Unsure of my plans, it seems a good starting point. It'll keep me out of Rusty's way if nothing else.

Rusty, my brother, brought me up after our parents died when I was little. With him already a Prospect, the club raised me for as long as I can remember.

Rusty rose through the ranks, and with every promotion, he became meaner and eviler. Initially not with me, but recently…

The way he looks at me is almost predatory. It scares me, like nothing else does, and I wish I'd applied for college in Minnesota instead.

As we sit down to eat, the phone on the wall in the kitchen rings. Mom jumps up to get it.

"Yes, Helen here," she answers.

I watch as her hand goes to her mouth. She pales and starts shaking.

"No!" she cries out. "We'll be there as soon as possible, leaving now. Look after him, Raven!" She hangs up the phone, looks at all of us, David, aka Slender, Noah, and me, taking a deep breath.

"There's been an accident. We need to get to the hospital!" Mom shouts while shooing us out of the door. We pile into her car, with David behind us on his bike, and race to the hospital. As we arrive, Raven sits in the waiting area. It's clear he's been crying. He looks at Mom, with silent tears running down his cheeks and just shakes his head, about the same time as a doctor comes into the waiting area and walks towards Raven.

"Mr. Saunders, you can see your father now. He is under guard, but you'll be admitted." He looks at Mom. "Mrs. Greenwood?"

I interrupt him. "I'm Miss Greenwood. William Greenwood is my brother."

He nods. "Ms. Greenwood, you can see your brother. We've removed the bullets to his legs and hips. He's just out of surgery. If you ask the nurse on the orthopedic ward, she will show you to him." I return his nod and am about to turn, as Raven grabs my wrist and holds me in place.

"Mrs. Nixom?" The doctor looks at Helen.

"Yes, I am Helen Nixom," she confirms.

"Would you like to follow me into our relatives' room for a moment?"

I can see the fear radiating from Mom and Noah as they follow him into the room. Looking at Raven, I ask, "What happened? Why are they taking Mom and Noah there?"

Raven sighs.

"Something went wrong today. Our team was ambushed, and some members got shot. Stone, Rusty, Clusseaud, Moggy, most of us. For whatever reason, Bear threw himself over Rusty to protect him. He didn't make it, Ellie; he died protecting your brother."

"No! No-no-no-no-no! Please tell me that isn't true! Please tell me he's alive! Poor Noah, poor Mom!" I sob and wail as the full impact sinks in.

◊◊◊

A Year Later

"Rusty, don't!" I plead with him. Like so many times before.

I don't feel guilty for thinking *I wish they had shot him, and Bear was alive instead.* The last year has been hell on earth, with my looking after Rusty and trying to nurse him back to his old self. His hip wounds have made him cold, evil, relentless, brutal, and turned him into my worst nightmare. My torturer.

With his weight crushing down on me, the only thing I can do is to transport myself to a different place, so I don't actively endure the disgusting things he does to me. I stopped crying months ago. It just makes him more vicious. It's like I am a bystander in my own rape. Like I'm looking down from above, watching him loom over me, holding his hand over my mouth, rutting.

When he's finished, he parts with a smirk.

"Frigid cow!" he calls me, zips himself up, and walks out of the door as though nothing happened.

Today is my eighteenth birthday. And the last time he'll have the chance to touch me. I get up, shower and dress, lift the mattress off my bed, grab my bags from underneath, which I packed weeks ago, and shove them in my car. The men are on a run, so the coast is clear. I should say goodbye to David. Sorry, Slender now, Mom, and Pennywise—yes, Noah patched in too—but am too scared that I'll cry and break down. Instead, I jump in my car, gun the engine, and leave the clubhouse property in the proverbial cloud of dust.

I'm embarking on a new life, liberated from the club violence, and above all, my abuser.

Minnesota, here I come.

◊◊◊

Present Day

My door crashes open and slams against the wall.

"Bitch, you tell anyone, anyone at all that I was here, I swear I'll kill you!"

Rusty's threats aren't idle. I experienced his wrath more than once. Sitting on my bed, I try to shake the oncoming flashback. Flashbacks are tough, and I can't afford to dissociate right now. His presence always brings them on. I need to stay in control and concentrate on breathing.

Payton Hunter © 2024

"Answer me, you whore!" he screams at me.

"I won't tell anyone, I promise," that comes out sassy. It riles his already frayed temper. He pushes me until I am on my back. Oh no, not again. I manage to scramble off the bed. He's around to my side in a second, and I'm caught between the nightstand and the wall. When the first punch lands on my face, I almost black out. He grabs me by my hair and pulls me further into the room. Losing all sense of time, I have no idea how long the beating and kicking continues for, but it seems like forever. I'm lying on the floor, curled into a ball, arms over my head to protect it, simply taking what he dishes out. He's never been this bad. He's losing his mind for sure.

A single thought penetrates my mind: *I'm glad I called Raven earlier, when I went to the toilet.*

I never thought I'd have to escape twice in my life, but I should have known that his irregular checkups wouldn't stay like that. I was a fool to believe he had changed. A proper idiot. That animal will never change, and today he proved that I'm one hundred percent unsafe. I crawl to my nightstand and dial Raven's number.

2 — Slender

Unbelievable! The shit I just heard in church has me raging. Fists clenched, I want to punch the first asshole getting in my way.

Rusty's always been a dick, but threatening his sister?

I know Ellie and remember her well. We went to school together and for a while she was my little shadow. She followed me around, sat on the bleachers, watched me train. Such a cute, sweet girl, her reddish-brown curly hair bouncing around her naturally pale face, always smiling at me, always a kind word for everyone. Her skin tone made her look like a porcelain doll. I crushed on her badly in those days, but when I became a Prospect, she became completely out of reach, being the VP's sister. Me, the lowly Prospect, and Ellie, my dollface.

Things changed after the family party.

We'd spent the evening talking and laughing. Stayed outside by the fire when most others returned inside. She stole her hand into mine and looked at me with so much trust, I couldn't help myself and kissed her. It was the single, most formative moment in my life. She was nearly eighteen, and I was nineteen and willing to move the earth for her. Wait for her, if that's what she needed. A few days later, she just disappeared. She took my heart with her when she left.

That was twelve years ago. I've grown up since then, risen through the ranks and am now the Sergeant at Arms for my club. The person who keeps the club safe. I run Lightning Security with Ferret, our IT guy, and Pennywise, our Enforcer. Pennywise and I are best friends, have been since school. We're like blood brothers and often communicate without words, which others find creepy. Together we make a dangerous team. He's the funny one. The clown with a penchant for horror, hence his road name.

Ellie is back, hiding from her own brother. After the last few months, I want that pig in the ground, but this? This is not helping to keep my temper under control. I'm glad she reached out to Raven. Ashley being her former best friend and all. And I'm relieved she'll stay with Vegas and Ashley, as their house is ultra-secure. Within half a mile reach of the property, the cameras spot anyone coming in, no matter from which direction. She'll be safe there. Thank God.

My mind is in turmoil; I'm torn between the residual feelings for her, the feelings that never disappeared, and the resonance of the pain when she just upped and left without so much as a goodbye.

I took it as I was not important to her and left her well alone. Now I'm fighting with the unrealistic need to find her at Vegas', shake her, and demand her to explain why she left, and the sane reaction of ignoring her as best as I can, saving my sanity.

After today, Rusty's demotion to Prospect—since Moggy vetoed the vote to throw him out bad—means I must be on my guard one hundred percent of the time. We all know Rusty is gonna take the rope we gave him, figuratively speaking, and hang himself with it, but not before causing major aggravation. That is his way.

Remind me to slap Moggy. I was looking forward to burning the club tattoo off Rusty's back. Now I just feel cheated, and annoyed that I'll have to continue to put up with his shit.

◊◊◊

The Poker run so far is running smoothly. All riders made it back safely, with the auction now in full swing. Everyone is having a grand time. Until Masher, the SAA for the Restless Slayers, our dominant club, walks up to me.

"Slender," he growls at me. "Get that fuckwit Prospect of yours under control. He just touched up Snakes' Old Lady!"

I'm certain that steam is coming out of my ears right about now.

"Sorry, Masher, I'll grab Greg and kick his fucking ass!" I tell him.

"Wasn't Greg, man, it was Rusty," he informs me. My blood pressure goes from normal to about a gazillion!

"You're fucking joking, right?" I ask Masher between gritted teeth.

"No, man, get him into line before I do it for you!" Masher is posturing, understandably pissed. I whistle at Pennywise between my fingers to get his attention. He must have seen my thunderous face as he jogs straight over to us. I fill him in, and he apologizes to Masher as well. We wave Dawg over to us, and we all go hunting for our *Prospect*, Rusty.

"There he is, the fucker!" Dawg spots him between stalls. He's deep in conversation with Caleb, one of Greg's friends, who's been helping out and following Ratchet around. We sneak up behind them.

"Caleb, go find Ratchet. I'm sure the Bone Marrow tent needs more raffle tickets," Dawg tells him. Caleb nods and darts off.

"Who do we have here?" Rusty sneers. "The three Amigos, huh?"

Before any of us can react, Pennywise grabs him by his cut, drags him behind the stall Rusty was standing at before punching him several times. Rusty's on the floor, getting his ass handed to him by Pennywise while we watch. We obviously didn't pay enough attention, because Rusty throws a large handful of dirt into our faces, and another one in Pennywise's eyes. While we're trying to clear the grit, he stumbles up, limps to his trike and rides straight out of the gate.

"I'll find Raven!" Dawg seethes.

"Fuck, you alright, Slender?" Pennywise asks.

"Fine, man, just pissed that the motherfucker got away!"

"You're preaching to the choir. Can't believe he got one over on me, fat fuck that he is!" Pennywise growls.

Just as Raven appears with Chloe in tow—Dawg's already put him in the picture— a familiar voice screams. I turn around, and what I see has me clenching both fists. Rusty is dead! Absolutely no question.

Ellie is running towards us. Running, well, more like limp hobbling. Her face as black and blue as her arms. The way she holds herself tells me her body is bruised to fuck. I'll kill him for that!

"He knows, Raven, he knows I'm here!" she bawls. "Rusty called my cell. He's going to find me and kill me!"

Instinct, and my ice-cold intent to kill his ass, take over.

"No one is going to touch you sweet thing, I guarantee it. I'll put a bullet in his head first."

Ellie shakes with pure fear.

"I don't want to stay at Vegas and Ash's anymore. I'd never forgive myself if they get hurt because of me!" she wails.

"It's the safest place for you, Ellie," I tell her.

"He doesn't know where Vegas' place is, and they have the best in top-rated security. He wouldn't be able to get closer than half a mile without all the security systems alerting. I'll speak to Vegas and see if it's okay for one of us to stay there as well, just to make sure there is backup, and you're never alone." My questioning eyes lands on Raven, who nods at me in agreement. The deep furrow between his brow clarifying that he's had enough of Rusty's shit too.

I turn and wrap Ellie in my arms. She's shaking and sobbing, completely out of her depth.

Seeing her like this makes me realize that there must be more to this than *just* the beating she received a couple of days ago. I guide her through the clubhouse, and take her up to my room, where I sit down on the bed and pull her into my lap, her head resting on my chest. With her tears soaking my T-shirt, I want nothing more than to take her fear and pain away, but it's out of my hands. All I can do is sit there with her, give her a chance to cry it out, providing a little safety.

Rusty will have to go through me to get to her. That's not a threat, it's a promise. A silent promise I make right here, right now, to myself and Ellie.

With her slight body against mine, she feels thin and bony. Her face, red and swollen from crying, she hiccups, looking exhausted.

"Hey, Dollface, I promise, nothing is going to happen to you here. Not while I'm around. I'll protect you, sweetness." I speak to her in a soothing tone, trying to calm her, running my hand over her hair and back, repeating the same motion over and over again.

"You are safe. Nothing's gonna touch you while I'm here!"

Slowly she calms, and after a while her breathing evens out. She's fallen asleep on me, and I'm damned if that doesn't make me feel ten-feet tall.

I slide us both gently down the bed, move her to her side, and wrap my arms around her. She feels good in my arms. Warm, soft, she fits against me perfectly. Her five-foot something frame almost eclipsed by mine. She looks like a tiny, exhausted pixie with her green eyes, curly chin-length reddish-brown hair. Not that I can see her eyes, as they are closed, but their light green, almost hazel color is etched forever into my memory.

I reach for my phone, pull it out of my pocket and call Vegas.

"Hey, man, you heard what happened with Ellie just now?" … "Yeah, the bastard phoned her. He knows she's here, threatened to kill her. She's here with me, in my room, just calmed down and fell asleep. Do you mind if I stay with her at yours? Separate rooms, of course, am happy to take the couch" … "Thanks, man. I'll see you later at yours" … "If you need me, find me. Other than that, we'll take her car to yours later" … "Great, see ya later, buddy."

The need to protect her is overwhelming, and no way will I trust anyone else with her safety. Not a chance is he getting to her again. Over my dead body!

◊◊◊

By Sunday, the pig is still missing, and I've endured a handful of sleepless nights on Vegas' couch. Seeing Ellie again hit me like a punch in the gut. Not just because of the state she's in, but it brings old feelings back to the surface. I thought I was over her leaving, but, yet again, she's the only thing rampaging through my brain day and night. You'd think as a grown man I'd have grown out of my crush, but obviously not.

She's never alone. When Vegas and I are working or on runs, Greg or Dougal are outside, keeping eyes on Ellie and Ashley. Greg is a strong Prospect. Six months in and he's solid brother material.

Church tonight is not something I'm looking forward to. Rusty will be the chief item on the agenda, aside from Spen's update. Ellie seldom lets me out of her sight. Her nerves get the better of her. So, I'll take her to the clubhouse. She can stay in my room and watch TV while we're in church.

"Come on, man, we need to go," Vegas reminds me.

"You ready, Ellie?" I turn to look behind me, where I last saw her getting ready. As she looks up and nods, my breath stutters in my chest. She's gorgeous. Tight blue jeans on her slim, tight body, snugly clad butt cheeks, porcelain skin, and man, those eyes of hers!

Ellie's not wearing any makeup. She doesn't need it. She's smoking au naturel. Her tight top emphasizes her not-too-big tits. Just a handful, but that's enough for me. My size dwarfs her. All she needs is wings and she'd pass as an Irish fairy.

We walk to the bikes, and Ellie climbs on straight behind me. No hesitations. I grab her knees and pull her body closer into mine. I need to touch her, despite it making me hard. She wraps her arms around me and holds on tight as we set off down Vegas' long drive and filter into traffic.

At the clubhouse, I make sure she's securely installed in my room before joining the others in church.

3 — ELLIE

Spending so much time near Slender feels weird. It reminds me of days long gone and that one kiss we shared, playing on repeat in my mind, begging the question, if he felt the same about it, or whether I was just a quick interlude. Not that it matters. It's been years since then.

Slender and Ferret took my phone and gave me a burner, so Rusty can't trace me. It reduces my nervousness; however, my hypervigilance is driving me, and everyone else around me, crazy. How they put up with me, I don't know. I can't help the fear. It triggers me in ways I find difficult to describe, so I try hard not to think about it. Several times a week I wake up screaming, not knowing where I am. When Rusty used to appear, I had flashbacks, often losing time and memory. Unfortunately, not the memories of *that* past.

The only time safety settles into my soul, is by Slender's side. I struggle to call him David. It seems he has outgrown his boyhood name.

Not having a routine isn't helping me either. A regular job would help. Aside from the income, I need to concentrate on something other than the mess I'm in.

I make my decision. Tomorrow, I'll start looking for a job.

The sound of bikes rumbling into the property is nothing new. Whoever's late for church is subject to Raven's ire.

Shit- shit- shit, were those shots? I'm sure I heard at least two outside. Knowing I should stay where I am and lock the door, my legs decide it's a good idea to run out of the room and down the stairs, where I can see the guys racing out of church with their weapons drawn. I follow them outside. Peeking from behind the men, I see Greg, on the ground bleeding, and a host of Restless Slayers surrounding him, pointing their guns at us.

The one who shot Greg, asks for Rusty to be handed over. I realize Rusty must have caused this. My gasp draws Slender's attention, who shoots me an angry look.

Right now, I really don't want to be the center of the men's attention. I begin to shake, panic crawling up my spine. *Holy shit, what did he do now?* The mere thought of Rusty makes me shiver. Vomit rises from deep inside me, and I'm working hard to subdue the intense nausea. I've tuned out the surrounding noises. It's like I'm watching a silent movie. I see their mouths open and close but can't hear what they say. Another minute and I'll have gone altogether.

Slender grabbing my arm, putting his around me, pulling me into him, jerks me out of my visceral reaction. He walks me inside with everyone else following and sits me at the bar.

"Don't move! No matter what, do not come into church!" his urgent tone impresses on me.

Nodding, I sit on my bar stool like a statue, watching his urgent strides disappear into church and the door close behind him.

I grab the whiskey he left for me and sip it slowly, hoping the burn will calm my nerves, which are stretched taut; the risk of dissociation isn't far off. This, I cannot afford to let happen. I need to stay present.

My thoughts wander to the past.

I ran away at eighteen, went to Minnesota, signed up late for the secretarial course, adding an editorial one, more for myself than anything else, since I love to read, and grammar fascinates me. I'm a nerd like that. Leaving Minnesota was easy. The move to Superior was my first and biggest mistake. I worked as a temp for a while, then found a job at a publishing house, as an editorial assistant. It paid enough for me to buy a house and live without having to count every cent twice. Not rich, not well off, but comfortable enough for me.

Feeling safe in my home was my second mistake.

It took four more years before Rusty found me, but find me, he did. Despite the rape never happening again, his volatile temper and ever-growing mean streak had me shaking in my boots. Luckily, he never appeared more than once or twice a year. Until recently, that is. Then his visits became more frequent, and his temper rose with each visit, until he beat me bloody, and I had to seek shelter with the club. Once again on the run from my brother.

The noises emanating from church, rip me out of my musings. I jump as the door flies open. A guy I've never seen steps out, walks towards me, grabs my arms, and leads—well, more like drags—me into church. Certain I shouldn't be here; the mass of angry looking men frightens me senseless.

"No, let me go! Leave me alone! Fuck off and let go of me!" I scream as he drags me onwards, kicking his shin hard, with zero effect. Instead, he grins, showing me his rotten teeth. I continue to struggle as hard as I can, but it's useless.

I watch in horror at the sight unfolding in front of me. Slender, brows drawn in fury, tries to jump over the table to get to me. Two Slayers bring him crashing down, subduing him in a choke hold.

"Calm down, man," Masher bellows at him. "We only want to ask a few questions!"

He stops struggling so much and gives me an encouraging smile.

Raven snarls at Fury.

"What the hell is this about? You come into my house, shoot my Prospect, hold me at gunpoint, no explanation, now you drag a girl in here who isn't even an Old Lady and pull her into club business. At least I presume that is what you are doing? Conducting club business in front of civilians. What's next? All the old ladies being subjected to this?"

Fury spins, foaming at the mouth, cocks his arm, and before Raven can react, his fist flies straight towards his head and he crumples to the floor unconscious.

In that same moment, Chloe, Ashley, and Dawg storm through the door, guns blazing trained into the room, where half an army of Slayers stands around the table.

"Step away from my old man, Fury!" Chloe screams at Fury, who stares at her puzzled, while her gun is trained on his head.

Ashley pulls me behind her. "What the ever-loving fuck is going on here?" she demands.

The whole situation screams utter chaos. Guns all around, everyone pointing at everyone; a situation which will only take the slightest trigger to escalate into a bloodbath.

Dawg makes a start, holstering his gun. Followed by Ashley. Vegas nods at the rest of the Souls, who all holster their guns in a show of goodwill. Masher puts his gun away next, and everyone else follows suit, apart from Fury.

"Fury, don't make me shoot you! I like you and the guys, but I'll not tolerate being threatened by you after just having patched up the first victim of your trigger-happy soul!" Chloe growls at him. Her growl makes me shiver, and there is no doubt in my mind that she would actually shoot Fury.

I watch, scared out of my mind, as a Slayer walks out of the room, winking at a furious Chloe as he passes, before returning with a bucket of water and tipping it over Raven, who comes round coughing and spluttering.

"Your old lady just saved your ass, man! Best say thank you later!" Masher tells him.

The two Slayers holding Slender release him and forcefully push him into his chair.

"Where's Rusty?" grates Fury.

"That's the million-dollar question," Ash throws in before anyone else can open their mouth. "If we, fuck… if *I* knew that, I'd put a bullet in him myself!" Her voice sounding as cold as ice and slightly bored.

"That fucking bastard raped my Meghan! At the rally!"

Pandemonium ensues at Fury's wild-eyed explosion.

I can't contain the sob any longer. My head explodes with fear, grief, sorrow, anger, and hatred for my brother.

"Oh my God, I am so sorry, so, so, sorry!" I sob as I sink to the floor. My head's spinning, and inside I want to scream, but my mind traps the screams, t--urning them into sobs instead. The anguish paralyzes me, while Chloe and Ashley walk up to Fury, tears running down their own faces, and try to comfort him. Fury seems to calm a little at their gesture.

He orders everyone but the high-ranking officers into the bar. As the door closes behind them, I sense Slender coming to sit next to me on the floor.

"Hey, Dollface, come here." His soothing voice breaks through my scrambled brain. He wraps his arm around me, pulling me towards him.

"Shh, darlin', everything will be fine. No one will hurt you. We'll find him, Dollface. I promise. Everything will be okay." His constant murmuring calms me; focusing on his voice and his arm around me, helps to keep the emotions from breaking me completely. He has no idea what Fury's declaration just did to me. How the guilt of not having spoken up years ago eats me alive.

Could I have saved Meghan from my own fate?

The second Fury spoke, it transported me back in time. Visions of Rusty above me and his sneering voice, overwhelms me. Slender remains thankfully oblivious.

Unable to follow the exchange between Raven and Fury, Fury's hard, humorless laugh jolts me to the core.

"You bet your ass you are! He raped and abused my daughter in more ways than one! She's broken and may never recover from this. Scarred for life by that fucking animal," he rants.

I stand, shake off Slender and walk to Fury.

"I am so sorry for my brother's actions. Rusty's changed in the last year or so, beyond recognition. He deserves to be put down for what he did to your daughter and the women from this club. He's crazy and has gone off the deep end. Rusty beat me and threatened to kill me. This club took me in and protected me ever since. Please don't take your hatred out on them. It's not their fault. They would never condone this kind of treatment towards any woman, and they definitely would never protect him for doing this."

Fury looks me up and down. Some not fully healed bruises catch his attention.

"He did that to you?" he questions.

"Yes, he did." Ashley steps up to Fury, phone in hand, showing him pictures she took when I arrived. Fury's eyebrows rise as he scrolls through Ashley's phone.

"I know he is your brother, but he raped my little girl. He'll die for this!" he hisses.

I look him straight in the eye and nod. "I won't stop you," I assure him with heartfelt sincerity. My hatred obviously runs deeper than I'm aware of. "I understand, but don't take it out on the entire club for one man's actions. They didn't know, and if they did, they would have taken him out."

An hour later, Greg the prospect is stitched up, everyone has eaten, and I follow Vegas and Ashley home, with Slender, Ghoul and Masher, as well as the VP and SAA from the Restless Slayers, who'll stay at Vegas' overnight. I'm kinda glad Slender is with us. So many people would scare me even more otherwise.

We all park outside Vegas'. Ashley leads us inside, where she disappears with Ghoul and Masher, showing them the man cave, where they can sleep on the couches.

Still shaking a little and clinging to Slender's arm, he leads me to my room. I should be scared to be alone with him, but I trust him explicitly. He guides me into the attached bathroom, turns on the tap on the bath, adds some bath salts from the shelf, and tenderly undresses me from behind, even making sure I'm facing away from the mirror. His gentle hands divest me of my shirt and jeans, tapping my leg to lift my foot, one side, then the other, until I step out of them. He pulls off my socks too. There is nothing sexual about his touch, only gentle, tender care.

He holds out a towel between us and encourages me to get out of my bra and panties. Such a gentleman. Finally, once I've lowered myself into the bath, he takes the towel down and kneels on the floor next to me. He just sits and strokes my hair.

"Please, Slender, stay with me tonight," I catch myself whispering. "I can't be alone in my room."

His gaze locks on mine. "Are you sure, Dollface? Anything you need, but be sure," he murmurs in return.

"Yes, I'm sure," I reply.

4 — SLENDER

It takes all my restraint to just be the friend Ellie needs. Helping her undress for getting into the bath was easily the most difficult thing I've ever done. Give me drunken fools in clubs any time, easy. To manage the club's safety, easy. To deal with this fragile woman, who's shaking and clearly overwhelmed, still relatively easy. Touch her skin without touching her the way I want to? Man, that's almost impossible. My dick just hasn't gotten the friendship memo. Holding the towel in front of me so she could divest herself of her bra and panties was more for my sanity's benefit than for Ellie.

Stroking her hair seems to calm her, and to be honest, it soothes me too. So, I almost miss her whisper, "Please, Slender, stay with me tonight." My heart pounds like a hammer drill. Anything but that. No way can I be in the same room or bed with her and not touch her.

"Are you sure, Dollface? Anything you need, but be sure," I murmur.

Damn it, Slender, you are such an idiot! That was your dick talking, not your brain. But as our gazes lock, I can't bring myself to take back my words. '*Looks like it's going to be a helluva long night, Slender, and you only have yourself to blame,*' I silently reprimand myself, with my dick jumping inside my jeans as though having a victory dance. If I could, I'd slap him right now. Maybe that would make him go down and behave?

I leave the bathroom and draw back the comforter and sheets from the king-size bed, root through the drawers until I find an old T-shirt and shorts for her, leaving them on the bed.

Opening the bathroom door and sticking my head in, I let her know, "Ellie, I'm gonna go find Vegas, get a clean T-shirt and some water. Do you want anything?"

"Just some water, please."

"Okay, Dollface. I left a T-shirt and shorts out for you for whenever you're ready." I nod at her and close the bathroom door on my way out.

Finding Vegas in the front room with Masher and Ghoul, I motion for him to follow me into the kitchen.

"Hey, man, just letting you know I won't be on the couch tonight. Ellie is freaking out, and she refuses to be alone," I explain to Vegas while grabbing two bottles of cold water out of the fridge. "And before you say anything, it isn't like that," I add, knowing full well what Vegas' dirty mind is like.

"If you say so," he snorts at me, pissing me off.

"Yes, actually I do say so. She doesn't need that shit right now." I huff, turn around, take the stairs two at a time, to the sound of his chuckles following me.

What an asshole! But hell, he can't help it. He's Vegas, after all, thinks he's the class clown and has no clue how annoying that actually is. Sighing, I shake my head at his antics. I hope she's dressed and under the sheets when I return to the room.

That thought has me dithering outside the door, before I take a deep breath. *Here goes nothing. God, please let me make it through tonight with my sanity intact. Not asking for much here.* I doubt the big man will be open to my plea.

Payton Hunter © 2024

To my relief, she's curled up under the sheets when I open the door. She looks lost and forlorn, and there's something else… Something I can't quite put my finger on. Not that I'll try to dig into what's bothering her tonight. Tonight, I'll just comfort and hold her. I'll be the man she needs, not the man I've become.

The man I should have been when we were younger. Not the self-centered asshole, still green behind the ears, believing that life is just about having fun. I learned the hard way; didn't see it until she was gone. But that changes today.

"Are you okay, Dollface?" I ask her. The way she's holding herself bothers me.

"Not really. I feel as if I've been freight trained, chewed up, and spat out the other end in the middle of the tracks." The wobble in Ellie's voice makes my heart clench.

She's suffered too much recently, and today must have been the worst shock of all. Everyone knows what a dick her brother is—I can't even get myself to think of him as *my brother*—but to find out he's so much worse than she believed is a kick in the teeth.

Slowly, I stroll over to the other side of the bed.

"Are you sure you want me to stay with you, Dollface?" Offering her the option of changing her mind; secretly hoping she does.

"I'm sure, David. I can't be alone tonight." She stretches her shaking hand out toward me. In fact, she is trembling all over.

I throw back my side of the sheets, divest myself of my jeans and socks, exchange my T-shirt for one of Vegas' I borrowed, and crawl into bed. It takes some shuffling until I'm comfortable. When I turn to face her, I pull her close to me.

"Ellie, I'm only a man and you are an extremely hot woman. I have no intention of seducing you tonight, but if my dick plays up, please don't be scared. He can't help it. It's a physical reaction," I explain as my cock twitches. Half chub is putting it mildly.

To my surprise, Ellie snorts.

"Hey, Dollface, my discomfort amusing you? Not nice," I tease her.

Her giggles make me smile. If that is the reaction I elicit in her, I'll take it.

"You're a dude, so I expected nothing less. Just keep your dude tool to yourself." She laughs at me.

"Dude tool?" I repeat in mock consternation. "Dude tool? I have you know this is my pride and joy, not some tool. He has a brain all of his own. Fair enough, his IQ isn't very high, but he's an intelligent life force." Her laughter only grows with my fake huff.

Hearing her giggle, laugh, and sensing her smile against my chest as she's snuggled against me makes me feel like a hero when I'm as far from it as anyone can get.

Nevertheless, her obvious trust is spectacular, and has me grinning from ear to ear. Then suddenly she stiffens and fidgets against me, which has me wondering what's going to wipe that smile right off my face. I brace.

"What's up, Dollface? What's got you so antsy and stressed out? You can tell me, you know. I'm here for you, and you're safe with me," I murmur, holding her tight.

"I can't." Her defeated and broken voice makes my skin crawl. Squeezing her tight, I run my hand up and down her arm to calm her.

Quietly I tell her, "Ellie, you can tell me anything. I mean it, I'll always be here for you, no matter what," hoping to God she'll open up.

When she finally starts talking after a few minutes of quiet contemplation, my heart sinks.

"R… R… Rusty," she stutters. Never have I heard her stutter before. Fury courses through my veins, and I want to riddle him with bullets. I lock my jaw, so I don't grind my teeth.

"I left because of him," she continues.

"Go on, Dollface, I'm listening," I tell her in a low, calm voice I'm not feeling, fully expecting to hate what follows from here on in.

"He did things to me," she admits, her voice almost inaudible.

"What did he do to you, Dollface?" My calm belies the raging tornado of temper and emotions inside of me.

"First, it was only teasing and goading me. It escalated to slapping, shoving, sneering, and bullying. But the worst came around my eighteenth birthday," she continues.

Please God, don't let it be what I fear the most!

"He raped me. My own brother raped me, then threatened to kill me."

Ellie's sobs break my heart and soul into a million pieces. Realizing I can't, despite wanting to jump out of bed and kill the fucker, I pull Ellie even closer, running my hand over her back and let her tears soak through my T-shirt. Trying hard to think of what to say to her, I come up empty. All I can do at this moment is to hold her and keep my fury under control. She doesn't need me freaking the fuck out.

"Shh, Ellie, … I'm here, Dollface… Shh, I promise he'll never get near you again. I swear on my life." My eyes burn with unshed tears. For the little girl who suffered, for the eighteen-year-old Ellie of the past, and more so, for the deeply affected Ellie of the present.

Ellie wriggles out of my arms and throws herself onto her side.

Payton Hunter © 2024

"Can I hold you, Dollface?" I ask her gently.

When she nods, I shuffle closer, pulling her back into me, her back to my front, trying to transfuse my warmth and strength into her.

"Thank you, Ellie, for trusting me enough to tell me, for accepting my comfort," I murmur while kissing the top of her head.

"I'm so sorry this happened to you, and you felt you had no one. I'm also sorry for having been such an ass when I was younger. Keeping away from you was… difficult. Then when you disappeared, questioning why was not in my repertoire of abilities. My selfish streak was a mile wide and no match for my maturity, or rather lack thereof. Please, Ellie, let me be here for you. The one thing I regret more than anything, is not having tried to explore the friendship we had then.

"I'm aware I can't ask for anything more, but please, Ellie, let me be your friend. Let me be here for you. Let me help you through this and support you in any way I can."

As I speak to her slowly and softly, her breathing evens out. Leaning up on my elbow, I watch her relaxed, albeit swollen face, realizing she's fallen asleep. When? I'm not sure; not sure she heard what I had to say either, but hell, I'll just repeat it when she wakes, making certain she hears me.

In the meantime, I consider all the horrible ways I'm gonna make Rusty pay. Killing isn't enough for that bastard. He needs to suffer and suffer big! He must suffer like Ellie has for years; suffer like I do right now. It feels as though someone ripped my heart out, tore it to shreds, pulled my soul out, threw all of it up, and scattered it in the wind. The pain is indescribable. My mind runs itself ragged at hypersonic speed, unable to cope with my anger and need for revenge. All I can think of is this beautiful, pixie-like creature in my arms and the furious hatred her brother inspires in me.

5 — ELLIE

The sun streaming through the window, warming my skin, wakes me. *Did I have a vivid dream, or did Slender stay with me last night?* Carefully moving onto my back, I note the indentation in the pillow next to mine. *No dream then.* I guess me spilling my guts, him listening, me sobbing, him holding me, talking about what an ass he used to be, and how sorry he was for what Rusty did, wasn't a dream either. Reality punches me in the gut with crumpling force.

For the first time in ages, I slept without a nightmare or flashback. Whether it's that, or my late-night word vomit, I'm noticeably lighter, calmer. The more I think about it, the more I admit to myself that talking to him was hardly a word vomit at all. I only said two or three sentences before I cried my heart out. I'm glad Slender is nowhere in sight. That embarrassment can wait for a few minutes.

With a sigh, I swing my legs over the edge of the bed, run my hands through my hair, walk in the bathroom, and get ready for the day. When facing him, I need to at least appear sane.

◊◊◊

After breakfast—well really more like brunch since it is getting on for midday—I snuggle deeper into Ashley's deep couch, Kindle in my hand. I'm trying to read and focus my thoughts on anything but the church meeting happening right now.

Ashley went to work this morning. A note on the kitchen table tells me. While I look out of the window, a Restless Slayers MC brother sits on his bike in the front yard, watching the house and surroundings. It increases my nerves tenfold. Giving up on reading, my feet pace on their own accord. My brain works in overdrive. Thoughts of Rusty, echoes of memories, imaginary pictures of what he may or may not have done to others as well as me. Fury's harsh words to me yesterday, and the realization of Rusty's sealed fate flit through the chaos of my mind in wild flashes. Confusing me as I struggle to distinguish between flashback and reality. What's the long gone past, and what's the present? It all rinses into one as though going through the spin cycle of a washing machine.

Unsure of when I hear the bikes, I stare out of the window, looking down on the familiar sights of Vegas and Slender riding into the yard. Their somber faces strike a lightning bolt of fear through me. I watch them slowly scale the few steps to the front door, fixating on their lips as they talk, as if I could lip read. I trudge into the hall, as they enter. Slender's solemn look and Vegas' eyes, downcast to his boots, warn me that a bomb is about to go off. I steel myself.

"Dollface, you're gonna have to come with us."

The pain in Slender's voice lances through me. And yes, right in this moment, it's the club's Sergeant at Arms speaking to me. Which is quite disconcerting as I find it difficult to reconcile the SAA and David in my mind.

"Where are we going?" I whisper, my fear increasing every second we stand here, looking at each other.

Vegas turns to me, taking over the conversation. Maybe to spare Sender the act of giving me bad news.

"Ellie, listen to me." His tone stern, befitting the VP of the Stormy Souls, not my friend Vegas. "Your brother has done a disappearing act. Search parties are looking for him. Unfortunately, circumstances have changed. Fury got a call. His daughter tried committing suicide last night. He now wants assurances we're doing all we can to find Rusty."

His serious tone has me throwing my hands over my mouth.

"Oh God, is she alright?" I ask him, and when he nods, relief fills my heavy heart.

"Oh, thank God," I breathe. Vegas, however, uncomfortably shuffles from one foot to the other.

"Ellie, he wants you and Slender as '*security*'. He's set a time limit for us to find Rusty. If we don't, he'll shoot Slender in a week…" his voice trails off, and I realize what he left unsaid. I'd be next.

"Don't worry, Ellie, we'll find him. We called in every favor owed to us and a few more. We'll find him." Vegas tries to reassure me, and I pretend to believe him.

They send me upstairs to pack a bag, where Slender joins me, before he leads me back downstairs and wordlessly hands it to Vegas.

I follow them out to the bikes. Vegas straps my bag onto his, and Slender hands me a helmet, motioning for me to get on behind him, which I do, enjoying the sensation of his body against mine, for what could be the last time, not allowing myself to think further than this trip.

As we get to the club property, both clubs are waiting for us. Without ceremony, the Restless Slayers shove Slender and I into the waiting, blacked-out van, a couple of Restless Slayers Prospects behind the wheel, and then we're on the move.

All the while Slender is talking to me, trying to calm me, but I don't even hear the words. My mind has separated from my body, and I'm watching the scene below me, as though it was a horror movie. I couldn't say how long we've been on the road when we stop at a service station to fill up. They lead Slender and me out to the side of the building to the restrooms, allow a toilet break and, on our return, hand us a bottle of water each. Slender watches me with concern.

"Hey, where d'ya go?" he softly asks.

Unsure how to answer his question, I shrug my shoulders. "I'm fine," I push out, my voice sounding much stronger than I feel.

Slender laughs humorlessly when he states: "Oh, Ellie, you are so far from fine, it's not even funny anymore. But I won't probe further. Just know I'm here for you."

I can't help myself. "Well, we got all of seven days," I snip at him, my voice dripping sarcasm, as the Prospects lead us back to the van and we continue our journey.

◊◊◊

We arrive at the Restless Slayers MC compound, which couldn't be more different from the Stormy Souls'. A gray, multistory warehouse-type building greets us. Concrete, everywhere you look. Their version of an outside area is AstroTurf by the side of the building with raised brick fire bowls, which I guess double up as grills. I couldn't see much out of the blacked-out windows, but we seem to be in the middle of an industrial estate concrete jungle, making me glad that this compound is highly secure, since the neighborhood seems more than questionable.

Slender tried to talk to me throughout the journey, and I let his quiet voice wash over me, without paying attention to words, just following the sound of his voice, which surprisingly has a calming effect on me and keeps me from dissociating again. Having been on the road for five long hours, including gas stops, I'm relieved to get out of the van.

We're marched into the building and up two flights of stairs. When a door opens in front of us, we're shoved into a small room with our bags thrown in after us. I only exhale when the lock clicks. We're locked in from the outside. A door on the far wall leads to a shower and toilet. More a stall than an actual room. A few bottles of water and some Saran-wrapped sandwiches are on a small console table, and a small flatscreen TV hangs on the wall.

I don't know whether to laugh or cry hysterically. This all seems so unreal. I hate Rusty. Our situation all started with him and will only end with him. Once again, someone else is paying for his behavior.

Slender rifles through his bag and pulls out a bottle of Jack Daniels and a bottle of Coke. He tips out one of the pint water bottles, quarter fills it with whiskey and tops it off with the coke.

"Were you in the boy scouts?" I ask him with a lopsided grin. "You seem to be prepared for all eventualities."

A deep chuckle rises from his chest.

"No, Dollface, just thought we could probably both do with something to take the edge off." He smiles at me. He's right. I need to relax and not ruminate over the reason we are here, especially if I want to retain my sanity and stay present.

"Might as well get comfortable," he states, before taking off his boots and throwing himself on the double bed in the room. The Restless Slayers MC searched our bags before we set off and threw our phones to Raven. We have no means of contacting anyone. Not that contacting anyone would be of any use in our situation. Not knowing what else to do, I shuffle onto the bed and sit next to Slender, at the head end of the bed with crossed legs, trying to digest today's events. He stretches out beside me, laying on his side, watching my twisting hands for a beat, before he takes them into his, to stop my repetitive motions.

"Where did ya go? I know I said I won't probe, but I lied. I watched you earlier, in the van, you were there, but you weren't… present. It was as though someone had switched you off." His serious eyes bore into mine. Realization hits me hard. He needs to learn the truth about my stress induced coping-mechanism.

My voice is almost a whisper when I tell him my story.

"You already know that Rusty raped me. During that time, I dissociated. Not that I realized what that meant back then, but I've read up on it since; it means that part of my brain— my conscious self, if you like—splits off when I get into certain situations to protect myself. It happens when I'm stressed out, lose control, am threatened, or experience physical violence as well as when I try to be close to someone. Like naked close," I add, just to make sure he gets what I'm trying to say, without me having to spell it out for him. Since he was upfront and told me what an idiot he was, I need to be upfront myself to prevent misunderstandings. I'm never gonna be a notch on his bedpost. Looking at my feet seems to be the best thing to do, since Slender's gasp didn't go unnoticed.

"Dollface, look at me!" His voice is a command, not a request. Slowly I turn my head and look at a furious Slender, his eyes shooting daggers, and if he could, I don't doubt he'd be spitting fire.

"You can keep your anger, David, and stick it where the sun doesn't shine," I growl at him; I don't need guilt heaped onto me for my mind's instinctive safety-net reaction. It's not as though I can help it.

"Is that what you think?"

Slender's disbelieving voice hits me like a slap.

"Do you seriously believe I'm mad at you? Are you crazy?" He takes a deep breath.

"Of course, I'm angry, I'm hopping mad, but not at you, Ellie, never at you. I'm mad at that piece of shit brother of yours, for hurting you, damaging you, physically and mentally. If I could, I'd kill him with my own bare hands!" his voice rises to near shouting. For the first time since I sat on the bed, I think I made a fool out of myself in front of him. It's testimony to my hypervigilance and self-criticism.

Inhaling deeply, I lean back against the headboard.

"Sorry, David, I didn't mean it like that. It just came out. Dealing with my suspicious mind isn't easy. Not for me, nor for anyone around me. At some point I turned from a normal human being to a nervous wreck, always watching over my shoulder, always reminding myself to be cautious, to not trust, making situations my fault, even when they are not. I don't deal with loss of control well, it comes out as anger sometimes, other times I switch off," I tell him with what I hope is a small smile but fear it's more of a grimace.

6 — SLENDER

Vibrating with anger, I listen to what Ellie has to say. '*I'm gonna kill him*,' is the mantra repeating in my brain, making it difficult to concentrate on her words. Despite not understanding what's going on when she '*switches off*' as she put it, I realize the truth in her words, having witnessed it firsthand. The attempt of a smile that doesn't reach her eyes tears me in two. My pain, in that moment, is indescribable. All I know is I want to protect her from the world, be her barrier, her protector, the one who makes everything better, despite knowing that the situation is not as simple as that.

"Dollface, none of it was your fault. I know you know it, but you need to believe it. '*Sorry, this happened to you*' isn't enough, and it's the wrong words. I admire you for your strength, resilience, ability to survive what would have broken most, the courage to break free and carry on with life as best as you can. Do you grasp what I see when I look at you?" I ask her.

She looks at me, wordlessly shaking her head.

"A warrior, a beautiful, strong woman, capable, loyal, and loving, with more resilience than I ever experienced in anyone. I see beauty, courage, strength, and green eyes that could burn a hole in my soul every time I stare into them. I see honesty, compassion, empathy, tenderness, but I also see passion and an incredible protectiveness over others. You, Dollface, are a superstar in my book. A truly amazing woman, more so now than what you already were at seventeen. You deserve only the best in life, to be honored, protected, and loved." Her hand covers my mouth, cutting off my impassioned speech. Make no mistake, there is more where that came from.

What she says next floors me completely.

"I believe you."

Her serious voice makes me believe her. Then, to my surprise, she scoots closer, curling up next to me, placing her head on my shoulders. The gratitude for her trust is overwhelming and makes my eyes sting.

"May I hold you?" I ask, realizing that her permission means everything to me.

In answer, she lifts her head, looks straight into my eyes, and says, "I'd like that. I know I'm safe with you, and nothing can touch me."

"Nothing is ever going to touch you again, Dollface, I promise on my life," I tell her, while wrapping my arm around her shoulders, pulling her closer, letting the silence wash over us.

Her body notably relaxes against mine after a few minutes. I almost don't hear her murmur, "Slender, when I switch off, it's like being outside of my body. Like I watch what's happening to me, to my surroundings, but I'm not physically attached. Like being protectively frozen out. Does that make any sense?"

"Thank you for trying to explain it to me, Dollface. I believe you but, if I'm honest, I have no experience with this kind of thing. I promise, though, I'll support you as much as I can, and I'll research when we're back. How does that sound?" I ask her, placing a gentle kiss on her hair.

"Thank you," she whispers.

We spend the next hour in silence, each of us in our own thoughts, with my hand slowly stroking her hair, trying to soothe both of us.

The banging on the door startles us. Not that either of us can open it, since they locked us in.

"Can't open the door, it's locked!" I shout, making Ellie flinch.

"Sorry, honey," I apologize with a wince.

"What the fuck, Prospect!" a woman shouts outside the door.

"Open the door right the fuck now, before I decide to come and relieve you of the keys myself!" More grumbling behind the door, before the lock clicks twice.

A very tall blonde with seriously short hair walks in, carrying a tray of food.

"With no idea what you wanted, I ordered in; didn't want to risk poisoning you with the food the club girls make. Hope you like Chinese?" Her eyes twinkle good naturedly as she puts down the tray.

She sticks out her hand to Ellie.

"Hi, I'm Tanya, not met you before. Sorry that I wasn't there to roll out the welcome wagon when you got here." Ellie grips her hand and shakes it.

"I'm Ellie, hi, Tanya," she replies evenly.

Tanya looks at me. "Now you are Slender, aren't you? Met you at the rally. I'm Masher's daughter."

"Hey, Tanya, wish I could say it's good to see you again, but given the circumstances, please excuse me if I don't," I respond.

She throws her head back and laughs, while Ellie watches with wide eyes.

"No offence taken, Slender. Can't say I blame you. I wouldn't be happy either. Just wanted to ask if you two want to come downstairs for a bit, have a drink at the bar with me, move your legs for a while?"

Ellie's reaction surprises me.

"Sure, I'd love to." She wriggles off the bed, pulling me along with her, not letting go of my hand she grabbed as she started moving.

As we get downstairs into the bar area, nothing but ice-cold hostility greets us, I watch Ellie immediately withdraw into herself. Tanya guides us to a table and disappears to get some drinks—a beer for me, orange juice for Ellie. She sets the drinks down in front of us and takes a seat.

"Don't let them oafs intimidate you." She conspiratorially leans towards Ellie. "I don't agree with you two having been *'invited'* and I'll personally guarantee that nothing bad is going to happen to you here, Ellie. Dad told me about the photos he saw of you. Let me assure you; you'll be safe here."

She looks at me with regret. Clearly she can't guarantee the same for me, but then that doesn't surprise me. As long as Ellie's safe, that's all I ask for. So, I wordlessly give Tanya a small nod, showing I understand what she's saying without words.

"I was the one who found Meghan. She outwardly looked okay, a couple of scratches, where she told me she fell over in the dark, and a bruise on her face, she claimed was from a branch hitting her. It wasn't until after the Poker Run, I found her crying and she confessed. She was scared she'd be pregnant. Once everything came out, I had no choice but to tell the club on her behalf."

Once again, Ellie surprises the shit out of me. She takes Tanya's hand as though it was Tanya in trouble and tells her, "It's okay, I understand. I'd have done the same." Her empathy proving how much she identifies with Tanya's predicament.

"How is Meghan?" she asks.

Tanya looks at her, deep sadness in her eyes.

"Meghan's like my little sister," she replies. "I love her like one. She was lucky I came into the room when I did, though she doesn't appreciate it just yet and is angry with me for having called the ambulance. It was scary. The doctors felt it was necessary to keep her in the hospital and arrange for support, including consulting a psychologist who specializes in trauma."

I watch my woman clasping Tanya's hand as if to transfuse her with empathy, and I'm so very proud of her.

Wait, what am I thinking? My woman? Holy shit, where the hell did that come from? The thought should scare the crap out of me, but for whatever reason, it doesn't. It feels good. It feels right. I realize then that I'm caught. To be honest, it probably happened years ago. No other woman brought out the protector in me, like Ellie. What can I do but give into my fate? Now I just gotta persuade Ellie and make sure we're on the same page.

I pull myself back into reality, noticing that my beer is empty, so are Ellie and Tanya's glasses. No idea what else they talked about while I was lost in thoughts. But whatever it was, Ellie seems lighter and even beams an actual smile at me. God, she looks amazing with a grin on her face. I'm gonna make sure she has many more of them in the future, in fact, I intend to make it my personal goal to extract a full-blown laugh out of her, if it's the last thing I do.

Her tiny frame stands from the table, giving me a chance to admire her amazing body. She's petite, but well proportioned. Her ass is tight in her light blue jeans, and her tits are perky, not too big, just the way I like them, just showing under her white blouse. My cock agrees with my assessment and uncomfortably butts against my zipper. *Down, boy!* Not the time, nor the place. He'll just have to wait and be happy with my hand for now.

As her hand grabs hold of mine, pulling me up, I smirk. She can lead me around by my hand anytime she likes. Eventually, I hope she'll lead me by my dick if I'm lucky. I'm a patient man. I can wait for her.

Tanya takes us back to our room, where we find the forgotten tray with now-cold Chinese food. Doesn't bother us, we tuck in and clean the tray in no time.

"Would you mind if I took a shower?".

"No, of course not, go ahead, Dollface, I'll go when you're done," I encourage Ellie, watching her every move as she bends over to grab clothes out of her bag. It takes extraordinary efforts to suppress the groan crawling up my throat, watching her tight ass swaying in front of me. '*Must not think about her ass, must not think about her tits, must not think about tapping, must not think about that ass'*, I repeat to myself at least ten times until she disappears into the bathroom.

With a sigh of relief, I open the top button of my jeans, undo the zip, and readjust my painfully hard dick. It could pound nails right now. Then the shower comes on and my mind wanders back to Ellie—a very naked Ellie—in the next room. I grit my teeth and switch the TV on. Anything to distract me. A deep groan escapes me as the picture comes on. Someone has it in for me up there. *Seriously? Real Housewives of New Jersey? God, what did I ever do to you to deserve such punishment?* I throw myself onto my stomach like a petulant child, instantly regretting when my rock-hard boner hits the mattress. *Damn, that hurt.*

The shower stops, making me hurry to close my zip, as to not give poor Ellie an eyeful. With my still raging hard-on, I scrabble through my bag, getting a clean T-shirt and sweat shorts. When Ellie finally emerges, I can't get in there quick enough, leaving her with a slightly confused look on her face as I rush into the bathroom, as though chased by the FBI.

Closing the door tight behind me, breathing a sigh of relief for small mercies, I turn on the shower. Thankfully, the water is nice and hot. Stepping in and soaping myself, I can't banish the picture of a naked, wet Ellie from my mind. No way can I spend the night in the same bed with her without going insane in my current state. So, as needs must, I grab my cock and give it a couple of hard strokes, squeezing the tip. My eyes almost cross. My thoughts are on Ellie, on her hot, slim body next to me in the shower, grabbing my throbbing tool and guiding her hand slowly up and down. Her hands are so small, she can hardly close them around my girth. She leans in, pulling my head down to hers, sealing my lips with a demanding, passionate kiss, while she increases the speed of her strokes, gripping me tighter, making a groan rumble from deep within my chest. Her tongue strokes mine in time to her hand stroking my dick, which twitches in her hand.

"David, please fuck me," she whispers, turns, and bends, holding onto the shower wall. Not needing to be told twice, I place myself at her soaking entrance and slowly push in. God, she is tight. I push in little by little, giving her an inch at a time, allowing her to adjust around me. Her tight, hot wetness is overwhelming, and I have to stop for a moment in order to regain some control.

"Please, move," she moans, and that's all it takes for me to break. Not taking any prisoners, I push into her hard, until I feel myself bottoming out. She pushes right back into me.

"Harder!" she demands. That does it. I fuck her hard, each stroke getting me closer to the goal. I reach around her and pinch her clit. She shatters on a scream, and I follow right behind her, groaning as I shoot my load again and again. My breath stuttering, coming in pants, I lean my head against the tiles, trying to get back to reality. Unbelievable, I just jerked off to thoughts of Ellie, proving just how big of a jerk I am. Excuse the pun, but it feels rather disrespectful, since she's in the next room. The woman I want more than anything but cannot have. Not now, and maybe not ever, but I'll wait. Damn it, she's worth waiting for.

7 — Ellie

My mind roils in turmoil. If I thought the shower would calm it, I was sadly mistaken. If anything, the alone time in the shower focused my mind on Slender even more. He's more Slender than David, now he's grown up, much as I have, and admittedly, I like the man I see now more than the boy of the past. It unsettles me because he makes me feel things. Feelings I've never had with anyone else.

After the disastrous loss of my virginity, I stayed away from men. They're scary entities to me. Yet, with Slender, I feel safe.

When I look at him, I get butterflies in my tummy, and something more. There's a tingling in my most private area. Moisture collects in my panties, and I get antsy. Yes, I've been to sex ed classes. I know it's called arousal; however, I experience it for the first time.

Intellectually knowing and feeling it with overwhelming intensity are two different things. Thing is, he doesn't need to do anything to make it happen, it just happens. All I need to do is look at him, his dark blond hair, hanging down his back, his high cheekbones giving him a Viking-like appearance, as does his nose. He looks like a warrior. Someone who can keep me safe, and that's how I feel every time he's in sight. Add to that his broad shoulders, the corded muscles in his arms, the large, usually jeans-clad thighs, telling of powerful legs and you have one fine, sexy male specimen. Even now, just thinking, not seeing, I tingle and my pussy drenches.

Slender is a harsh man, but never with me. He's a gentle giant, easy to anger with others, and I've realized, he can be a very vindictive, evil enemy, yet he doesn't scare me at all. Deep down, I'm certain he'd never hurt me. His kindness and care for me are always on the surface with him, always protecting me. Which is more than what anyone else has done for me. Even though it may sound unbelievable, I consider it a valuable gift.

The bathroom door opens, and I stare like a deer in the headlights, unable to take my eyes off the man who strolls out the bathroom, hair hanging wet around his shoulders, shaking his head as though he was a diet coke advert from the eighties! My mouth dries up, my tongue is sticking to the roof, which is the only thing keeping it from hanging out. His sweat shorts reveal more of his muscular legs and thighs. They're even better than I imagined. Those tight shorts leave little to the imagination. Not that I imagined what his thingy looks like.

Yes, I know it's called a penis, but my brother saw to it that using this word disgusts me. And disgust's the last thing churning through me when I ogle all that is Slender. His chuckle confirms my beet-red flushing.

"Enjoying the view, Dollface?" he teases me, his voice dripping with amusement.

"Sorry," I have to clear my throat, "didn't mean to stare." My admission has me gazing at my hands. His fingers lift my chin so he can look me in the eye. There is heat in there, amusement, and something else I can't quite put my finger on.

"Never apologize, not for that anyway. For you to like what you see is good for my ego." He smiles down at me.

"As if your ego needed any more inflation," I scoff with a grin.

"Ouch, you wound me." He throws his hand over his heart, pretending to crumple to the floor as though my words cause him mortal injury. I hear the thump of him hitting the floor behind the bed. A weird sensation works itself all the way up from the depths of my tummy. My lips curve into a silly grin, then my mouth opens, and a roar of laughter comes out. A sound that surprises me. I've not laughed in so long…

Now that I've started, I can't stop. Just when I think I've calmed a little, his head pops up from the side of the bed with a pretend look of anguish, making me laugh even more. It's like a live puppet show. My stomach hurts, my sides are cramping, and I'm so out of breath, I'm coughing, yet still unable to stop. Until he scrambles off the floor, throws himself on the bed next to me, and pulls me close.

"God, it is good to hear you laugh," he murmurs near my ear, his face beaming with the biggest smile I've ever seen on him.

"Thank you, Slender, I needed that. Laughter has been absent from my life for a long time." I turn my head and kiss his still-smiling cheek.

As soon as my lips touch his skin, a zing of static flashes through me. The look in his eyes when my green ones meet his blue ones assures me he felt it too. His eyes have darkened with something almost predatory, yet it doesn't scare me. If anything, I'm excited. Fear entirely absent from my current swirl of emotions.

"Dollface." His tone holding a warning and his face suddenly serious, when he sits on the edge of the bed, staring at me, his eyes piercing me as though he can see right down into my soul.

"I'm only human. It's taking everything I have not to kiss the living daylights out of you right now. I don't want to frighten you." He sighs and sits, leaning against the headboard. "We gotta talk."

Well, that sounds ominous. I'm aware I'm damaged goods, undesirable to a man like Slender. So, I just nod and wait for the bomb he's gonna drop on me.

"Ellie, look at me," he pleads. When I do, he continues, "I already told you what a schmuck I've been. The past is the past. I can't undo the mistakes I made.

"I like you, Ellie. I know you feel this thing between us, too. Your eyes tell me so much more than your mouth ever could, but I'm worried. Worried that I'll do more damage than good. I want to see where this goes, Ellie. Take the chance I messed up when I was young and an asshole."

That makes me giggle.

"Yes, that you were, for sure. A grade-A asshole." I smile, hardly able to believe what I'm hearing. *Could this be? Could this be real?*

"I want to explore this thing with you, have a relationship with you, support you in all things, protect you, care for you. I want you to be mine, Ellie. But I realize that nothing worth having is ever easy. I won't push you, wanna take it real slow, at your pace." He looks into my eyes, and I can see the honesty and truth radiating out from him.

"Slender, yes, I feel this thing between us. Of course I do. How could I not? It's hard to ignore. Yes, I'd like to see where this could lead too, but… be prepared to live without sex for a long time, maybe forever, which isn't fair on you. I want more for you than that. I want you to be happy Slender, truly happy, and I don't think that's going to be possible with me." The sadness overwhelming me as I make this statement is staggering. I know it to be true. Being around any other man takes an extreme effort not to dissociate. So how could I possibly have a relationship with him, tie him into my very own cycle of hell? It wouldn't be fair.

Everything inside me hurts and I'm as stiff as a board when I try to shuffle off the bed. His hand shoots out and grabs me. I start to panic and fight against the force holding me on the bed. Then I freeze. He notices instantly. His voice gentles me, so at odds with his powerful grip.

"Shh, Ellie, it's me. Shh, honey, don't leave, please, stay with me."

His calming tone soothes me, allowing me to subdue the panic and take deep breaths, gripping onto his arm to steady myself, to ground myself in the present.

"I'm sorry, Dollface, I didn't want to frighten you," he apologizes. Which is crazy because he did nothing wrong. It's me that's the wrong one, the damaged one, the crazy one.

"Have you ever spoken to anyone about all of this? About how you switch off?" His tender tone brings tears into my eyes. Tears, I thought I was long done crying.

A humorless laugh leaves my mouth before I can stop it. "Talk to anyone? Who to? No one knows but you, so if you like, yes, I've spoken about it. To you!" Agitation clear in my rising voice.

"It might help you speak to a professional," Slender suggests.

"How would I even find one? And just the thought of baring my all to a complete stranger gives me the hives," I reply honestly.

"Ellie, I told you I wouldn't push, and I meant it. Only you know what's right for you." His statement pacifies me, leaving me vulnerable but unthreatened.

"Can I hold you, Ellie?" His question surprises me.

In answer I shuffle closer to him and place my head on his chest. His arm comes around me, holding me tight, his body heat relaxing me, wrapping me in a cocoon of safety.

"Slender?" I almost whisper, praying my voice will hold for what I need to tell him.

"Yes, Dollface?"

"Slender, I want all that with you, too. I like you a lot, always have, ever since my mad crush on you in high school. But I'm broken. You'll need to be patient while I try to fix myself. You may wait for a more intimate relationship for a long time. I trust you and am willing to take a chance and leap with you, as long as you're certain and won't seek relief elsewhere. I couldn't bear that. It'd break me for good."

His arms tighten around me even further, if that's at all possible, as though he's holding onto me for dear life.

"Ellie, listen and hear me. I would never do that to you. I want you, all of you. Mind, body, and soul. However, the body can wait. We'll take it at your pace. For now, just being here with you is enough. You're worth waiting for, Ellie; you are such an amazing, strong woman, your beautiful mind and soul take my breath away every day.

"Never mind what your spectacular body does for me. You are my little pixie, my dollface, and sex or no sex doesn't change that. I'll be the proudest man, just walking by your side."

That does it. This sweet man moves me to tears, and with them streaming down my face, I come to my knees, straddle him, and pepper his face with kisses. He's that special.

He snorts with laughter as he pushes me back a little and hands me a tissue. No idea where it came from, and don't care either. I grab it and noisily blow my nose. Then slowly I close the distance between us. It's like gravity is pulling me toward him.

Gently I place my lips onto his, enjoying his warmth and the softness of his lips against mine. Instinctively, his hands go to my head, burying themselves into my hair, massaging my scalp. This feels so good. I flick my tongue out against his lips, getting a first taste of him, making him groan and grip my head tighter. He's fighting to let me have this kiss without trying to deepen it, and I value that more than I could ever put into words. Slowly, his lips move against mine, gently and carefully. It's the most amazing, breathtaking experience. Chaste, but oh so sensual.

The sensation of heat it causes to bubble within me has me gasping in surprise.

"Dollface, are you okay?" His worried eyes seek mine.

"Yes, Slender, I think I am." I smile at him, get off his legs, and snuggle up next to him, or rather more, into him. For the first time in years, I'm utterly at peace.

8 — SLENDER

I still can't believe what just happened, as I hold this beautiful creature in my arms. Cuddling is not my thing, but with her, I'll happily change my habits. It's what she needs, and what my woman needs, she gets. I'm man enough to admit that she means something to me. Something more than I've ever experienced before. It's new, feels right, and I'm no less of a man for it. Though I can't deny that my dick is throbbing uncomfortably in my shorts, and these shorts were not made for hiding erections. I sport a considerable tent, which makes me hyperaware and cautious to not let our lower bodies touch. The last thing I want is to frighten her, or make it look as though I can't control myself. I roll to my side, so we are face to face, keeping enough distance between us so my erection doesn't touch her.

"Dollface, I'd like to touch you, may I?" I ask her, my voice serious, trying to convey that I won't take advantage. She looks at me and nods.

"Words, sweetheart, I need your words," I encourage her softly.

"Yes, Slender, you can touch me, but if I tell you to stop, you need to stop."

"Of course, Dollface, you have nothing to worry about," I reassure her. Without pulling her any closer, I run my hand across her hair and face, holding her hand with my other one, stroking my thumb over her fingers. It's a tender, soothing kind of touch, so far removed from sexual it's not even funny, yet electricity travels up my arm, spreading outwards from my fingers. Moving from her hair and face to her back, I slowly run my hand up and down her back to her waist, above her clothes. Her sigh makes me smile, and I've never been happier than when her foot tangles with my leg, as she pulls herself closer to me.

"So good," she mumbles, her eyes closed, our noses touching. Her breathing evens out as she falls asleep with a gentle smile on her face. With the last few days taking their toll on me, I too drift off with my arm still around her waist.

◊◊◊

Fists drumming on the door wakes us up; I have no idea what time it is.

"Get your ass out of bed and dressed. We'll be back in ten minutes!" Masher's growly voice yells through the closed door. I sigh. The fact that they are waking us in this manner tells me that nothing good is coming for us this morning.

"Hey, Dollface, wakey-wakey, our presence is required." I shake Ellie gently, which has her sitting up in bed, rubbing her eyes.

"Wassup?" she says with a cute yawn.

"Masher just banged on the door; we're to be collected in ten minutes," I tell her, while grabbing my clothes and disappearing into the bathroom to take care of business.

"Oh, great, maybe we're going home? Maybe Raven found Rusty?" Ellie's hopefulness and excitement is sweet, but since it's only been twenty-four hours, this is highly unlikely. Much more likely that we'll be questioned, particularly Ellie. I don't answer her query though and pretend I didn't hear, while flushing the toilet.

She uses the bathroom after me and comes out fully dressed. Jeans and T-shirt, with flat pumps, makes her appear smaller than she is, fragile almost.

Payton Hunter © 2024

I hear them coming to the door and just manage to warn her, "Ellie, just answer their questions, they won't hurt you," before the door opens, and Masher and Ghoul step in. When Masher struggles to look me in the eye, and Ghoul remains silent, both just indicating to precede them out of the door, I sense something isn't right.

Downstairs Fury, three Prospects, and Tanya, who shoots Fury and Masher angry looks, meet us. Man, if looks could kill, both of them would be a pile of ash on the floor.

We follow the officers into the room where they usually hold church. When the Prospects follow us, I gather that this is not just a question-and-answer session. Made all the clearer by the two Prospects stepping up behind me, dragging me into the center of the room, and Tanya stepping up to Ellie, murmuring softly to her.

I watch Ellie's eyes open wide in horror, then begin to pull against the Prospects holding her.

"Let him go, now!" she screams, kicking and scratching the Prospects with all of her might; spitting, hissing, clawing like a feral cat.

I look at Masher.

"Let me go speak to her," I request. Fury, Ghoul and Masher nod. They know I'm aware of what's gonna happen here. I'll be taking one for Team Stormy Souls. Anger vibrates through me in ice cold waves of fury at their decision to drag Ellie in here to watch, I try my hardest to keep it reined in.

Walking up to her, I take her face in my hands and kiss her gently.

"Ellie, please, calm down. I was expecting this, and it'll be okay. I'll be okay. I need you to be strong. Close your eyes and switch off if you have to. I promise everything will be okay. We'll be okay, Dollface; we'll get through this, whatever it takes."

Payton Hunter © 2024

The tears rolling down her cheeks are killing me, but I know I don't have options.

"I tried to stop it," Tanya whispers, looking at Ellie, eyes full of compassion and regret.

"Keep her with you; keep her safe," I plead with her. When she nods and I step away from Ellie, Tanya steps forward, into Ellie's line of sight, so at least she doesn't have to see everything. I can tell she's struggling behind me.

"No, let me go, you bastards!" she screams and hisses at them, and after a nod from Masher, she calms, so I take it the Prospects are no longer gripping her.

"Tanya! She's your responsibility!" he shouts at his daughter. "Don't make me regret this."

As I stand in the center of the room, I watch Ghoul take out his phone and nod at Fury.

"All set, Prez," he tells him.

With that, Fury steps forward, and with a pair of knuckle-dusters, swings and punches me straight in the face. My skin splits on impact and crushing pain explodes in my face. Within seconds, his other fist hits me, with much the same effect. Then Masher steps up next and punches me in the ribs and abdomen, making me double over and grunt. That's all they're gonna get from me. If they hoped for begging or cursing, or any other reaction, they'll be disappointed. Ghoul hands the phone to the other Prospect, pulls me up and lands several punches of his own.

I can't see shit now. My right eye is swollen shut, and my left is covered in so much blood, it makes it difficult to see anything at all. I try hard not to register Ellie crying while they continue to give me a beatdown. Not knowing what is up or down by the time they're done, I just smirk at the camera held up to me, showing Raven that I'm okay. I can take it all day, as long as they leave Ellie alone.

Ghoul and Masher grab me under the arms and drag me upstairs, while Fury follows with Tanya and Ellie, who, I only notice when we're back in the room, is carried by Fury and catatonic. Good girl, she did what she had to. She switched off.

One look at Tanya confirms though that Ellie saw, she witnessed everything. Tanya's face is a grimace of anger, worry, sadness, and compassion. Every conflicting emotion rolled into one is dancing across her face. A hiss escapes me as Ghoul and Masher lay me on the bed and Fury places Ellie next to me. Tanya goes into the bathroom and returns with a bowl of water and a wet cloth.

"Get out, let me get on with it," she tells the officers. Fury growls at her but receives a warning glance from Masher. Seems like strained relationships. None of my business though, and the throbbing in my face and the rest of my body makes it easy to not give a fuck.

Once the door closes, Tanya sits on the bed next to me, cloth in hand.

"I'm sorry, I tried to talk sense into them, but…" Her voice trails off as she cleans my face gently with the wet cloth, before rinsing it in the bowl.

"Your eyebrow needs stitches," she states matter-of-factly. "I'll send the Medic up to see to it."

"No thanks, darlin', it will be fine," I insist.

"Don't be an idiot. Right now, it's flapping in the wind. It needs stitching. I'll send the Medic," she repeats in a tone allowing no argument. About halfway through, she stops and sits next to Ellie, who stirs on the bed.

"Hey, welcome back, Ellie, are you alright? One minute you were there and the next you sank to the floor, not reacting to me, not hearing me or answering, just staring into space. You scared me. I thought you passed out at first," Tanya murmurs to Ellie, who lifts her eyes and looks at her.

"I'm sorry I scared you. It's something that just happens when I'm overwhelmed. I can't control it," Ellie whispers, still obviously fighting to orientate herself.

"How did I get up here?" she asks.

"Fury carried you up here for me," Tanya simply states, causing Ellie to shiver.

"I think I need to bathe in bleach." Ellie's acerbic answer makes me hiss, as grinning hurts.

"If there's anything, Ellie, anything at all, I can do for you, please tell me." Tanya's sincere words ring through the room.

Ellie nods, turns her face towards me and gasps.

"Oh my God, Slender. What have they done to you?" she sobs, gently putting her hand against the side of my head, just about the only part of me that isn't beaten to fuck.

Grabbing her hand in mine, a piercing pain shoots through my arm.

"Darlin', I'm okay, takes more than that to get rid of me. I'll be fine in a couple of days," I try to reassure her.

"This is all my fault!" she cries. "I should have stopped them; I'd rather they'd beaten me. I'd have taken any of what they dished out. It's unbearable to see you hurt like this over my insane brother. If I'd only spent more time with him, maybe I could have prevented all this!" Her tone now bordering on hysterical, I can't do anything but hold her hand. Tanya surprises me when she climbs on the bed next to Ellie, puts her hands on Ellie's shoulder, and gives her a gentle shake.

"Ellie!" she calls out to her. "Stop it! None of this is your fault. You, blameless in all of this, need to remember that we can only choose our friends, but are stuck with our blood relatives. Had you spent more time with that fucker of a brother of yours, you'd have likely gotten more beatings, and he'd have taken advantage in other ways too!"

Ellie stiffens at Tanya's perceptive words.

"This is not your fault, Ellie, it's Rusty's. I know he's your brother and I hate to be harsh, especially with what you just went through, but as far as I'm concerned, he needs to die, and painfully so. A man who is violent towards women doesn't deserve to breathe the same air as the rest of us."

To my amazement, Ellie sits up straighter, takes a deep breath and looks Tanya in the eye.

"I know all of that, Tanya, but it doesn't lessen the nasty aftertaste in my mouth. He's an evil man, but he wasn't always like this. The last year has been the worst. As much as I sometimes wish death on him, he's still my brother. Yet, I'm fully aware of the consequences of his actions and am not asking for him to be spared. Thank you, though, for being so frank with me, for being supportive of me, despite of Rusty being who he is and what he's done to your family."

Tanya nods at Ellie, leans in and hugs her, receiving Ellie's reluctant hug in return. Ellie takes the damp cloth out of Tanya's hand.

"I'll finish cleaning his face so your Medic can stitch him up." She literally dismisses Tanya, who nods, gets up, walks to the door and leaves.

My little pixie is a warrior, and I couldn't be prouder of her.

Payton Hunter © 2024

A few moments later, there's a knock on the door. A guy carrying a medic kit walks in, and without fanfare, puts three stitches in my eyebrow. No numbing. It hurts like a bitch.

"Your nose is broken, needs to be straightened," the Medic states.

"Fuck off, you touch my nose and I'll rip you a new asshole! Literally!" I growl at him.

Ellie curls up to me when he's left and we both must doze off, as the next thing reaching my consciousness is Tanya walking in with a tray of food, some ice for my face, and more bottled water. She nods at us and leaves us to it.

Ellie cuts up my food into small bites. Chewing is not the easiest thing right now with my busted lip. She hands me pain relievers the Medic left and helps me to get to the bathroom.

Getting up is excruciating and breathing deep is difficult. Clearly, I was an ass when I refused to be checked over properly. Looks as though some of my ribs may be cracked. Ellie fusses until I'm back on the bed and comfortable. God, her fussing makes me feel so good. I allow myself to admit that I fell for this woman years ago and am only falling deeper with everything she does.

9 — ELLIE

To watch Slender being beaten for my brother's sins was probably the hardest thing I ever had to endure. The only way to cope was to leave my body until it was over. Anger churns in my gut like poison. Anger at the world, anger at the Restless Slayers, anger at Slender for allowing himself to be beaten like that, anger at myself for not being able to stop it, but most of all, anger at Rusty. No, anger isn't strong enough a word. I hate him. His stupidity will cost him his life and make me lose the last family member I have left.

Lost in my thoughts, I watch Slender sleeping, keeping my distance so as not to hurt him. He must be in agony, even with the pain relievers. I hate not being able to be physically close to him. I've fallen for this man again, hard and deep. That fact alone scares the living bejesus out of me. How is this going to work? How will we ever be able to have a physical relationship?

Slender is hot, and touching him, excites and arouses me, to a point where I want to do more than have a kiss and a cuddle. I want him inside me, want him to take away the terrible memories and replace them with new ones. I'm desperate to be with him, properly, as a couple. But how do I even start?

Slender starts fidgeting next to me. It's the middle of the night, so I guess the pain relief is wearing off. I take a deep breath and scuttle closer to him.

"Are you awake?" I murmur.

"Hmm hmm." His rough voice reaches me.

"Are you in pain?"

"Not too bad right now, Dollface, as long as I don't move," he answers quietly.

With all of my courage, I whisper, "I'd like to try something. Will you let me?"

"Sure, Dollface, what have you got in mind?" He turns his head and looks at me.

"Just let me explore you, no talking. I want to find out what I can do, whether I can be physical with you," I tell him, my voice shaking with nerves.

"Sure, sweetheart, no taking advantage of me, though." He smirks at me. "And only if you're sure," he adds that last bit with serious eyes, all joking gone from his voice.

"I am, now, try to relax, and no talking," I tenderly admonish him.

"Okay, boss." He winks while making the universal sign for zipping his mouth, which has me grinning. This man, even when in pain, he tries to keep things light for me.

Nervous is not quite descriptive enough for my emotions. Sitting up, stretching my hand out, I run it over his bruised arm. His skin is hot to the touch, under my cool fingers, velvety soft and hard at the same time. I trace every muscle, every vein on his brawny arms. Picking up his hand, I kiss each knuckle, not missing his tenting shorts.

Wow, I affect him as much as he does me. My mouth dries up at the thought of causing such a visceral reaction in him. Becoming braver, I move up his T-shirt, which is still blood spattered, and slowly and lightly run my fingers up his chest, trying not to hurt him. He hisses when I touch his rib cage, so I move up further to his chest. His nipples pebble hard under my fingers. I never knew that those are a sensitive part for a man.

He watches me as I continue to explore his body. Leaning forward, I place a gentle kiss on the corner of his mouth, avoiding the split side. So far, I'm all good, and my private parts ache in agreement, wetness building inside my panties. I direct my fingers down towards his waist and down further to caress his thick, muscular thighs, running my hands across them and all the way down to the calves and feet, where I grip one of his feet firmly and attempt to give him a foot massage, which has him groaning and his erection jumping in his shorts. Wanting him to feel good, I press my lips to the inside of his lower leg, kissing my way up to the inside of his thighs, making him fidget and groan.

"You're killing me here, Dollface."

I want to do more for him though, so ignoring my beginning discomfort, I run my hands higher up his leg, and inside the leg of his shorts. He hisses out a breath.

I close my eyes and urge myself onwards, though the buzzing of excitement is replaced by the prickling of anxiety. When I accidentally touch his cock, it's hard, pulsing, and the veins stand out on it. I stroke him before panic rises to the surface.

"Dollface, stop!" His stern voice reaches me.

"You need to stop. It's getting too much for you. You don't have to touch me. I'd rather have you present with me than anything else," he speaks to me as though soothing a small, scared animal.

I remove my hands with an equal balance of disappointment and relief coursing through me at the same time. He rolls on his side and watches me.

"You are the most special, beautiful thing I've ever seen." His husky voice breaks through my haze and puts me in some sort of trance. Suddenly, my arousal roars back to life and crashes over me like a wave. When I meet his eyes, they show nothing but heat, understanding, and something I can't quite put my finger on…

"Did you enjoy touching me?" he asks, keeping his eyes locked on mine.

"I sure did. It made me feel all warm, tingly, fuzzy, and a little moist."

He laughs at my description.

"Moist?" he snorts, as though he's never heard that word before. "Oh, darlin', you are so special. I love your innocence," he states, smiling at me.

"I'm not that innocent," I throw at him, sounding like a spoiled child.

"No? Will you experiment with me then? Trust me to guide you right and only do, or make you do, what you can handle?" Slender asks, his eyes twinkling with mirth, but heat flares through them, making me breathless.

Nodding, I train my eyes on his, focusing solely on him.

"Undress for me, sweetheart."

Entranced by his voice, I stand, take off my T-shirt and bra, letting both drop, encouraged by the flash of desire in his eyes, and the hiss of his breath through his teeth.

"So beautiful," he groans, making me stand up straighter, proud I have this effect on him. Becoming braver, I slowly lower the zip of my shorts and shimmy them down my legs, watching as his eyes fix on my dark blue lace panties. I catch the edges with my fingers and drag them down my legs, swaying with each move as though guided by music only I can hear. His breathing comes faster, and his eyes darken with his need for me, encouraging me, keeping my self-doubts and angst at bay.

"Touch yourself, caress yourself with your hands, as though they were mine. Remember, you are safe. I won't touch you."

His hands are clenching next to him, and despite my nerves, I trust him completely. He'd never hurt me. I close my eyes and run my hands over my small breasts. Squeezing them, discovering how sensitive they are when I pinch my nipples lightly and an electric shock goes straight to my clit, making liquid heat pool between my legs. *Damn, this feels so good.* Running my hands over my torso, wishing they were his, I can't keep back the moan, drawing a low groan from Slender. I raise my leg and place my foot on the bed, not able to stop my hands from wandering lower. The heat emanating from between my legs is scalding. As my fingertip touches the hard nub of my clit, a bolt of need runs straight through me. Collecting some of my wetness on my finger, I spread it across my clit, stroking in circles. My breath comes in sharp pants, and I can't suppress my own whimpers.

When I open my eyes to look at Slender, I see him stroking his enormous erection. His girth is immense. Instead of scaring me, it just makes me hotter. I lick my lips, watching him, my eyes locking on his movements. A deep rumble leaves his chest.

"Don't stop, sweetheart, let me see you touch yourself," his hoarse voice tells me.

I spread my knees a little wider, giving him a better view of my finger, no longer satisfied with just circling my clit, but dipping deep inside of me. I can feel my walls tightening around me.

"Yes, baby, that's it. Fuck yourself for me." His crude words don't disgust me, they only drive me crazier. I'm burning bright and my whole body is tight. I pinch and roll my nipple with one hand and push my finger deep inside me while my thumb pushes down on my clit. Then the world explodes.

"Oh God…" I groan while my orgasm crashes over me, robbing me of all sense of time and space.

Once the waves calm, I open my eyes, watching Slender. His body tightens, the muscles in his neck cord as he hisses: "Yes…" releasing reams of his essence over his abdomen. I crumple on top of the bed.

"Wow, just wow!" is all I can string together. I'm relaxed, tired, sated, a tad embarrassed, too. I've never done this before. Yes, of course I've masturbated, but all that stopped after Rusty… *nope, not letting him ruin my moment!* I never knew orgasms could be like that, nor that I'd ever let anyone watch.

Unable to meet his eyes, I get up, walk to the bathroom, and dampen a washcloth with warm water. Still naked, I move next to Slender and gently wipe away the residue of his own explosion from his stomach before throwing the cloth into the small hamper in the room.

Crawling back onto the bed next to him, his arm comes out to wrap me up and hold me tight to him. Careful not to jostle him, I snuggle up.

"Damn it, woman, that was the single most sexy thing I've ever experienced. You are so beautiful, even more so when you're aroused," Slender whispers in my ear, carefully kissing my cheek.

"I can't believe I just did that." I groan, embarrassment gaining the upper hand.

"Babe, it was beautiful and natural. Finding pleasure in yourself is a normal thing, and you gave me so much pleasure, without the threat of dissociating. It was gorgeous to watch, and you were ravishing. Never be ashamed of your amazing body and the way it reacts, no matter what. Don't feel self-conscious, not with me, sweetheart." Slender's soothing, calm words melt my heart. *God, I love him.*

That thought hits me hard. But it is true. I might have had a crush on him years ago, but this goes so much deeper. So deep it scares me that if he changes his mind one day, it'll leave me crushed and my heart and soul ripped into smithereens.

◊◊◊

It's afternoon when the lock clicks from the outside. Ghoul steps inside, with Masher in tow.

"Get up, get dressed. Your club came through for you. You're going home. You have ten minutes, then we leave!" Masher hollers, turns and walks out. Ghoul looks at Slender.

"Do you need help to get downstairs, man?" he asks.

"Sure as shit do," Slender grates out.

Ghoul nods and leaves the room. I help Slender sit up and get dressed, while he struggles to keep his pain in check. His face is pale, as he grinds his teeth together, just sitting on the edge of the bed. Once he's dressed, I put his boots on for him.

"Thanks, Dollface, couldn't have done this without you," he grumbles. It pains me to see this big, powerful man reduced to needing my help. I just finish stuffing all our clothes back into our bags when the door opens. Tanya, Ghoul, and another member I've not seen before step into the room. She helps me with the bag, and Ghoul and the other guy carry Slender downstairs and to the waiting van. Tanya hops in with us.

"Are you coming with us?" I ask, surprised.

"Yup, Ellie, I am. I need to be there when your brother gets his just deserts, I promised Meghan," she replies and then turns her face towards the window as we roll out of the Restless Slayers' property.

Payton Hunter © 2024

10 — SLENDER

Every bone in my body throbs and I'm about twenty seconds from barfing with the pain in my ribs and lack of ability to take a deep breath. I watch Ellie and Tanya, hating that Tanya is with us. I've been around the MC world long enough to know that when she said she promised Meghan, she's not along for a pleasure outing. She's here with a purpose, and no matter how it could affect her, she's gonna do what she needs to. She is the SAA's daughter, after all, and has clearly inherited Masher's traits. Most of all, a penchant for keeping her friends and family safe. I, and most bikers relating in some form to the Restless Slayers MC, have heard about her. Her reputation as a hardass with her family precedes her. Rusty is not the first to be at the receiving end of her revenge. Which is known to be swift, uncompromising, and mostly gruesome. Probably why Pennywise was so impressed with her. He's got an equally gruesome streak a mile wide.

After five hours from hell, including rest stops and a few incidents of me nearly passing out whenever the road was uneven, jostling me around, we reach Arnold's town limits. Ellie watched out of the window, sighing. The closer we got to home, the quieter she became. I can't imagine how knowing that Rusty's time is running out must affect her.

"Slender," she addresses me.

"Yes, Dollface, what ya need?" I answer, wondering what's coming and whether I'm mentally prepared for the next few hours. I'm pretty much out of action for now, so the major portion of dealing with Rusty is in Pennywise's hands.

"Do you think I can speak to Rusty?" Ellie's voice cuts through my thoughts.

"I can't see why not, Dollface, but why would you want to?" I reply.

"He's my brother, Slender, and although I am not the kinda person who needs revenge, I need closure. Don't get me wrong, I don't wanna watch him get his… punishment. I just want to talk to him. I need to know if there's even the slightest bit of my brother left. It's important to me and hopefully will help me deal with the outcome."

Right, this second, I want to drag Ellie over to me and place her in my lap, comforting her, as her voice is so full of pain. Unable to do anything about it, physically hurts me. "Dollface, if that's what you need, that's what we'll do. I'll be there with you one hundred percent of the time." Reassuring her rewards me with one of Ellie's smiles. A small one, but I'll take it.

The turn into the club property is up ahead. Thank God this hell ride is almost over. The first bikes are pulling in and we're jostled yet again, causing me to hiss, my vision fading around the edges. Ellie casts me a worried glance, which I try to soothe with a small, forced smile of my own. Finally, the van stops. Tanya gets out and shuts the door behind her. The Prospects engage the central locking. I get it; they must make sure Rusty is present. Just then, one of our vans enters the compound and pulls up a little closer to the clubhouse than us. Vegas, Dawg, and Pennywise jump out. Dawg, smirking; Vegas, tired and pissed looking. Raven and Dougal are standing with the Restless Slayers' officers in what looks like a tense standoff. Dawg and Pennywise open the rear Souls' van door and drag Rusty out into the sunlight.

Ellie's horrified gasp makes me turn my head towards her. Hands clasped over her mouth in shock and horror, she watches as her brother, looking much worse for wear, is dragged out and pulled forward. Fury, Ghoul, and Masher turn around to their crew and one of them lets out a whistle. The locks click, the van doors open, and Ellie jumps out. We're home, thank God.

Two Slayers help me out of the van, Ellie stays by my side, Pennywise invites Fury to accompany him to take Rusty to his new quarters, and a few Slayers follow them as Rusty is dragged up to the dugout.

"Ellie!" I call sharply, as I can see her eyes glued to Rusty.

"Don't watch, Dollface. Stay with me, sweetheart." I gentle my voice as I get her attention. She keeps her eyes on me as they lead us into the office. Raven looks me over, furious, as Fury and Pennywise enter.

"You bastard!" Raven hisses at Fury. He looks as though he'd like to put a bullet in his head.

"You knew we were on the case; you knew! I kept you up to date on everything that happened!" Raven rants.

"Calm your tits!" Fury states. "Chill! We haven't done much damage; his pretty face will heal! You needed an incentive!"

Raven stands and walks toward Fury, looking ready to lay him out, as Pennywise steps in front of him.

"Don't do it, man, keep your head!" he hisses at Raven, who gives him a curt nod.

"Pennywise, can you take Ellie and Slender up to his room? I'll ask Chloe to come and see to them," Raven instructs. Pennywise nods and leads us out of the room.

Upstairs, Pennywise and Striker make me comfortable on the bed. Well, as comfortable as can be. I just try to breathe and close my eyes. The bed dipping next to me has me clenching my teeth, so as not to let a hiss of pain out. Ellie shuffles down the bed and lays down next to me, grabbing my hand and holding onto it for dear life. I know she's at the limit of what she can take, and the slightest thing will push her over. She rolls onto her side, facing me, and carefully moves closer, like a small, frightened animal, seeking comfort in my body heat. I wish I could hold her the way she deserves, but that is impossible. Instead, we're both quiet, just breathing and trying to comfort each other the best we can. Ellie's shoulders quietly shake, and I feel like shit that I can't dry her tears.

A knock at the door has Ellie sitting up.

"I'm so sorry, man!" Raven apologizes as he walks in.

"No need, Prez. He'd have taken it out on one of us. Rather me than her," I grind out, hissing in pain, looking at Ellie.

"Watching what they did was not easier, believe me." Her voice trembles as she speaks.

"They made you watch?" he growls.

She nods and confirms: "They wanted me to see what they'd do to Rusty and to me if you didn't find him in time. They would have shot him!" She gestures to Slender, still shaking.

The door opens and Chloe walks in with a bottle of whiskey, her medical kit, and a few glasses. Taking one look at Ellie, she pours a good measure and encourages her to drink it. She repeats the same with me and Raven, then gets to work. Thankfully, Raven takes Ellie outside. As she straightens my nose, I try not to throw up. It hurts like a bastard. Chloe cleans me up a bit more, before handing me a bottle of water and a couple of tablets.

"Take those now, Slender. It'll help with the pain. I'll leave some more with Ellie. Try to sleep. When you wake up, hopefully the worst of the pain will be over," Chloe says, stroking my hair, like I was a little boy.

Raven and Ellie return.

"We'll leave you be now," Chloe tells us, grabbing Raven's hand.

"Ellie, my number is on the dresser. If you are at all concerned about him, ring me. He might have a concussion, so don't let him up until the morning. I left some pain relievers on the dresser. Give him two every four hours. He's already had some, should sleep with them and feel better in the morning. But, as I said, call me if you think you need me. I'll come over, no matter what time."

Ellie nods gratefully while Chloe gives her a one-armed hug and drags Raven out of the room. I try to smile at Ellie and focus my attention on her when she crawls onto the bed next to me again, but the medication kicks in, and a wave of fatigue rolls over me. All I can do is close my eyes, as Ellie strokes my chest and whispers: "Sleep, baby, see you in the morning."

◊◊◊

Not sure what time I wake the first time. All I sense is that I'm on my side, with Ellie curled tightly around me, her arm thrown over my side and leg entangled in mine. I ease her arm away, as it's pressing against my ribs, lean forward, grab some more pain relievers, which she placed on my bedside table with a bottle of water in easy reach. *God, I love that woman.*

Even exhausted herself, her first thought is for my comfort. She deserves to be worshipped, and it'll be my priority to show her just how much goodness she deserves. With that thought firmly embedded in my tired brain, I lean back and try to go back to sleep.

Payton Hunter © 2024

The smell of coffee, bacon and eggs finally wakes me. Helen, aka Mom, is in my room and is setting up breakfast for us on the dresser.

"Good morning, sunshine," she chirps with a smile. I never thought I'd be so happy to see Mom first thing in the morning.

"You two better get up. Raven said Chloe is on her way over to look in on you," she tells us. I nod but am unsure whether I can get up, or whether I even want to get up just yet.

"Sure, Helen, we'll get ready. Thanks for bringing breakfast up. You didn't have to. I'd have come down and got it," Ellie replies.

"That's quite okay. I don't mind. I'd rather be up here anyway than put up with that lot downstairs." Mom wrinkles her nose when nodding her head downstairs. She's never been keen on the Restless Slayers. They are a different breed to us.

"Thanks, Mom, you're the best," I say, blowing her a kiss.

"Well, they've not beaten the charm out of you yet, and I'm a sucker for an invalid." She laughs at me.

"Invalid?" I ask her in mock horror. "Really? Invalid?" I shout after her as she leaves the room, laughing. Ellie is giggling, and man, it's a wonderful sound in the morning. I get off the bed, shower, with Ellie's help, and get dressed. Chloe re-stitched my eyebrow last night, releasing the pressure, and having my nose straightened has helped. My ribs are still extremely painful, but I'll manage with the pain relievers she left last night. We eat our breakfast, and just as we're ready to go downstairs, Chloe walks in.

"Hey, you guys, I just wanna quickly check on Slender. Hmm… your nose looks a little better, and your eyes aren't as swollen now. How are the ribs?" she asks.

"A little easier; I'll live," I tell her. She slants her head, draws up her brows, and gives me the stink eye, obviously not believing me.

"Yeah, right, if you say so, Slender," she scoffs at me.

"Ellie, want to come to Ally's with me this morning? All the girls are meeting up there, Sarah and Tanya included," Chloe asks Ellie.

"Well, I'm not sure about that. I don't wanna leave Slender like this," she protests promptly.

"Don't worry," Chloe replies. "Striker is on Slender duty today, so you can come with me. The men will be er… busy… most of the day. A bit of fresh air would do you good," she finishes.

"Chloe is right, Ellie; you should meet with the girls. I'll be busy this morning with the others."

"But I—" she begins to say, and I know what she's thinking.

"I'll make sure you get to speak to Rusty," I promise her, hoping it's a promise I can keep. But staying here while things are going on isn't good for her, so I'm taking a chance here.

Finally, she gives in and follows Chloe out of the door. A few moments later, Striker ambles in.

"Morning, man. I'm here to help you downstairs to church," he grunts. I try to stand from the bed but must grab his hand and let him help me up. He stays beside me as I slowly hobble down the stairs, where everyone is congregating. I watch as Ellie and Tanya leave with Chloe.

"You had breakfast?" Raven asks Fury, who replies: "Yup, had breakfast an hour ago." Raven turns and calls to the men: "Let's go!" and everyone, me included, files out and follows him up the path to the dugout, the bunker where Rusty is held.

Payton Hunter © 2024

11 — ELLIE

The door chimes at Ally's as Tanya, Chloe, and I walk in. Ally, Sarah, Ashley, and Caroline are already in a booth.

"How are you feeling, Caroline?" Chloe looks at Caroline with concern. She's still recovering from smoke inhalation she sustained when the house she and Dawg lived in, burned down. They only just made it out.

"Much better, Chloe, thank you. Dawg picked me up last night and waited on me hand and foot. Thanks again for letting us stay at your apartment." She smiles at Chloe, her voice only slightly croaky.

"That's fantastic!" I add, clapping my hands.

Sitting down, I listen to the old ladies chatter about their men, wishing I could join, very aware of my shortcomings.

"I don't know about you, girls, but I have to say, with Dougal, absence makes the heart grow fonder, was definitely true!" Sarah wiggles her eyebrows.

"Oh, come on!" laughs Ashley. "They've only been away a couple of days!"

"And? I bet you got it good from Vegas last night!" Ally pipes up, and I snort, trying to suppress the laugh bubbling up. It feels good to almost laugh, though.

"Don't make the single girl jealous!" I snort, wringing my hands subconsciously, earning me a weird look from Chloe, Ashley, and Sarah.

"Well, I sure couldn't complain last night!" Caroline interjects, causing Ally to howl like a dog, while Tanya roars with laughter.

"You're all too funny! I'm gonna choke to death on my coffee!"

At that precise moment, Ashley changes color, gets up, and sprints to the ladies. Ally, Caroline, and Chloe look at each other, smirking knowingly.

"What? What have I missed?" Sarah looks from one to the other, with Tanya following with interest, same as me, not understanding. Chloe shrugs her shoulders.

"Not our story to tell, Sarah!" Chloe tells her, knowing that Sarah will now be like a bloodhound on a trail. Ashley has zero chance of getting out of this one now.

A very pale Ashley returns to the table.

"You alright?" Ally asks.

"Hmm-hmm." Ash nods.

"Spill it, sister! What's going on?" Sarah growls at Ashley. Me? Well, I watch the drama unfold as Sarah gets her hooks into Ashley, who helplessly looks from Ally to Chloe and back to Ally, a big *"HELP"* sign flashing above her head.

"What's happening?" Tanya whispers to Chloe, who just shakes her head.

"Just watch," she sniggers.

Ashley is shifting uncomfortably in her chair as we all watch her and Sarah.

"Ashley Saunders! You tell me right this moment what's going on or I won't let you have Leo next weekend!" Sarah's full-on glare hits a helpless Ashley.

We can see the moment she capitulates.

Payton Hunter © 2024

"I'm pregnant," she whispers.

"You what?" Sarah jumps up and looks at her best friend as though she'd grown two heads.

"I'm pregnant!" Ashley says louder and then, "Oh my God, I'm pregnant!" she screeches, smiling from ear to ear.

Sarah jumps up and down, smiling the biggest smile I've ever seen.

"That's great news. Congratulations! Does Vegas know? What'd he say? When are you due? I'll be godparent, right?"

"Stop!" Ashley yells at her friend. "I only found out yesterday and am so sick every day I haven't thought about anything yet. Other than tying up my hair in the mornings so I don't get vomit on it. I've not had it confirmed with the doctor, and no, I haven't told Vegas yet, I'll do that tonight. So please, keep that gigantic trap of yours shut! Otherwise, I'll withdraw godmother privileges." She smirks at Sarah.

"Oh, you wouldn't dare!" Sarah replies in mock outrage that has us all falling over each other, laughing.

"Watch me!" sasses Ashley. "I need some fresh air. Mind if we walk through the park for a bit?" Ashley looks green around the gills.

"Sure, let's do that. Be nice to stretch the legs a little." Tanya smiles and shuffles out of the crowded booth.

The park is just around the corner, and we stroll around the large pond in the center.

Ally brought some bread, so she, Caroline, and Chloe feed the ducks, while Sarah talks Ashley's ear off. Tanya approaches me by the benches. I know she'll talk to me about things I want to ignore for as long as possible. It makes me extremely uncomfortable. Only yesterday I was a hostage of Tanya's father's club and had to watch Slender being beaten.

"Hey, Ellie, can I talk to you?" Tanya asks. She's one tough cookie. She obviously grew up in the club, lives and breathes it, and I can't help thinking *'When I grow up, I want to be like her.'* But instead of using my words, I just nod at her. While I admire her for her strength, she also intimidates me a little.

"I'm sorry for what happened to you and Slender at the hands of my family. Men like ours often act first and think later. You should never have been in the situation where they considered making you pay for your sewer rat of a brother's sins. I need to explain why I condone them going after him. He raped Meghan. Meghan is an innocent, sweet eighteen-year-old, and let me tell you, he wasn't gentle about it. She was bruised and scratched, but mainly in places invisible, covered by her dirty and ripped clothes. When I asked her about it that night, she lied, told me she fell and that's why she looked a bit of a wreck when she got back. It didn't explain the tears and her one-word answer. Meghan is usually a chatty Cathy. If anything, it's difficult to shut her up. Of course, I couldn't let her get away with it and she told me the whole sorry saga when we got back home. It was me who told Fury. He was understandably out of his mind with worry and anger—"

"Tanya, stop," I interrupt her, knowing full well she only did what was right. I don't want or need her apology because I understand.

"Maybe, if I'd done the same, this wouldn't have happened to Meghan. You did the right thing," I continue. I can't help the tears stinging in my eyes. Guilt crashes over me like a wave, trying to drown me.

Tanya steps up to me and wraps me in the biggest bear hug ever.

"Don't you say that, Ellie, don't you ever blame yourself! It wasn't your fault then and isn't your fault now. He'd have done it, anyway. Hindsight is a wonderful thing, Ellie, but we all live in the present. Don't put blame or guilt on yourself. No one else does, certainly neither me nor Meghan," she murmurs to me whilst hugging me tight. For the first time, having voiced the thoughts I've had since everything came to light, eases me, and loosens the knot inside me a little. I hug Tanya back just as tightly.

Chloe, watching us from a distance, looks surprised at our hug. She's been watching our exchange with wrinkled brows, obviously not trusting Tanya, and who could blame her? Chloe is Raven's Old Lady. Tanya is from the Restless Slayers, who took me and Slender hostage.

Slowly, Tanya and I walk towards the others in silence and join the duck feeding frenzy, listening to Ashley and Sarah continuously bicker. If you didn't know they were best friends, you'd not believe it.

"Are you alright, hon?" Chloe looks at me and asks in a gentle voice.

"Yeah, I'm okay. Tanya talked to me and apologized for what the club put me through. I cannot believe that Rusty raped that poor girl. I met Meghan, you know; she came to see me when we first got there and talked to me. She is such a sweet girl. I wish I could reverse what he did, but I can't." I sigh.

"The poor girl will carry this with her for the rest of her life! I wish I had the guts to make him pay myself.

"I know he needs to pay, and I know he'll pay with his life. He deserves it, Chloe. He's my brother, and at some point, I loved him unconditionally, but he has changed beyond all recognition. Turned into a wild animal. No one can put him on the right path anymore. He deserves what he is getting. He did it to me too, you know?" My eyes haze with unshed tears as I speak to Chloe.

"Please tell me you are joking, Ellie, I thought you said he didn't touch you that way?" Chloe looks at me in abject horror.

"Well, I lied. I was too scared he'd find out and kill me. Please, Chloe, don't tell anyone about this. I have nightmares every night and almost all men scare me. But most of all, *he* scares me. I know I need help, and I promise I'll get it when this is over, but I can't deal with all of it simultaneously."

The truth of my statement suddenly hits me like a dump truck. Falling deeper for Slender, the knowledge that my brother is gonna lose his life over this, and my own constantly returning memories and dissociations really are more than I can deal with on my own.

Chloe swallows hard and puts her arm around me.

"Ellie, no one can tell you how to deal with this, and I am so sorry this happened to you. You know I'm here for you, right? You can talk to me any time, any place. And of course, I'll keep this private. Just promise me you'll come to me if you need me."

No one is more grateful than me in that moment. Chloe offered to be my anchor, to help me, which is more than I ever had. Not finding the right words to express myself, I simply breathe a quiet, "Thank you, I promise."

We spend another hour walking aimlessly, chatting, until we return to the diner, where Ashley wolfs down an enormous piece of carrot cake and an order of chamomile tea, which has all of us shuddering in disgust.

"Don't argue with the pregnant lady," she sasses.

◊◊◊

Payton Hunter © 2024

Shortly afterwards, Tanya receives a phone call and asks to be taken back. As one, we leave together, and are now sitting in the clubhouse bar, strangely absent of men. I have a vague idea of where they are, but despite my feelings about Rusty, I wish I was wrong.

When the door opens and the men file in, all it takes is one look at their grim faces and blood-splattered clothing. Now, more than ever before, I wish the police could have dealt with this matter, instead of sullying the souls of these men, Slender amongst them, still looking much worse for wear and a tad fragile. I walk over to him, gently hugging him.

"Are you okay, Dollface?" he asks me, holding my eyes captive with his.

"Yes, babe, I'm fine." His eyes twinkle as I call him babe, making me smile. Good to know I affect him just as much as he does me.

"Slender, you know I said I wanted closure? I need to talk to Rusty. Is he still alive?" My voice trembles as I ask this important question. The need to confront Rusty is burning hot in the pit of my gut. I can't ignore it anymore.

He sighs.

"Yes, Dollface, he is. And from what Fury, Masher and Ghoul were saying, he'll stay that way until Tanya has her own chance to exact revenge for Meghan." The tone of his voice clarifying that he doesn't believe women should get involved in physical retribution, but in a way, I understand Tanya, and she'd warned me in not so many words.

All around us are couples in discussions. Rusty's filthy hands touched many of the women here, dirtied them. Chloe and Raven are in deep discussion too. Judging by the back and forth and the way they look at each other, it can't be a comfortable one. Sarah and Dougal's exchange is heated. Sarah finally loses her temper.

"I know, I don't want to see him, asshole. I have nothing to say to the scumbag, but you won't stop me from being there for Ashley. If you think that's how this will work, you can fuck right off!"

The room goes silent as Sarah stomps over to Ashley and Vegas.

Dougal rolls his eyes, throws his arms up in defeat and spits, "Damn women!" before stomping off in the opposite direction, causing Dawg and several others to chuckle under their breath.

It lightens the overall mood a little. Fair enough, at Dougal's expense, nevertheless where there was silence, there are now quiet, somber conversations. A few trays of sandwiches appear on the bar. Everyone helps themselves and has a beer or two.

◇◇◇

An hour later, we follow the men up to the place they call the dugout. Another word for dungeon, I guess. The men walk in first, dispersing through the room, and put out a few chairs for us.

Only Tanya remains standing, hands shaking, and face contorted in fury and anguish, wrapped in Masher's arms, who talks soothingly to her. I watch Vegas care for a shaking Ashley. Slender wraps his arm around me, sitting me on his lap. The whole situation is almost too difficult to bear, and I bury my head in his chest, while Sarah sits next to Ash, with Dougal and Vegas bracketing them. We're all pale but hanging in there. Chloe stands up front with Raven, holding his hand.

Fury steps into the middle of the room.

"Ladies, we wanted to give you an opportunity to tell Rusty whatever the hell you need to tell him. Or exact your own vengeance, if you like. It's an opportunity. You do not have to do anything if you don't want to, and we'll understand if you'd rather leave. We'll carry on our vengeance here, so if you are squeamish, I suggest you leave now. No one will think any the less of you."

This is my chance, so I step forward, holding Slender's hand, tears falling freely down my face. Leaning heavily into Slender, my eyes go wide in shock when I finally step in front of Rusty.

"Oh my God, what happened to you?" I sob.

Rusty pulls off a condescending grin, looking more like a grimace. "Why? What do you care? I obviously didn't teach you my lessons well enough!"

Slender steps forward, and punches Rusty in the mouth. I grab his arm and pull him back.

"Stop, Slender! Don't let him goad you," I beg him before standing up straighter and looking Rusty in the eye.

Despite my tears, my voice is stronger as I speak to Rusty again, for the last time.

"Rusty, you are my brother. I loved you so much when we were younger. I don't know what happened to you, what made you become the evil, vile, travesty of the person you once were. You're beyond help, and without remorse. Beating me does not make you strong, just a sad shadow of a man. Goodbye, Bill," I finish, sure I said all I needed to, turn, and let Slender lead me away. His eyes are on Rusty, promising hell to come.

Ashley is next, holding Vegas and Sarah's hand with Dougal supporting Sarah. There is no mercy in Ashley's eyes, only anger. Her voice is ice cold as she looks Rusty in the eye.

"Not so strong now, are we, Rusty? Got any more threats of gang rape and killing me? You're the filthiest cockroach I ever had the misfortune to meet." She wrestles out of Vegas and

Sarah's grip and steps towards Pennywise. "Give me the hammer!" she demands. Pennywise sends a questioning look towards Vegas and when he nods, passes the hammer to Ashley.

"This is for my mother!" She tells him calmly, raises her arm and slams the hammer onto the toes of his right foot. The noise of the bones breaking a satisfying crunch.

Rusty's face turns red with the effort not to scream.

"And this is for me and the hell you put me through!" She lets the hammer fly onto his left foot. This time, he cannot suppress the scream. Sarah steps up, ripping her hand out of Dougal's.

"You filthy bastard, rot in hell!" she bawls at him before spitting in his face. Dougal pulls her back. He and Vegas lead the two women away, and I follow. I can't bear to watch his demise. Tanya and Chloe are the only ones staying behind.

12 — SLENDER

The past three months have been quieter, but difficult. Fully healed after being at the receiving end of the Restless Slayers' wrath, I returned to work installing security systems for private and corporate clients. Lightning Security also provides security staffing for clubs and bars in the local area. We have a great reputation, no small thanks to Ferret, our IT and tech wizard. Working with Dougal, Pennywise, Dawg, and Ferret can be good fun, and throwing troublemakers out of bars suits me nicely.

Things with Ellie have been difficult. Our relationship seems to take two steps forward and then one or two back. Though I don't mind waiting for her.

She's worth it; however, it is getting more difficult each day to support her through her anxiety, self-doubt, and self-deprecation. She sees herself as this ugly, horrible person, not worthy of love, affection, friendship even, and nothing I do or say can persuade her otherwise. I wonder if a person who experienced other forms of violation can be equally vulnerable to what is said about alcoholics. Whether she must hit rock bottom first, before she'll seek the help she so desperately needs. I've tried to talk to her about the subject, but she shuts me down every time. Yet, I'm so in love with her that none of it matters, not to me anyway. And if it takes years for her to find her way out of the hole she is clearly stuck in, I'll wait and be there for her the whole damn duration.

Today is a day I'm not looking forward to. I've been nominated, alongside Ferret, Dawg, Vegas, and Neil, our bar manager, to interview the new talent. We have six hours of back-to-back interviews to look forward to, having openings for at least four bar staff and six dancers to start with. Meanwhile, there is still a discussion going on as to what the bar, or rather strip club, is going to be named.

Ellie, meanwhile, is helping Ally at the diner. She's looking for a job, but, so far, nothing suitable has come up. She still lives with Vegas and Ashley, an arrangement I'd like to change, especially since they are expecting their first baby. I've got some money saved and would like to buy a house for us or have one built. The Stormy Souls' property is extensive enough to facilitate houses.

There are over one hundred acres, partially covered by brush, shrubs, and a small woodland. All it would need would be an access road and services distributing. I like the idea of a self-build. A friend of mine in Duluth has a construction company, so I'll try to see him later to find out what would be possible before I bring this to the table.

I watch the others exit the clubhouse and stroll to their bikes. We all saddle up and follow Vegas out of the gates. Neil will meet us at the completely rebuilt club we own and are trying to open as soon as possible.

Vegas punches the keys on the security keypad by the back door and lets us in. The space is unrecognizable. There's a new teak wood bar with a mirrored backdrop for all the bottles of liquor, taps, and fridges everywhere for bottled soft drinks and beers. To the right is a big stage with four poles, a heavy chair in the center, lighting racks on the ceiling, large speakers everywhere. But my favorite is the rest of the interior.

A plush, dark-red carpet, with round black sleek lacquered tables and comfortable half-back chairs dotted in front of the stage and main area. There are also more private black and red booths further towards the back of the room. At one end of the space, a sleek chrome and black staircase leads to the VIP area, which is behind closed doors and has mirrored windows, so you can see out, but not in. There are tables and comfy chairs for ten in each, and anyone holding a membership can book one of the five private VIP rooms. Membership costs a thousand dollars per year and includes waitress drinks service via an online order screen. Lap dances are private and discounted, whereas other patrons have gotta dig deep at fifty dollars per lap dance. Ten of that goes to the Club, the rest the dancer keeps, plus tips.

You can book tables for bachelor and bachelorette parties, and the general admission fee is forty dollars per person. There are going to be special ladies' nights every month, where we'll host male dancers for the ladies' enjoyment. I could do without the interviews for that, though. Couldn't think of anything worse than watching men shaking their ass. A shiver of disgust creeps up my spine just thinking about it.

"Come on, Slender, get your ass moving!" Vegas shouts over from the area in front of the stage, where three tables have been pushed together for us. Hurrying to catch up, I hadn't realized I was gawking around. Neil comes up to the table, bringing beers.

"Here, try these. Those are craft beers from a local microbrewery who would like us to take on their product."

"Hmm… would be nice to support some local businesses," Vegas agrees, carefully taking a sip. If it's not Bud, it's usually not Vegas' deal. We all stare at him in utter surprise when he smacks his lips and decrees: "Man, this is damn good." We all follow suit, and he's right, it's an amazing bottled beer.

"I'd go for it, Neil. See if we can get a good deal here," I say, with everyone else nodding in agreement.

Neil unlocks the front door and ushers the first girl into the waiting area. She emailed a résumé and Ferret checked her out. Her name is Lauren, she has bar experience and glowing references. Best of all, she's local. A cute blonde, with her hair in a messy bun and a friendly smile, approaches when Ferret calls her over. Neil explains the duties, and she tells us about herself. She's thirty-one, a single mother of two, and needs an evening job as both her kids are in elementary school, and the boyfriend she lives with works during the day, so childcare is only available on an evening. Which is fine by us. We hire her and after a cacophony of thank yous, she's gone.

Next is a guy called Evan, twenty-two years old and obviously batting for the other team. Not that it bothers us. Not at all. He's polite, funny, well-groomed, and hired on the spot by Neil.

Crystal is next. She's a beautiful, twenty-seven-year-old, Philippina, with gorgeous huge almost black eyes, and deep dark-brown straight hair, reaching down her back, almost to her ass. She is witty and not intimidated by us burly bikers, not afraid to speak her mind. I like that. She, too, gets the job.

Last is a guy who Neil knows. He used to bar tend with him for years, so doesn't really need interviewing. It's just a formality. His name is Chris. He's thirty-five, a Marine vet, and motorcycle enthusiast. Needless to say, he's got the job. Since the interviews flew by and it's only lunchtime, with our first dancer not auditioning until two p.m., we lock up and pile into Ally's.

Ellie spots me walking in, comes up to me, wraps her arms around me and says: "Hey, handsome, finished already?" Offering me her lips. Kissing her makes me crazy. My cock is instantly hard, skipping half chub entirely.

"Hmm," she mutters against my lips. "Someone's pleased to see me." With a beautiful smile in her eyes.

"Yes, Dollface, he and I both." I smirk at her. Intimacy is great between us. Kissing and cuddling as well as light petting are no longer an issue, but anything more than that happens on a play-by-play basis. Which is fine, I don't mind waiting. I've never felt like this before. Willing to wait, that is. Since Ellie's come back into my life, I've not been with anyone, not even the club girls. I just don't have the urge. Only when Ellie is around me. She carries my dick and balls in her purse.

I groan and discreetly readjust myself, still kissing her. When we pull back, I answer her: "No, Dollface, not finished yet, just taking a lunch break, sweetheart."

The need to pull her against me and show her just how much I want and adore her fizzes strong in me, like a battery of fireworks on the fourth of July, waiting to be released. And, by the way her eyes shine and darken, she reflects her want and need back at me.

We both walk to our booth and Ellie smiles at all of us.

"What can I get you guys?"

After placing our orders, we wait for her to return with a large pot of coffee and a tray full of mugs.

"I'll be back when your food is ready," she tells us.

"Thanks, doll," Vegas replies.

As she walks away, Vegas turns to me.

Payton Hunter © 2024

"You gonna claim her already? You're joined at the hip, practically both living in my house. Not that I mind, dude, but as her landlord, I have to be sure your intentions are honest!" He furnishes me with a serious look, whilst Dougal, Neil and Ferret almost fall over themselves laughing.

"Dude? Seriously, Dude?" I stare at Vegas, my eyebrows almost hitting my hairline. "Brother, don't make me come over there and kick your ass," I follow up, causing Ferret to choke on his coffee.

"Yes, I have every intention of claiming her. It's just not that easy," I confide in the others, who are now looking at me with interest and something akin to empathy. They know about Ellie's past. Recent and distant.

"Man, that woman is so strong. I have nothing but admiration for her," Dougal adds, with Dawg nodding in agreement.

"I know. Unfortunately she doesn't see it in herself. She sees herself in an entirely different, very warped light," I admit with a sigh.

"You tried talking to her about maybe seeking help, therapy, maybe?" Dawg asks.

"Yes, bro, I've tried, but she shuts me down every time. It's tough. I want a life with her, to build a family, but she's avoiding the whole thing like the pestilence. There's no talking to her."

Vegas looks behind me, his eyes widening. As I turn, I see Ellie standing behind me, her eyes wide, her face a grimace of anger and sadness.

"Ellie, I'm s—"

"Here are your burgers, fries, ribs, chicken, and pizza. If you need anything else, come and let Ally know," she cuts me off, turns on her heel, takes off her apron, and disappears into the back. The back door slams, and next thing we know is Ally is standing at our side grilling us, giving us the third degree of what the hell we did to chase Ellie out of the diner.

"Ally, stop! You're relentless!" I growl at her. "I messed up, okay? But I told nothing but the truth. Unfortunately, she overheard me talking to the guys. Ellie needs help, professional help. I love that woman and support her as best as I can, but this doesn't seem to be enough anymore. Every time I speak to her, she shuts me right down." My frustration and pain bubbles out of me, straight into Ally's lap.

She stares at me wide eyed, as clearly, she hadn't expected me to answer honestly. Well, I've got nothing to hide.

"Oh wow," Ally answers. "You are a dumbass, aren't you, Slender?"

As if I didn't know that already.

"But I see your point. She's not right, easily spooked, always fidgeting, and her eyes are always darting here, there and everywhere. I agree, she needs help. I'll talk to Chloe when I see her later. We'll try to take Ellie out, speak to her on our own. Maybe she'll listen to us."

"Thanks, Ally, right now I'm beyond grateful for any advice and help with this," I tell her, get up and give her a hug, before leaving with the others to return to the bar.

Three hours later, I want to shoot myself. The number of girls applying with zero talent is mindboggling. I've seen everything by now, and Dawg made several gagging noises during the process. From tits hanging down to the knees, to girls who really shouldn't be wearing thongs to an audition. We've had the good, the bad, and the downright ugly.

With only three more girls to see, we have a shortlist of four. Madison, a cute busty blond, sweet as pie, but man can she work a pole. And her burlesque chair dance had us sat with our tongues lolling, unable to look away.

Lucy, a tall, well-proportioned girl with the fieriest auburn locks I've ever seen and very pale skin; she's a regional pole dancing champion.

Avery, a native-American-looking beauty, tall and model thin, and Lilly, the picture of an all-American blonde innocent girl.

Innocent my ass. Her almost emotionless eyes give away her jadedness.

Next up is Victoria.

A tall African American girl, with peroxide bleach blonde, very short, cropped hair, enters the stage.

"Hi, I'm Victoria," she introduces herself confidently.

"Hey, Victoria, did you bring your music?" Neil asks, and when she nods, he adds, "Go on, the stage is yours."

By the time she swings on the pole, our mouths are hanging open. She just dropped headfirst halfway down the pole, only to catch herself and follow with a show-stopping combination of daring formations. Her muscles have such a memory that her movements appear easy and fluid. I can see Neil adjusting himself and can't help myself.

"Neil, you dirty fucker, she's too hot for you," I tease him. "Bet I'm more to her taste."

All heads shoot round when we hear a loud gasp. I jump out of my seat as I see Ellie, with her hand clasped to her mouth, staring at me and giving Victoria the death stare.

Oh, holy shit. What did I just do? If only I'd kept my gigantic trap shut. Ellie turns on her heel and walks to the door. I sprint after her and catch up in the parking lot.

"Hey, Dollface, I'm sorry, I didn't mean it, was just teasing Neil; he has the hots for this girl. You gotta believe me. Ask the others, they'll confirm," I plead with her.

She throws me a look, full of hurt, anger and something else I can't quite put my finger on. Regret? Validation? I can't quite work it out, but it kills me.

She takes a deep breath and when she speaks; I wish she hadn't. Her words have my tiny universe exploding right in front of my eyes.

"Slender, you seem to have a problem with me. I'm disappointed that you've not spoken to me. It's okay to find other women attractive. I'm obviously not enough. Not as faulty as I am. Newsflash! I may always be faulty. This is so not fair to you. I can't, and won't, ask you to put your life on hold any longer. I came to tell you I was sorry for running out on you. However, having witnessed you staring at a half-naked girl hanging from a pole with your tongue hanging out, I'm now telling you: Go ahead. You don't have to worry about me anymore because I'm gone. Don't try to find me, Slender, don't call me, don't text, don't put anyone else on my tail. I need to get back to my life and sort my mess out. I can't do that with you. Goodbye, Slender, have a great life," she says with the most broken voice I've ever heard, turns on her heel, walks to her car, gets in and drives off. Me? I stand there like a salt statue and watch her taillights disappear around the corner, stunned. My world just came crashing down around me.

"FUUUCK!" I scream into the wind.

13 — ELLIE

I couldn't believe what I saw walking into the bar, all ready to apologize to Slender. I behaved like an ass at Ally's. He's right, I do struggle. I shut him down constantly, because he makes me confront what makes my skin crawl, what brings back horrendous memories and uncontrollable flashbacks. I know I need help, and I'm going to find it, but it has to be on my terms. My terms entirely, no one else's. Pain shot through me like a bullet through my heart when I heard him talking about that woman, hanging from the pole upside down, her over-inflated boobs nearly falling out of her top. I realized then that I had to let him go. It wasn't fair to either of us. I know he wouldn't walk away, so I had to do it for him, leaving him to get on with his life, while I'll try to put mine back together.

When I arrive at Ashley and Vegas', I do not remember how I got there. Unable to recall the journey, I'm slightly disorientated. This can only mean one of two things. Either I dissociated while driving or was on complete autopilot. Neither is good. What if a child or animal had run into the road? What if there was another car and I couldn't stop in time? What if I blacked out and crashed? What if…

I'm pulled unceremoniously out of my rising panic when Ashley rips my door open wide, hand on hips, fire in her eyes.

"What the hell are you doing, Missy? Vegas just called me. Slender is with them, destroyed. What the hell did you do? I know he can be an ass, but Slender is a good man. What did he do to deserve you running out on him?"

I begin to respond, "I didn't..." but then it hits me. That's exactly what I did. I ran out on him, away from my problems, pushing all the blame onto him. I was royally unfair. Must have a clear twenty seconds when these thoughts bubble up, because as soon as they appear, they have gone just as suddenly, leaving me feeling upset and angry.

"Let's go inside, then you can explain yourself," Ashley says, turns and walks to the front door, holding it open for me, rubbing her quite large baby bump as she lets me walk past her into the house.

Walking straight past her, through the lounge and into my room, I drag out my suitcase and bag, open drawers and start to throw everything into them. Ashley is standing behind me, watching.

"Ellie, what's going on with you? I love you like a sister. Please speak to me. If I need to rip Slender's head off, I will. You know that." Her gentle voice surprises me.

Sighing, I sit down on the comforter.

"Ashley, I wish it was that easy. My life's a mess. Slender supports me, yes, he's patient and kind, but there is no way to know whether I'll ever be able to have sex with him, without freaking out and leaving my body. It's not fair to him. He has needs. He's a man, after all." I drop my hands in my lap.

"Does he pressure you?" Ashley asks.

"No, not at all. He's so patient it's not normal, but one day, he'll resent me, and I can't deal with that. I love him, Ashley, and I don't want to hurt him like that. I know I've hurt him now too, but this will pass. He'll find another woman and can be happy with her," I tell her.

"I'm not sure who you are trying to persuade here, me or yourself," Ashley replies, looking at me with sad eyes. "You need help, Ellie," she continues, and I nod my head in agreement.

"I won't try to stop you, but please let me call Chloe and ask her if she knows of a good therapist. Where are you gonna go?"

I laugh mirthlessly. "Back home, to Superior."

Ashley's eyes are as big as saucers as she asks: "Are you sure that's a good idea? Is there nowhere else you can stay?"

I shrug my shoulders. "Nope, not really. It's my house. I won't give *him* the power to drive me out." My reply sounds strong, but her face tells me she doesn't believe a word I said. She knows me well. But without giving me any further shit, she turns on her heel, and a few seconds later, I hear her talking to who I assume is Chloe.

Packing my meager belongings doesn't take long. Less than an hour later, I'm in the kitchen, dragging my packed bags behind me. Ashley is waiting for me, wrapping me in a big hug. I loved my time with her. Catching up with my former best friend has made our relationship bond so much stronger. She's about the only person I trust.

"Thank you, Ash, for letting me stay, and I'm sorry I brought trouble to your door," I whisper, trying hard to hold back tears.

"Don't be stupid. It was great having you here, Ellie; anytime you need to get away, come and see me. And promise me you'll be here when the baby comes. Only three more months."

Now here comes the hard part.

"Ashley, I'm not sure if I'll be ready enough to come to your wedding next month, but I promise I'll be there for the birth," I assure her.

"Okay," she tells me, to my surprise. "But you have to promise me you'll contact this lady here." She hands me a note with the name Darcie written in capital letters and a phone number with a Superior code. Chloe came through.

"Chloe warmly recommended her. She knows this lady personally and says she's a trauma specialist," Ashley continues.

"I promise I'll call her as soon as I'm settled," I reassure her, while picking up my bag, giving her a last hug, grabbing my suitcase, and walking away to my car.

◊◊◊

Pulling my car into the drive, I sit quietly for a moment, thinking about the evening I hastily threw some clothes in my luggage and ran in a hurry to keep myself safe. There is no danger now. I'm finally safe. So why can't I believe it?

It takes all my courage to get out of the car, walk to the door and unlock it. The smell is the first thing that hits me. Not only the stale air, from weeks of not opening the windows, but when I enter the kitchen, it is strewn with rubbish and what at some point was half-eaten food.

Rusty obviously came back here first when he ran and left everything behind him. The contents of the plates on the table are unrecognizable and covered in flies. I dry heave and gag, run to the window, and throw it wide open. Next, I grab the rubber gloves from under the sink, a trash bag and throw everything left on the counters and table into it, disturbing a host of flies who rush in a dark cloud out of the open window. The smell is so severe, it makes my eyes water. Holding the trash at arm's length, I throw it in the outside trash can, closing the lid swiftly to keep the stench in.

Next, I tackle the rest of the rooms, throw all the windows wide open, and empty at least two cans of air freshener in the kitchen and front room, before I even dare go upstairs.

Here, the chaos is not as bad. My room, luckily, he left alone, so it just needs airing. When I open the guest room door, the scene in there is an entirely different matter. I can smell his body odor everywhere, and that spurs me into action, throwing open the windows and picking up dirty underwear and socks off the floor, together with a blood-stained shirt and jeans. I throw them into the trash can and carry it down with me. They'll go straight outside too. Not as if he needs them anymore.

Next, I strip the beds and load the washer before remaking mine.

A trip to the grocery store later, I've filled all the cupboards and can finally make myself a cup of coffee, resting for the first time in hours. With the washing out on the line, I'm at a loss of what to do with myself. For the first time in months, I'm truly alone, with too much time for thinking. Having stayed in touch with Andrea, I let her know I'm back and arrange to meet her for coffee.

◇◇◇

"Hey, girl," she greets me. "How are you? Are you back for good?"

I take a moment to think. *Am I?* I nod. "Yes, girl, I'm back."

"Oh good, have you got a new job yet?" she asks.

"No, not yet, have only just gotten back into town, but I need to find one, and fast," I answer, which is true. My savings are dwindling away every day and will do so quicker now that I'll be using more energy in the house again.

"Hey, I saw an advert in the paper, Office Aids is hiring. I know it's a temp agency, but it might be a good start if you're desperate?"

Andrea digs through her purse and holds out the paper to me. I open the job section and there it is. I grab my phone and dial the number on the advert. After a brief conversation with a friendly woman, I've got an interview secured for tomorrow morning. Start would be in two weeks' time, if I'm successful, and the pay is decent.

After enjoying another hour of Andrea's company, I drive home and order some pizza. Cooking just for me suddenly seems like a big chore. I grab my purse and dig for the number Ashley gave me. Taking a deep breath, I dial the number.

"Darcie Fargo's office, good afternoon, how can I help?" a kind voice answers.

"Hello, my name is Ellie Greenwood. I got this number from a friend of mine, Chloe Saunders. Is it possible to make an appointment with Mrs. Fargo please? She is a trauma therapist, I believe?" My hands are sweating, my heart races, and my mouth is so dry it's difficult to get out the words.

"Ah, I remember Chloe. Great shame she left the hospital. I'm Darcie Fargo, and please, call me Darcie. Mrs. Fargo is my grandmother." She laughs. "How can I help? Can I call you Ellie?" she asks. Her kindness and fun attitude puts me immediately at ease.

"Sure, Darcie, Ellie is fine," I reply, taking a moment to think about what I'm gonna say, and as though she knows, she doesn't press further but just waits for me to speak.

"I've got issues stemming from sexual, physical, and mental abuse, and need help," I finally get out.

"Okay, sorry, Ellie, but I have to ask, is it recent? Or in the past?" Her calm voice comes through the speaker.

"A bit of both, I guess, sexual trauma in the past, and the rest in the past and more recently," I answer her question.

"Okay, not a problem. I can tell you a little of what I do, if you like? Then we can see if you want to make an appointment. How does that sound?" she asks.

"That sounds fine, thank you." *Could my voice be any more robotic?* "I need you to know that I have no health insurance at the moment, so I will have to pay you privately."

"That's no problem and something to worry about later. Let me tell you about myself. I'm twenty-nine and have been practicing as a trauma therapist for a few years now. Generally, I see clients who have suffered abuse of some form, usually sexual, physical or mental. Sometimes I work with ex-servicemen, who have PTSD. I tend to take an individual approach, so there are no hard-and-fast rules as to what type of therapy you'd get. It will be tailored to your needs.

"There will be homework assignments between sessions, and I usually try to start with one session per week, but we can review that. Everything we do or say is strictly confidential. You'd have to come to my office, or in exceptional circumstances, I'll make house calls. How does that sound to you?" she asks.

"Sounds great. I'd be happy to come to your office," I reply, unsure whether I can, but not wanting to admit to that.

"Okay, I have an opening tomorrow afternoon at four, if that suits you? You can come to the office, and we can make a start at getting to know each other if you like?" she offers.

"Yes, thank you. That'd be great." My heart is beating out of my chest.

"Okay then, Ellie, I'll see you tomorrow at four. Have a lovely rest of the day and be kind to yourself," she tells me, before we say goodbye and hang up.

14 — SLENDER

Nothing can pull me out of my rotten mood. Ellie is gone, and I'm so mad at myself, I'd like to punch something. Myself preferably, which is only what I deserve. Fair enough, so I joked when I spoke about Victoria. Still, it was thoughtless, not to mention tasteless. Now I'm paying the piper. My sanity kinda left with Ellie. Speaking to Ashley didn't help. She wouldn't tell me where Ellie went at first, but I nearly paced a hole in her floor, so in the end she let slip that Ellie went back home, if you can call it that, to Superior. She also strongly advised me to leave Ellie alone, and that Ellie was gonna get some professional help. That, at least, made me feel a little easier. I'd like to put a man on Ellie but have no reason to request this from the club. Her immediate threat has disappeared, and she is an adult. Plus, the club can't spare a member to sit outside her house for nothing. Not to mention Ellie would be utterly mad if she found out.

I've fucked up. Twice in one day. Now all I can hope is that she'll come to her senses and that her feelings for me are the same as mine for her. In my heart is a huge empty gap, where she took part of it to Superior with her. I need her back but am unsure how to accomplish my goal and give her space simultaneously. She specifically asked me to not call or text and to leave her alone.

"Hey, misery guts, what's got your panties in a twist?" Raven slaps my shoulder as he walks up. I find it hard to look at him, the picture of domestic bliss with Chloe, a shit-eating grin on his face, which I'd so like to slap into nonexistence. He's my Prez though, so no chance of that.

"Fuck off, Raven, leave me alone," I grunt at him and try to turn to walk away when he grabs my arm and pulls me back.

"Hey, fuckface, you may be my SAA but trust me, you will not disrespect me and get away with it." Raven's fists are clenching, and he's pissed.

I sigh. "Sorry, Prez, I'm an asshole. Won't happen again. Punch me if you like," I apologize.

"No, 'cause that's what you're fishing for. Here's your chance to speak up or unbunch your thong and behave like a brother."

Suitably chastised by him reading me the riot act, I point at the bar. "I need some liquid courage for that," I admit, and walk over.

Picking up a beer for Raven and a whiskey for myself, I make my way to the table Raven is sprawling at, waiting for me to spill. Taking my seat and a deep breath, I hand him his bottle, raise my whiskey to him, and shoot it down in one go. The burn in my throat turns to warmth in my stomach, which I relish as the only thing in there has been an icy knot since Ellie left the Club.

"I've been a grade-A ass, Prez," I start. "First, I spoke about Ellie to Vegas and Dawg, which of course she overheard and walked away, then I joked with the guys about one of the new dancers, Victoria, which Ellie also overheard. That second fuck up in the same day made her end it. She's gone, Raven, gone back to Superior, asked me not to contact her."

Payton Hunter © 2024

I actually feel a little better for spilling this out loud. Raven whistles through his teeth. "Shit, man, I'm sorry, that's rough. I know you were in deep. Anything we can do to help?" he asks.

"Chloe already helped, according to Ash. She's given Ellie the number of a trauma therapist, and Ellie promised to get help."

"Not surprised about Chloe. She's like that. Cares for everyone, often more than herself. But I rather meant the club as a whole. Anything you need or want us to do for her?" Raven questions.

I try to think.

"Actually, yes. Could we fit an alarm system to her house that Ferret can remotely monitor?" *Why didn't I think to ask that before?*

"Sure, you got it, Slender. No problem. I'll get Ashley to speak to Ellie and make the arrangements. Maybe not tell Ellie, though, that it's connected to our monitoring," he suggests.

"Thanks, man, that would take a load off my mind. I want her back, Raven, with everything I have, but I can't crowd her now. She's got to get the help she needs, her own way. And if that doesn't include me for now, then I'll deal. Her mental health is way more important than I am. But mark my words, when she's better, the fight is on. I want her back with me, as my Old Lady," I growl with my frustration.

"Expected nothing else." Raven grins at me.

"Oh, by the way, Raven, I meant to ask you something before I take it to church on Sunday. I want to build a house. We are sitting on over a hundred acres, would the club let me build somewhere on the property? I've got a friend who owns a construction company. He'd be able to plan and build for me. I don't wanna move into town. I wanna stay here. Close to the club and the brothers, but in a place of my own. I want to put down proper roots, maybe build a family, have kids someday."

I hold my breath as I watch Raven, deep in thought.

"You know what, Slender? That's not a bad shout. I was thinking about building or buying a house myself, and I'm sure there are other brothers who'd want that too. Might be ideal for Dawg and Caroline," he muses.

"Bring it to church on Sunday. I'll support it." He looks excited at the thought.

"And hey, man, if you need anything, call me. I'm here for you, brother." Raven stands and man hugs me.

"Sorry that things are tough for you. We'll do anything to help. You know that, right?" he quietly tells me while slapping my back.

"Yes, Prez, I know. Just need some time to get my head around all of this. Thanks, man, for putting up with my shit." I swallow hard, taken aback by the emotional side of me being in high gear. I love my brothers.

"No problem, man, that's what brothers are for. To support each other," Raven replies, before letting go of me and walking into his office.

I need to clear my head, so ignore everyone and everything else around me, walk outside to my bike, gear up, and throw my leg over my treasure. With the engine purring and rumbling underneath me, it seems my equilibrium returns, so I follow my gut and roll out the gate for a good hard ride, to settle my restless mind and soul.

◊◊◊

Church is packed, every seat taken. It's an important meeting, deciding on a new name for the bar, prior to reopening. Several names went in the hat. Storm Shelter, Coochie Hut, Cooters,

Leather and Lace, Saints and Sinners were the favorites. Today we'd settle on one through an anonymous vote. Each member votes for a name on a piece of paper, thrown into a box, and then votes are counted. Or at least that was the plan.

"Settle down!" Raven bellows through the cacophony of talk and laughter. Church meetings are the one time where we all get together, other than Prospects, who aren't allowed, hence the beginnings can be a bit… boisterous, shall we say?

Once silence descends, Raven starts the meeting officially. He sits at the head of the table, with Vegas and Ferret to his left, me and Pennywise to his right, Dawg and Clusseaud next to Ferret, with Spen next to Pennywise, opposite Dawg. Anyone else just parks their asses where there's a free chair. I struggle to concentrate, my mind wanders to Ellie, how she's doing, and pain lances through my chest. Pennywise jabs his elbow hard into my side, Raven's stare cuts through me. Damn, I missed my cue, didn't even realize I was up first.

"Right, update. Club is secure no threats, no problems, still recovering from the recent events. It seems we have a breather. We've recruited a guy for the new club, who might want to moonlight for Lightning Security, Ferret checked him out. Ex-marine sniper, goes by Chris. Big dude, crew cut, typical veteran type, and bike enthusiast. Only thing wrong with him is his bike." I snigger. Watching him get on that Triumph Nightstorm amused me to no end. He looks way too big for his ride. But to each their own.

Spen follows with business and financial updates, Dawg scribbles everything in his book. Zippy is next with an update on the new tattoo shop he opened.

"Man, I'm swamped. Got appointments coming out of my ears and only been open two weeks. I can't sustain this; despite the good money it's making the club and myself. I'm literally flat out from eight, sometimes seven in the morning until nine, ten at night," he groans.

Admittedly, Zippy looks like shit, with dark bags under his eyes, from burning too many candles at both ends. We learned a valuable lesson losing Flakey, whose picture hangs behind Raven, next to the other past members who are now riding the rainbow road.

"How can we help?" Raven asks. "No way do we want you to burn out. Tell us what you need." He looks at Zippy expectantly.

"Well, since you're asking, I need an apprentice and someone who can deal with the front desk, answer phones etc. Anyone know a budding artist? Or front desker?" He looks around.

Sparks sits up straighter. "Well, I might know someone. Must speak to Ally, though. Leave it with me. Same person who did Ally's last tattoo. Talented artist. I'll talk to her and get some details, if that's okay?" he says, looking straight at Zippy.

"Sure, man, no problem as long as it's not Ally herself, I see what she does to the muffins in the diner." Zippy winks at Sparks, who pretends to be outraged on his Old Lady's behalf, but we've all seen Ally decorate muffins and cakes, so we know that her artistic side is nonexistent. Laughter fills the room.

"Vegas, how far along are we with the bar's reopening?" Raven asks his second-in-command.

"Dancers and bar staff are recruited. Neil worked out schedules. The bar is stocked; everything is ready to go. Well, everything but the name, we need that for advertising and the signage. Even got an MC and DJ. So, let's sort out the name. We could be up and running in two weeks. Printers are on standby, as is the neon sign company," Vegas says.

As if on cue, Dawg sends around the list of names, rip-off style. All we gotta do is rip our vote off the tab and place it in the box. When the box goes around, everyone is ready for it.

Payton Hunter © 2024

Dawg and Spen get together in a corner of the room, sorting the names into piles and then set about doing the all-important count.

"Drum roll please!" Dawg announces, and everyone drums their hands on the table.

"The winner is: Leather and Lace!" he shouts over the drumming on the table.

Apparently Coochie Hut came second and Storm Shelter third. *Coochie Hut? Seriously?* Leather and Lace seems more fitting, especially with regular ladies' nights. It has a slightly more upmarket ring to it.

My eyes rest on Spen as he announces: "I'll get the order in as soon as we're finished here. We'll catch up next week, but let's set the opening day for Saturday in two weeks."

Cheers erupt. Everyone's income took a hit when we had to close our bar Stormy's three months ago, so we're eager to have a new watering hole, as well as an income stream. The meeting carries on from there, talking about menial stuff, where my attention drifts and my thoughts are back with Ellie. *What is she doing now? Is she okay? Will I be able to get her back? How is she feeling?*

All those questions roll over continuously in my head. Until Raven proclaims: "Any other business?"

Before I can open my mouth, Vegas is already standing.

"I'd like to suggest we patch in Greg at the earliest opportunity. I know he hasn't done twelve months yet, but he's been an excellent Prospect, not to mention he took a bullet for us, yet still tried to protect us and the old ladies," he makes his point.

"Hmm… I agree in part," Raven says. "However, if we patch him in now, that leaves us with only one Prospect, and we know that's not sustainable. Any suggestions?" Raven looks around the table.

Clusseaud raises his hand.

"Just talk, man," Raven growls. "We're not in high school here!"

Clusseaud lifts his hands in an apologetic gesture.

"I suggest we recruit. In the last year, the club has gone from strength to strength. We're in an excellent position, no incidents with the law, spotless reputation with the community, as the Poker Run proved, we have hangarounds, some would rip our arm off to be allowed to prospect." Clusseaud sits.

I stand. "Yeah, we do, but do we really want some of them? Some are weekend warriors, and the others, like Laffo, for example, who I'd really want to put forward, not to mention Neil of late, have no interest in prospecting. They love their freedom too much. They do brotherhood their own way," I point out the obvious.

"I suggest we table this until next week; allow time for everyone to come up with ideas. If we can find another Prospect, we'll patch Greg in, but not until then," Raven closes the subject.

"Now, I know Slender has something he wants to bring to the table," he continues, giving me my chance to speak.

"I'm wanting to build a house on club property. We have over one hundred acres of land here, most of it not used and just meadow or woodsy area. I'd like to ask for permission to build my house here, want to stay close to the brothers, not live in town, but have my own place to land. Settle, put roots down," I finish.

"That because of Ellie?" Ratchet asks.

"Yes, and no," I answer him truthfully. "I fucked things up there royally, not sure if I'll be able to put it right."

I watch as Spen nods in understanding, in a similar situation to mine. Deb's up and left him after a fight they had.

"However, I have every intention of trying to get her back and make her my Old Lady. Saying that, I've been thinking about this for a while, even before Ellie and the recent shit show. Just want to put down roots. As much as I love my room, it's not the same as having your own four walls. Especially with Pennywise entertaining and the walls being thin." I smirk at Pennywise, who grins and takes a bow, while someone in the room gives it the old "Ah, yes, Pennywise, yes, more, harder, faster!" routine, making all of us chuckle.

"Okay, anyone got anything to say? Any thoughts? No? Let's vote then," Raven cuts through the silly atmosphere.

"Everyone who agrees we should make land available for members to build their own houses on, say, aye."

Raven kicks off the vote and votes Aye, it goes around the table and when it reaches back to him, it's a unanimous vote. *Huh, would you look at that.* Seems I wasn't the only one with this thought.

"Anyone who wants to build on a parcel, see me or Spen; we'll get out a property map and start parceling off suitable sites. Now all of you fuck off and have a great Sunday." Raven ends the meeting, to hollering and hooting as everyone files out and either goes to the bar or makes their way home.

15 — ELLIE

It took me all morning to perfect my professional look before I walk into the temp agency foyer, where I'm greeted by a friendly, blonde, middle-aged lady.

"Hi, I'm Marissa, thank you for coming. If you'd like to follow me, we can get started," she says as she shakes my hand.

We walk to an office, where she gestures for me to take a seat in a comfy chair in front of her desk.

"Right, Eliza, have you got a résumé for me?" she asks.

As I nod, I correct her. "Yes, I have. Here you are, and please, it's Ellie. Only my parents called me Eliza when I was naughty." I smile at her. Marissa makes me instantly feel comfortable.

She looks over my résumé.

"I see you've got secretarial skills and have worked as an editorial assistant at a publisher." She looks at me bright eyed. "Can you take dictations and keep accounts?" she asks.

"Indeed, I can keep in-house ledgers, take dictations, either shorthand or digitized. My touch-type speed is eighty to ninety words per minute, with good accuracy. I can proofread, and in my previous job, undertook line editing," I explain my experience.

"That sounds great. How come you've not been snapped up by anyone yet?" Marissa leans back in her seat, waiting for me to answer. The one question I'd rather not answer at all.

"I've had some family problems. My brother died a few weeks ago, and I needed time off to deal with that." I try to sound as confident as I can, and by the expression on Marissa's face, which shows empathy and kindness, I've managed. I discreetly wipe my sweaty hands on my gray pencil skirt, glad she can't see my wringing hands from where she's sitting.

"I'm sorry to hear that, Ellie, my sincere condolences. Are you ready to get back to work?" she asks. I decide to be honest with her.

"I've arranged some counseling, which I'd likely have to attend once per week to help me manage, but yes, I'm definitely ready to get back to work, and to be honest, I need the money," I tell her.

"Okay, I like you, Ellie, I like your honesty. It is refreshing. So here is what I can do for you. We are a temporary employment agency, as you know. We offer health insurance and a salary of seventeen dollars fifty to start with. Which rises depending on your job-placement. As a new starter you'll be at the bottom end of the scale. I'm sure though that you'll work yourself up to a better hourly rate in no time, with your experience. I'll need to get all of your documentation in order, but I could have you start within the next three days. How does that sound?" Marissa smiles at me.

The hourly rate is rather low, but as it has health insurance I can deal with it. As Marissa said, I can work my way up and at worst I can still try to find a permanent job whilst temping.

"Thank you very much, Marissa. If you are offering me the job, I accept." I smile back at her.

"That's great!" Marisa exclaims. "I'm glad to have you on board. Is there any field you specialize in? Commerce, law, publishing, general secretarial work?" she asks, whilst making notes on her pad.

"No, I don't mind," I answer her honestly. "Be nice to have a change from proofreading and line editing," I add, as I stand, following her example.

"Let me sort you out, get you onto payroll and insurance. I already have a client in mind for you. How about I'll call you tomorrow with more information and a start date?" She looks at me questioningly.

"Sure, that's fine, no problem. In the meantime, I've got your number. If I can think of questions, I'll call you or ask you tomorrow," I answer, shake her outstretched hand, and follow her back into the foyer.

After saying goodbye, I'm dying to do a victory dance in the street but restrain myself. I'd look like a fool in my pencil skirt, white shirt, matching jacket, and heels. Instead, I just grin to myself, call Andrea, and sit in a cafe, treating myself to expensive coffee and a quick lunch, before it's time to attend my first appointment with Darcie.

◊◊◊

Walking into Darcie's posh office is possibly the most difficult thing I've ever done. On the sixth floor of one of the few high-rise buildings in Superior, it gives off the vibe of calm, minimalist spirit in the waiting area, where I'm sitting after giving my name to the receptionist. There are magazines on the table, but I'm struggling enough to keep myself together, never mind reading while waiting to be called.

After only a few minutes, a dark wooden door by the side of the reception desk opens, and a curvy woman with red wavy hair about shoulder length walks in. Her green eyes look directly at me when she states with a welcoming smile, "You must be Ellie, come on through," turns and walks back into her office, without waiting for me to follow.

Entering behind her, I notice that Darcie's office is entirely different from the waiting room. A collection of eclectic trinkets, photo frames and dark wooden shelves, filled with enough books to make up a small but well-stocked library. Instinctively, I want to run my hands over the spines of hundreds of leather-bound, antique-looking books, smell the distinct scent of aged paper and ink.

"Go ahead," Darcie encourages. "They're not for decoration. Sometimes it grounds me to just pick up one of those and smell the pages. It's very visceral." I follow her invitation and pick out a dark red bound first edition of Charles Dickens, *A Tale of Two Cities*, my breath catching as I know without a shadow of a doubt that this book is worth thousands of dollars.

Flicking through the yellowed pages instantly calms me, and I can't help myself but lift the book to my nose, inhaling its dusty old smell, which affects me like an expensive perfume would. Finally, after putting this rare treasure back into its place, I take a seat in front of Darcie's desk, from where she's been watching me.

"No couch?" I remark, looking around the homely feeling room.

"Nope," she replies, "I'm not a shrink, so no couch here. But if you'd prefer, we can sit in the nook on comfy chairs, and I'll have my secretary bring us some coffee?" she offers. She seems like a sweet lady, making me feel more at ease with every minute.

"Okay," I reply. "Could I have mine black please with one sugar?" Darcie nods and presses the intercom button, putting her request to her secretary. Five minutes later, the door opens and the lady I spoke with at the reception, enters the room with a tray. She puts it on the table in the nook, smiles at us, and walks back out.

Payton Hunter © 2024

"Thanks, Hannah, much appreciated," Darcie tells her warmly, before the door closes behind her.

I took the time to look around a bit more, take in the interior décor, and observe Darcie and her secretary's interactions.

Once Hannah leaves, Darcie gets up and walks over to the table.

"Come, Ellie, help yourself to coffee and a cookie. Must remind myself to give Hannah a raise," she jokes. My hands are shaking as I join her at the table, filling a cup with coffee, doctor it to taste, before finally taking a seat in one of those comfy armchairs.

"I don't know how to start." I look at Darcie pleadingly, needing her to take the lead.

"Okay, Ellie, I thought we'd spend today getting to know each other a bit more and see if we are comfortable with each other before we dive in at the deep end.

"My name, as you know, is Darcie Fisher. I've been a trauma therapist for a few years now. Anything we discuss here is going to be strictly confidential, so don't worry, I won't tell about the book sniffing." She winks at me. I like her sense of humor. It puts me at ease.

"Oh, thank God, I won't have to take a one-page advert in the paper to deny it then," I return her joke.

I start telling Darcie a bit about myself. About my parents dying when I was young, my brother taking care of me until I was eighteen, my moving to Superior after my secretarial course, my job at the publishers, and anything else I can think of, not touching the story between either Rusty and myself or Slender and me. When I surface, I realize forty-five minutes have passed, and I've spoken more than in the last two years.

My face must mirror my surprise, since Darcie quips, "See, wasn't as bad as you thought," waggling her eyebrows, making me giggle.

Payton Hunter © 2024

"Okay, Ellie, looks like you are okay talking to me. So, shall we take a step forward?" Darcie looks at me questioningly.

"Sure, that's fine by me. I'd like to see you again, Darcie," I confirm.

"That's great. Now then, can you tell me a bit about your immediate problems? Don't try to tell me the whole story. Just give me an idea of what affects you most in your day-to-day life, so we can work out what to concentrate on first."

"The worst are the dissociations." My voice echoes in my head before I even finished the thought.

"Explain to me what you mean by that," Darcie encourages me.

"Whenever I feel out of control, or something bad or unexpected happens, I seem to separate my mind from my body. It can be like watching whatever happens, like a movie from above, or sometimes I shut down completely. That's when I come round with time missing, unable to recall what happened. These periods vary in length, for the cinema-like and the shutdown part. Worst is when it happens in a car. I've arrived at places with no recollection of the journey. It's very scary, completely disorientating, and usually goes with a panic attack, though not always. Sometimes, a switch flicks and I'm out." I watch Darcie scribble, while nodding at me to continue.

"Then there is the panic and anxiety, which mostly leaves me unable to do normal things. Like going for a walk on my own, without turning into a gibbering wreck. Any situation where I'm not in control causes that now. It recently got worse, since my perpetrator… vanished. I see him behind every corner. Am constantly looking for him, despite knowing full well he ain't anywhere near me."

"Has it always been like that? Or is this hypervigilance something new?"

I take a moment to think.

"No, I think this is new, since he… disappeared."

As soon as I say the words, images flash through my mind. Images of Rusty, beaten and bloody, held in the bunker. I literally float above myself, watching myself talking to him, feel Slender by my side. I want to scream and cry but can't get out any sound. Slowly, a calm voice filters through to me.

Someone says, "It's okay, Ellie, you are safe, nothing is going to hurt you. You are safe with me in this place. Try to concentrate on my voice. It's Darcie, honey. Hear my voice. You are safe. Nothing can get you here."

She keeps talking and slowly I find my way back to reality with her guidance.

When I'm fully back inside of myself, I burst into tears. Embarrassment, stress, anxiety, and yes, grief, overwhelm me completely. Not knowing how long I cry, I just let the feeling of comfort and safety Darcie exudes wash over me, while she wordlessly hands me the box of tissues from the table. Exhaustion hits me like a freight train, worse than usual. Gazing at the wall clock, I realize I've gone over my time by almost half an hour.

"I'm so sorry, I kept you here, made you watch my outburst, when there are other clients you could see who probably need your help so much more than I do," I rush out my thoughts.

"Ellie, you are here now, and you are what is important. You are just as important as anyone else. Now, your reaction was completely normal. I'd have wondered if you hadn't reacted. It was good for me to see how fast you dissociate and how low your trigger threshold is. Now, don't worry, I won't ask about triggers today, but I am concerned that you have zero warning. I want to suggest something to you and am only asking you to think about it." She looks at me expectantly, so I nod.

"Good. Have you heard anything about PAWS? The initiative President Biden signed off on so that Veterans with PTSD can have service dogs?" Again, I nod. It was on the news, but what has this got to do with me? Not as if I've been in a war zone.

"My good friend trains psychiatric service dogs. No, before you ask, you are not crazy. Just hear me out." I listen to her say and nod.

"He rescues all sorts of dogs, small ones, big ones, but they all have one thing in common. They are protective, intuitive, tactile, and super loyal. They can help you by standing next to you when you answer a door, help you go out for a walk, help to alert you when your heart rate increases, to keep you present and so much more," she explains.

"I'd like you to consider contacting Alan, my friend. He currently has about ten different dogs. Just talk to him and see if he feels he has a dog that would help you."

I look at Darcie, completely aghast. I've always loved dogs, always dreamed of having one, but have I got the time to do this? And what about work?

"Before you say anything, as I can see thoughts literally racing through your head," Darcie giggles at me.

"These dogs are recognized service dogs. They can go anywhere with you and are permitted on public transport, in office buildings and places of work. They are the equivalent of a guide dog." *Damn, she's good.* Either that or I'm much more transparent than I'd like.

She hands me a business card with Alan's name and number.

"Please, call him, Ellie. I promise he's nice and harmless. He's a military vet who has dedicated himself to this cause. I'll leave this with you. So, how about you come and see me twice a week for now, you can come and see me after work, I'll give you a late appointment? How does that sound?" she asks me.

"Thank you so much, Darcie. I'm so grateful," I tell her.

"Okay then, Ellie, just make your next appointment on the way out with Hannah. I look forward to seeing you soon," she says as she holds out her hand for me to shake. Instead, I hug her. I can't even express how much better I feel leaving, compared to when I was entering this room.

16—Slender

The past three weeks have dragged, despite me being as busy as hell. Leather and Lace finally opened and has been swamped by customers. Most of us working in the security section of the business are on overtime. The new dancers, and even bar staff, are an absolute hit with the customers, and the private membership rooms always booked. We now have a waiting list for membership, and Leather and Lace's reputation is growing by leaps and bounds.

The thought of tonight has me groaning. The last place I want to be is at Leather and Lace, on the first ladies' night. Neil hired a popular group of male dancers and strippers. According to him, they are like "*Magic Mike*" only biker style.

Please, can I just shove and flush my head down the toilet already? *Miserable? Me? Never.*

Unable to concentrate on any one thing, leaves me tired and in a mood. So much so, the brothers give me a wide berth. Not hearing a word from Ellie is driving me insane. In my head, a thousand horrible things have happened to her, and I'm not there to help. I was a mega ass to her. Unfortunately, I realized too late what exactly I'd done—broken her trust.

The only thing keeping me halfway sane is that Ashley has taken pity on me. She's in constant touch with Ellie, and despite not sharing details with me, she tells me that Ellie is doing okay, has started therapy, got a new job and a huge dog. Never had her down for a dog person, but hell, what do I know? Ashley showed me a picture of Ellie and the dog. It almost reaches up to her hip! Ashley told me it's a Romanian Mioritic Shepherd Dog, I'd say it's a twenty-eight-inch high, one hundred-and forty-pounds hound from Hell! Put it this way, I wouldn't want him jumping on me. My initial thought was: She's lost it completely now. But when I looked closer, she looked more relaxed, with a smile on her face, mirrored by her dog's adoring glance toward her. If that's what this monster of a dog does for her, I'm grateful she found it. Not sure if it's a he or a she, so IT, it is.

I've asked Ashley to tell Ellie to contact me, if ever she needs anything, and surprisingly, Ashley did just that. The thought of Ellie and the dog makes me smile. Good to know she isn't completely on her own. I worry about her all the time.

"Earth to Slender," Dawg whispers in my ear at the same time as he head-slaps me.

"Damn it, Dawg, who do you think you are? Agent Gibbs from NCIS? I ain't Tony DiNozzo, so stop this shit, else I return the favor!" I mock growl at him.

He draws his head in, pretending to be scared. "No, please no, not a head-slap. I'm quaking in my boots. Please, have mercy, oh great one," he mocks me openly, which has Striker, Dougal and Clusseaud busting a gut.

"Ya looking forward to tonight?" Striker needles me.

"Like a hole in the head, man,"

"Such a shame I can't be there to support you all." Striker just can't help himself.

"You may be patched in now, grasshopper, but that doesn't mean I can't beat the shit out of you," I let him know, my evil grin leaving not much to the imagination. Striker raises his hands in a defusing gesture, and starts walking towards Stormy Customs, which is on the property now, in a purpose-built building, erected by my friend's construction company, within the space of a week. We've added sandblasting and a paint shop, so we now can do most things in-house for customers.

He's also drawing up plans for a house for me. After the discussion at the church meeting a few weeks ago, regarding building plots, a large area was portioned off behind the clubhouse. The clubhouse now has a five-acre perimeter and building plots behind that. Mine will be the first one. I've opted for a log cabin style, two stories with a wrap-around porch. There are mature trees on my two-acre plot, with an area assigned as a garden and, of course, there will be a double garage attached for bikes and cars. I'm planning on three bedrooms, two and a half bathrooms, with the option to extend if needed.

I'm unceremoniously ripped out of my musings when Chris's bike roars onto the property, as though chased by hellhounds. Gravel and dust flying everywhere. You wouldn't think you could ride a big Triumph Nightstorm the way he does, but hell, it's a sight to see. Unlike us, he does not own a Harley and does not give a shit if we wind him up. He's a cool guy and his own man. At six foot five, he's not short, that's for sure, and with his strong, muscular, gym-fit physique, cuts an imposing figure on his bike and anywhere else he goes. His light brown crew-cut hair still makes him look as though he's serving. I guess it's difficult to let go of some things. A Marine Corps tattoo graces his upper arm. He gives off an air of detached, quiet strength, and I bet my last dollar he can handle himself if need be. When we were talking, Chris mentioned he was a sniper and has been on several tours. Last in Afghanistan, before the big withdrawal. I watch as Chris parks his bike and walks over to me.

"Hey, Slender, how's it hanging? Just wanna make sure I got my security schedule, so just nipping in to see Ferret," he explains, when really no explanation is needed.

Raven comes out the clubhouse door, walking towards us.

"Chris, great to see you, man. What brings you here? You finally coming to get your Prospect patches?" Raven jokes.

"Nope, but have been thinking about it. Just told Slender, I'm here to see Ferret about my schedule," he replies.

"Well, you know we'd welcome you as a Prospect in a heartbeat. Just hurry and join already. I even promise no bike-cleaning duties unless you really fuck up bad," Raven tells Chris, his serious tone belied by Raven's smirk. Everyone is keen for Chris to join. He's a great guy and would be an even better brother. He's been hanging out a lot with us on his days off and seems to enjoy the brotherhood and comradery we have going here. Everyone likes him. Chris shrugs at Raven and walks into the clubhouse.

"How are ya doing?" Raven asks me.

"About as good as you." I sigh. Chloe struggled with the whole Rusty situation and left Raven, but at least they're in touch.

"Well, things are looking up for me," he admits. "Chloe messaged; she wants to meet in person to talk."

I want to smirk, but mustn't let on that I already know. Everyone knows but Raven. The weekend is gonna be one big-ass surprise for him, which was one of the things Clusseaud, Dawg, Dougal, Striker, and I were talking about to begin with.

Everyone has been busy behind his back, preparing for his wedding. No mean feat, especially since he doesn't know shit about it. I'm happy for Raven and Chloe. They deserve it. They are so good for each other. Her calm just gels with his wild. It leaves me wondering if Ellie and I would gel like that. Hitting me like a thunderbolt, I realize that it's what I want. For Ellie to be mine, for me to be hers, forever. Building a family with her, a home to come home to, is all I want and need in this life. Well, apart from being with my brothers.

It makes me throw caution to the wind. I get my cell out and compose a message.

Slender: Hi, Dollface, just want to tell you I miss you like crazy. I know I was an ass, and I broke your trust. Please forgive me. I'll spend the rest of my days making it up to you, I promise. I understand if you don't answer. Just promise to call me if you need me. Any time, any place, I'll always be there for you.

I shove my phone back into my jeans after sending my text, not holding out much hope for a reply. At least I tried. And I'll keep trying, every day, from hereon in.

◊◊◊

When I get to Leather and Lace, there's a queue almost around the block of excited, giggling women waiting for the doors to open. I can see what Neil meant by it being a good earner. We can expect a full house today. Riding past, I clock Ashley, Ally, Sarah, Caroline, and some of their friends. *Good grief, someone has it in for me today.*

After a quick chat about how we expect tonight to go, Dougal and I unlock the doors and let women in two at a time. A seemingly never-ending stream of women of all ages enter the club, and within no time, all tables are full, and it is standing room only. We have to watch not to clash with fire regulations at this point. Ally, Ashley, Sarah, Caroline, and friends are safely seated at a reserved table near the front of the stage. Their giggles and ruckus audible, even from here. Caroline is with them, which has Dawg groaning. He knows his Old Lady well enough to be fully aware he'll be carrying her home and listening to her rave about the show. I don't envy him one bit.

Sparks and some other brothers stand by the bar, obviously looking out for the girls without being too intrusive. Dougal watches Sarah from the corner of his eye, rolling his eyes at her antics but grinning with it. He doesn't mind his Old Lady having a bit of fun.

She works full time as a caregiver for children and they bring up her autistic son Leo together, which is hard work and stressful, I'm sure. He doesn't begrudge her a night of fun.

"She changed fifty dollars into one-dollar bills." He chuckles, looking at me.

"Oh, dear God, let's hope their G-strings hold that kinda money," I joke. "Not that I want to see the G-strings. Anything but," I hasten to add.

Finally, our limit is reached, and we have to turn women away or ask them to wait until someone else leaves, which in all honesty isn't likely. We booked two shows, an hour and a half each, and although I argued against Neil, now I'm glad we did.

The music starts and the first guys hop on stage. I'm actually surprised at just how good and expressive some of them are on the poles, unfazed by the backdrop of screaming women, hollering and hooting. Then the music picks up and the next lot of guys appear on the stage, performing a dance routine, which has the girls hollering and shouting, as the first lot of clothes fly towards the audience. I watch as Dougal hisses: "Oh hell to the no!" When one dancer comes down, grabs Sarah, and pulls her onto the stage, sitting her on a chair, giving her a public lap dance with his oily muscles popping here, there, and everywhere. Watching Dougal's face darken as Sarah laughs her ass off, smacking the dancer on the rear, and batting her eyelashes at him, is quite amusing. I have to grab hold of him and hold him back when Sarah sticks a few dollar bills in the guy's G-string before kissing his cheek as she gets up to leave the stage.

"Calm down, bro, it's just good fun." I try to calm Dougal, who takes a few deep breaths.

"Oh, she'll pay for that," he hisses, thinking I don't notice him subtly adjusting himself.

"She won't be able to sit tomorrow after I finish with her when we get home," he grumbles, more to himself than me, but it has me cracking up all the same. If looks could kill, I'd be a pile of ash at Dougal's feet for sure, which does nothing to temper my amusement. The girls are having a hell of a time. So am I, just by watching the jealous brothers trying to keep their cool while their Old Ladies shamelessly, but harmlessly, flirt.

During the intermission between the two shows, a bachelorette party books the private rooms, and our Old Ladies are finally making their way home. Sleepover at Ashley and Vegas', I believe. We ordered them a cab, and Greg and Caleb, our Prospects, follow them home.

For us, the night isn't over, not by a long shot. We're taking a quick break, getting a drink and some food, before we start the whole thing over again for the second show.

The second show is rowdier, as it seems the ladies have imbibed more given the later hour. To my surprise, we have to eject a few ladies who were getting way too handsy with the guys. I always thought a stripper's life must be good fun, but watching some of these dis-inhibited, inebriated chicks, I'm glad that stripper isn't on my career path. The entire night, I periodically check my cell for a message from Ellie. Unsurprisingly, I hear nothing back.

Counting my blessings when the night is over, I sit with Neil, Chris, Dawg, and Dougal at the now-locked bar, and enjoy the first beer of the day. We don't get to drink before lights out. We must be on top of our game.

"Fuck my life," Dawg lets out on a breath. "I've done lots of security. Bars, clubs, rallies, parties, you name it, but hell, this was something else!" he exclaims. We all agree.

"Man, those women were vicious," adds Chris. "One of them tried to stick her hand in the back of my jeans. Wouldn't take no for an answer." My cough doesn't quite cover my laugh, earning me a stern look from Chris, promising vengeance. *Oh, well.*

"Well done, team, I've just cashed up the entry fees." Neil comes back with a hefty grin on his face. "We had thirty-thousand dollars just from the entrance fees for both shows. Haven't cashed up the bar till or the private rooms yet."

Man alive, I nearly choke on my bear as Neil finishes his sentence. All of us look at him bug eyed.

"Did you just say thirty k just from entrance fees?" Chris is struggling to form actual words.

"Yup," Neil replies. "Told you it's a great moneymaker." He's not kidding. I check my cell for the last time as I walk out to my bike, ready for the way home. As I perch on the saddle of my faithful steed, I open the message app and nearly fall off the bike. There is a message from Ellie.

Ellie: Thank you, Slender, for the apology, and leaving me to sort out my life. I promise if I ever need to, yours will be the first number I call. Miss you too.

For the first time in weeks, I feel a little lighter and breathe a bit easier. Maybe all is not lost yet.

17 — Ellie

"Tucker, come on, boy!" Within seconds his claws click on the hardwood floor behind me. Getting Tucker has been a saving grace for me. As promised, I called Darcie's friend about a service dog. Darcie went with me when I first visited.

There were ten different dogs in the kennels, but Tucker stole my heart from the moment I saw him. His soulful eyes had me mesmerized the second I laid eyes on him. The way he seemed to smile at me, pushing his nose towards me, licking my hand, his shaggy light gray fur, which would require regular grooming, soft and thick. He looked as though he had bangs half covering his beautiful, hypnotic eyes. The only thing holding me back was his size.

Tucker is huge, stands twenty-eight inches from the floor, almost reaching my hip. His almost one hundred and forty pounds put me off at first. In my imagination, I saw myself being dragged along behind a dog the size of a small horse. However, his eyes haunted me, so I went back, took him for a walk, and the rest is history. I took Tucker home the very same day, and my life transformed. He senses when I'm close to dissociation, stubs his nose on my hand to divert my attention, presses against me, and, when needed, leads me in the opposite direction. In the rare times he couldn't stop me from dissociating, he sat next to me, keeping me safe, not leaving my side until I was back to normal. No matter where we were. Be that at home or outside. There is only one issue with Tucker. He hates my boss. I started work at a legal firm as a secretary. Since Tucker is a service dog, he comes to work with me and lays behind my desk.

It's a large office with several partners and contracted public defenders. Tucker is fine with everyone except Stuart Maxwell, one of the public defenders I keep the appointment book for. Doesn't matter what happens, or who's in the office, as soon as Stuart enters the room, Tucker's hackles go up and he starts a menacing low growl. Which is weird, as he's great with everyone else. At least it stopped Stuart's attempts at flirting dead in its tracks.

Today Tucker and I are following Darcie's advice and are taking a long walk in the Superior Municipal Forest. I've been there a few times, years ago. Then it was empty. It has great trails and plenty of backwoods areas. Not to mention that it has strenuous climbs and steep downhills in places. I love the quiet of the woods. Only birdsong and other animals, with the occasional walker, break the silence. Grabbing my backpack, which contains a map and compass—*yes, I can use both*—water, sandwiches, chocolate bars, and treats for Tucker. He needs a good long hike, and so do I. He jumps straight into the large crate installed in the back of my new SUV. My old car was too small for Tucker and his crate, so I bought a Ford Explorer. It's not new, just new to me. Once Tucker is settled and happy, I start the engine.

The only reason I chose Superior Municipal Forrest was Stuart's recommendation. In fact, he emailed me a map with trails rarely used by walkers. Proper trails rather than cultivated paths. I find the designated parking lot he recommended without difficulty, grab my waterproof jacket from the back seat, put my hiking boots on, grab my backpack, and let Tucker out. His massive tail wags and thumps against the side of the Explorer. He's grinning widely. At least that's what it looks like to me. I don't bother putting him on a lead, just grab my map, orientate myself, and start walking with Tucker right beside me. After a couple of hours, we take a little rest, having just trudged uphill for a good while.

Filling Tucker's collapsible water bowl and feeding him a treat, I sit on my waterproofs in the lovely flat meadow we found here. The sun is shining, it's lovely and warm, and life is great. I lay back with my arms crossed under my head, inhaling the woodsy scent, combined with the strong perfume of the meadow flowers and grasses, closing my eyes, listening to the birds' chirp, and high above I spot a raptor making rounds. Not sure what kind, but his wingspan is considerable.

Tucker comes and lays next to me in the sun when I spot a white-tailed deer. As soon as it catches our scent, it takes off. I smile to myself, feeling free and happy for what feels like the first time in forever. And in my heart, I wish Slender was here with me, sharing this peace, holding my hand, kissing me senseless. I miss him something fierce. Taking out my cell, I take some pictures of the beauty surrounding us, intending to send one to Slender. But when I try, there is no signal. *Typical. What did I expect on a backwoods hike?* Giggling, I shake my head at myself. Never mind.

"Come on, Tuck, lazy bones, time to get up and walk further before we turn back. There's a good boy!" I encourage Tucker. Not that he needs encouragement. He has boundless energy. He'll outperform me hiking for sure. I shoo him off, encouraging him to run, by throwing a stick for him, one he found earlier in the underbrush. He runs at least three times my mileage. Back and forth with this stick, looking as happy as, well, a dog with a stick.

Having only met two fellow walkers in hours, it's safe to say that we're well off the beaten track. Does it worry me? No, I have my trusted map and compass and a good idea of where we are, and I revel in the relative silence of the woods, soaking it in like a dried-up sponge.

For the first time in ages, my mind is at peace and empty. Well, apart from thoughts of Slender. Those are always there, in the back of my mind, tucked away in a corner, breaking free at inconvenient times. The difference is, now they put a smile on my face. My anger is receding, and after long discussions with Darcie, I see the world more realistically. Six sessions with Darcie doesn't seem much, but it's already helping to see things in perspective. Since she's not steered me wrong yet, I've signed up to self-defense classes at her local gym, and she's there with me. The first time I put on boxing gloves and hit the pads, it was cathartic. I know boxing isn't strictly speaking self-defense, but it's where I'm starting, with Darcie as my fierce supporter. As unprofessional as it may be, she seems to become more of a friend with each day that passes.

I'm ripped unceremoniously out of my thoughts as Tucker stands perfectly still in front of the trees, tail high, on alert.

"Hey, boy, come here!" I call him. He just ignores me and keeps staring at something that only he can see. *Oh God, he can't hunt a deer here, no way!*

"Tucker, heel!" I call him more forcefully this time. He turns his head and looks at me for a second and turns away again. I even wave his treats at him to get his attention, to no avail. Suddenly, he darts into the tree line and out of sight. *No,no,no,no,no! Damn it!* I run toward where he disappeared. There is no path, just thick undergrowth, as I follow the quietening noise of his running and growling. Whatever he's chasing, he's committed, and I dread to think what kind of damage my huge dog could inflict on a poor deer.

"Tucker!" I keep shouting. "Tucker, come here! Bad dog; no treats for you for a week!" I yell after him. I can just make out his gray fur disappearing in the undergrowth.

I pick up the pace. Twigs snapping in my face, scratching my skin as I try to follow Tucker. After chasing him for a good few minutes now, I realize I've lost my bearings completely.

Sweaty, pissed off with Tucker, and I'm sure my hair looks as though I've been dragged through a hedge backwards.

"I'll kill that dog," I mutter to myself, standing still, trying to listen and make out where he is, but all is silent.

Then I hear his low growly bark. Not just once, but constant. I follow the sound and step into a small clearing, where he is digging on the ground, barking continuously, without letup.

"Tucker, what the fuck has gotten into you? Bad boy, running away like that! No treats for you for a week!" I angrily shout at him. *Stupid hound.* He looks up at me, comes towards me, and gently grabs my hand in his teeth, pulling me towards where he was digging. Then I notice it. There's knocking and muffled sounds. It's coming from the forest floor!

Tucker is frantic, digging and scraping, and I fall on my knees beside him, helping him dig and sweep dead leaves and twigs to the side until his claws hit something hard. I forcefully push Tucker out of the way and clear the area. I can't believe what I'm seeing. Wooden planks sunk into the forest floor.

"Anybody there?" I call out, and again muffled noises and weak knocking from under the wood answer me.

"Hang on, I'll try to get this thing out of the way!" I call to whoever is stuck beyond the plank. Once I've cleared the soil, leaves and brush, I discover not only several planks but a pull

Payton Hunter © 2024

ring. *Shit, this thing is a trapdoor!* I'm not strong enough to lift it by myself, though. I try with all my might but can't budge it.

"Hang on, I'll get help!" I shout at the door, turn around and start walking the way we came. Surprised when I hear footsteps and leaves rustling, but also relieved beyond belief, I shout, "Hello? Anyone there? Hello? I need help!"

Pausing for a beat, listening for a reply that doesn't come, I call out again, "Help, please!"

The steps speed up. I keep calling to make myself easier to find. A tall figure with a large backpack and walking stick steps out from behind a tree, making me jump. Instinctively, I let out a scream. Tucker is instantly on high alert, lowering his front paws to the ground, growling. *Stupid dog, what's up with him today?*

Then I spot who's come to my rescue and suddenly understand Tucker's less-than-welcoming behavior. Stuart!

"Well, well, what a coincidence." He smirks at me with his cute smile. He's a good-looking man. The epitome of tall, dark and handsome. If I wasn't stuck on Slender, I'd totally enjoy his attention.

"Well, Ellie? Where's the fire?" He smiles down at me.

"I need your help, Stuart. Tucker found something in the woods," I tell him.

"Did he now? What, like a tree, a stick, a dead deer?" he asks with raised brows, mocking me. Anger boils inside of me at his dumb, insulting answer.

"No, you prick! Like something much worse! A trapdoor in the forest floor and it appears someone's under it!" I hiss at him. His face pales.

"Shit, Ellie, I'm sorry, show me where it this thing is, and I'll help you as best as I can," he tells me, calmly and with conviction. I grab Tucker's collar and lead the way, looking over my shoulder, making sure Stuart is following me.

I'm not surprised he's here; it's his favorite hike. He was the one who suggested the trails. He showed me lots of photos on his cell, of hummingbirds, deer and other fauna and flora, which persuaded me that this might be a place for me.

As we reach the clearing, Tucker whines and scratches at the trapdoor. Stuart drops his backpack to the floor and helps me pull on the ring. With an almighty creak and shudder, it slowly opens. I step back immediately, and my eyes water. The stench coming from below ground is vile. So vile, I retch. I notice stairs leading below ground and groaning reaches my ears clearly now, as I watch Stuart walk down the steps and disappear from view, after he tells me to stay put. The groaning stops, and I can hear muffled voices. Instinctively, I pull out my cell. We'll need help here. I've only got one bar of signal and that is coming and going in swift successions. Not enough to make a 9-1-1 call. Instead, I bring up Slender's number, switch my delivery reports on, and send a message.

Ellie: 9-1-1 am in Superior National F. Need help NOW! Bring the club.

I study my map and compass and give the grid coordinates and pray he gets the message. A huge sigh of relief leaves me when the delivery report chimes. Within seconds, his reply hits my phone.

Slender: On our way, what happened? Are you alright?

Ellie: I'm okay. Found a trapdoor in the woods. Someone is down there. Colleague found me and has gone down. Please hurry, the smell is disgusting coming from down there.

Slender: Hang in there, Dollface, Ferret pinpointed your location. We're on our way.

With a sigh of relief, I stick my cell back into my jeans, certain Ferret will find me, even without coordinates. Help is on the way.

18 — Slender

Leather and Lace kept me busy beyond belief and I'm glad I've got a day off today. Finally, time to get together with Paul in Duluth to discuss the final plans for my house and a construction schedule. I take the stairs to his office three at a time. Not having seen him in months, the only contact we had was over the phone. I'm keen to see my old friend in person. We're high-school buds, but life sent us down different paths. Last I heard, he was married with a couple of kids, living the citizen's life, and happily so. He was always the white picket fence kinda guy.

As I knock on his door, it gets ripped open from the inside and Paul greets me with a crushing bear hug. Man, I forgot just how strong that guy is. Remind me not to ever get on the wrong side of this guy. I might come worse off, and that is saying something.

"Hey, man, so good to see you," Paul grumbles at me while slapping my back repeatedly, and I hold back a cough.

"Mind letting me breathe? Don't fancy passing out in the doorway." I return his back slaps. Paul laughs and steps back.

"Sorry, man, I sometimes forget myself sometimes," he says, and I chuckle good-naturedly. Peeking around his office, I'm surprised at what I see. Dark brown leather and wood everywhere, plants and colorful pictures dotted around, obviously drawn by his kids. It is welcoming and, dare I say, homely.

"Take a seat, David. I've got your plans for you here." He invites me to sit in the huge leather armchair in front of his desk.

"Wow, Paul, looks like you're doing alright for yourself," I state, my eyes still wandering around the room.

"I can't complain, dude. Business is going from strength to strength," he replies.

"How's the wife and kids?" I ask, genuinely interested. His face darkens.

"Let's not talk about that. Not now, not ever." His icy tone catches me by surprise. I won't dig into things that aren't my business, so I just glance at him and nod.

Paul puts two rolled-up tubes of paper in front of me and proceeds to unfurl them. The first shows the beautiful frontage of an awesome log-cabin home, with full wrap-around porch, two stories, large picture windows on every elevation with bi-fold ceiling-to-floor doors at the back, leading to the porch and into the garden. I'm instantly in love. He captured my request exactly in his drawing. The next one contains more technical drawings, footprints, the building permissions, and everything else to do with the project.

"Man, this looks fantastic, just like I pictured it. When can you start, Paul?"

My excitement getting the better of me.

"Depends. Is the access road in yet?" he asks.

"Sure is, was finished a few days ago, only graveled for now, but access is there. Utilities are going in today and tomorrow," I answer.

"How does next week sound? I've just finished a project and can squeeze yours in now. Since it's a log cabin, the build won't take long. Couple of months at the most, about three weeks until first fix," Paul informs me. I'm as excited as a teenager getting his first blow job.

"Great, Paul, thanks. If I can ever do anything for you, anything, just ask, it's yours. I owe you one." I grin at him, taking out my checkbook and filling in a rather large check for the whole of the construction cost.

"You don't need to do that all at once," Paul tells me while looking at the sum with five zeros behind it.

"I know, but I want to pay upfront. I've been saving for years and can afford it. At least that way you won't have to front any materials," I insist.

"Okay, David, I'll call you tomorrow, just to make sure the utilities are on site, and I'll give you an exact time and day for us starting." He stands, shakes my hand, and reaches over to slap my back again.

"Can't thank you enough, Paul," I say as I turn and leave his office.

The ride back to the clubhouse feels different today. Paul's good news makes the day seem brighter, sunnier somehow.

Caleb waves at me from the gate as I pass through. He's proven to be a great Prospect and worth the effort of changing our bylaws. I like the kid. He and Greg are inseparable.

Having guided my bike into its space, I walk past Ferret's cabin and straight into his new office at the back of the custom bike garage we own.

"Hey, Slender, what can I do for you?" Ferret asks me as I drop into a chair.

"Just letting you know Paul is bringing his crew next week, starting at the house," I state, not listening to Ferret's reply as my cell dings with a message, I pull it out of my pocket, open it, and all the blood leaves my brain when I read what it says.

Ellie: 9-1-1 am in Superior National F. Need help NOW! Bring the club.

My blood runs cold. I hold a hand up to Ferret to stop him from talking and show him the message.

"Shit, where is she?" Ferret growls.

Just then she sends grid coordinates which Ferret punches into his laptop.

I send her a quick reply, praying she's okay. Anything happens to her, and I won't be held responsible for what I do.

Slender: On our way, what happened? Are you alright?

Ellie: I'm okay. Found a trapdoor in the woods. Someone is down there. Colleague found me and has gone down. Please hurry, the smell is disgusting coming from down there.

"Shit, shit, shit!" Ferret growls and is instantly on the phone to Raven, putting him in the picture.

"I agree. Sounds serious." I hear him say to Raven. "Best bring Chloe in case she's injured," he tells him and hangs up.

"Let's go, Slender, now! The others are meeting us at the gate!" Ferret shouts at me, whilst running at the door. I follow him instantly, but not before sending another message to Ellie.

Slender: Hang in there, Dollface, Ferret pinpointed your location. We're on our way.

When I get to my bike, running the entire way, I see every man possible, apart from Greg and Caleb, who are left to guard the clubhouse, on their bikes, and Chloe driving the club van. What a way to end her honeymoon. Her face is serious as it looks at me through the windshield.

Raven is already on his bike, shouting over the engines, "Don't worry, we'll find her!" With that he waves his arm and we set off, with Ferret and Clusseaud at the front as they have the coordinates, knowing where we're heading.

◊◊◊

Thirty minutes later, we're parked in a near-deserted parking lot. It's closest to where Ellie's coordinates are. We all have our guns ready, in case we need them, and continue our journey by foot. The undergrowth is thick and slows us down, but at least we're making a trampled path now, so the way back should be easier.

About fifteen or twenty minutes later, Raven holds up his hands and stops us, putting his finger over his mouth. In the ensuing silence, I hear it. The quiet whining and crying of a dog, and the sobbing of a person.

"Ellie!" I scream for her. "Ellie, where are you?"

"Slender!" her voice calls back.

"Oh, thank God, Slender, hurry! It's Tucker!" No one could stop me as I ran full pelt deeper into the undergrowth.

"Keep calling, baby, so I can follow your voice!" I shout out, desperately listening for her.

At last, we reach a small clearing in the undergrowth, and what I see makes me stop dead and has Chloe gasping. In the middle of the clearing sits a bleeding Ellie, covered in blood, holding a gigantic dog in her arms, that is clearly injured and bleeding as well. To the left of her lays the body of a tall, dark-haired man in hiking gear, his throat ripped out, gun still in his hand, his face unrecognizable, his eyes staring into space.

In one jump, I'm at Ellie's side. She's beside herself.

"Tucker is hurt. Please help Tucker!" she screams at me. Chloe steps forward with a first-aid kit. We pry Tucker out of Ellie's arms and immediately see the bullet wound at his back leg. Chloe puts pressure on it and applies a bandage to slow the bleeding.

"He'll be okay, Ellie, it's not a severe wound, and it looks like nothing important has been hit." She strokes Ellie's hair as she murmurs to her.

"Dollface, where are you hurt? Where are you bleeding?" I ask Ellie. Her sad eyes look up at me.

"I'm fine, Slender, it's not my blood," she tells me while pointing at the dead mauled guy to her left. She makes little sense when she keeps muttering, "Go and get them, you've got to save them. Please get them…"

Raven has spotted the trap door, left open, looks inside and wrinkles his nose.

"Whatever is down there, ain't gonna be pretty," he mumbles

He, Pennywise, Ratchet, and Sparks descend.

"Holy fuck in hell!" Raven shouts from down there. Moments later, Pennywise appears, bringing with him a woman who no longer resembles her former self, placing her gently in the clearing.

"She's alive, Chloe, she needs you," he says, and Chloe instantly jumps to where he laid the woman down.

"It's okay, you're safe now. I'm here to help you," she murmurs to the woman on the ground.

Sparks is next, with another woman in his arms. Then Ratchet with a girl clinging to him, no older than twelve or thirteen.

"Slender!" Raven yells, his voice shaking with fury.

"Get your ass down here!"

I take the steps down one at a time and can't believe what I am seeing. Cages! Fucking cages! Six of them. A table, with a backpack on it, full of water and food items. The stench is revolting. I can't help retching and heaving. Two cells remain occupied, but by the smell, I can tell we are too late for those girls. I walk closer. One woman looks like a once pretty Latina, staring blindly into nothing. Looks like she's been dead for a while.

"Oh fuck, no!" Raven growls, looking into the other cell. And then I see it.

Our tattoo on her left shoulder. The short blond hair, the tiny, emaciated body. A string of curses leaves my mouth.

"Oh, Debs," Raven says quietly. "What did you get involved in?" Tears run down his face.

"Whatever, whoever it is, we're gonna find him and do ten times worse than what they did to you," I vow next to Debs' dead body and mean every single word of it.

"Pennywise, Ferret, get down here!" Raven shouts, nearly bursting my ear drum. He's vibrating with rage. A multitude of feet stomp down the stairs.

"Oh shit," Spen says. "Smells of death and destruction down here."

I turn and walk towards him.

"Go back outside," I instruct, my eyes pleading with him.

"Why?" he asks suspiciously.

"'Cause you don't need to see this, Spen, just believe me and go back up," I tell him forcefully. Then I hear Pennywise and Ferret gasp.

I grab Spen's arm, but he twists with surprising speed and strength, wrenching his arm free and steps towards Ferret and Pennywise.

"Debs? Oh my god, Debs! Debs, wake up!" Spen falls to his knees shaking, screaming: "No, Debs, wake up, I'm here now, I'll never leave you again, Debs, please wake up!" He sobs as he holds the body of his dead wife.

Unbeknown to us, Chloe has followed them down the stairs. Gently she steps behind Spen, wraps her arms around him, rocking him, while he rocks Debs' body.

"She's gone, Spen, you need to let her go so we can bring her upstairs, sweetheart. She needs to be out of this prison, she deserves to be out in the sun and air, she deserves to be taken home." Chloe gentles Spen. repeating herself over and over again, while holding him and Debs in her arms, gazing up to Raven, tears streaming down her face.

"She'd want you to bring her home, and she'd want you to save the other girls, Spen," she keeps telling him.

It takes both Pennywise and me to pull Spen off the floor in the end and guide him outside, with a devastated Raven and Chloe following us. Raven quietly speaks to Ferret and

Sparks, who go back down and take care of the bodies, wrapping them in blankets they brought and bringing them up. The woods are our silent witness. No one speaks, and even the birds stop singing as the two women are gently laid onto the soft forest floor.

19 — Ellie

The scene repeats itself in my mind's eye again and again. Me putting my phone back into my pocket, hearing Stuart downstairs, but not being able to make out what he's saying. Me shouting down to him: "Stuart, I called for help. My friend is on his way." Hearing his footsteps ascending from below, and then feeling a gun pressed to my temple.

"Ellie, Ellie, Ellie, what am I gonna do with you? I hoped we could just come to an arrangement. You're a pretty girl. I'd get a pretty penny for you." He tuts, scoffing from behind me.

"But then you go, calling for help, ruining all my best laid plans. Now I'm going to have to shoot you, throw you in the hold and cover everything up good. Trust me, no trace of you will ever be found."

My mind is racing. *What the hell is he talking about? A pretty penny for me?*

"What the hell do you mean, Stuart? I... I... I don't understand?" I can't stop the stutter,

"Well, let me explain it to you, then," he sneers at me. "I buy and sell women and everything else that can be bought. Do you think I made my money as a public defender? That doesn't pay but is an excellent cover for my activities. No one would expect the strait-laced law graduate to get involved in this kind of activity." I wish he'd stop talking.

"Me and a few friends take orders on the dark web for anything our clients want. Satisfaction guaranteed!" His self-satisfied tone makes me sick.

He grabs my arm and propels me down the stairs. When my eyes adjust to the dim light, my mouth hangs open. There are six cells. Five of them with women and what looks like children in them, one remains empty. Obviously, that's where he thinks I'm going. I slowly gaze over at the women. The girl cowers by the back wall of her cell. One woman does the same, her hair and skin so dirty, I can't make out the color of it. The third woman leans against her cell wall, lips cracked, barely conscious. When I inspect the other two cells, both women in there are dead. What all of them have in common is that they are naked. I need to get the fuck out of here if I don't want to end up like them. I conjure my inner beast, just like my boxing teacher told me, apply the techniques he taught me, break free, and run for the door. Stuart lost his gun in the struggle, giving me a small advantage.

I hear his heavy footsteps behind me as I bolt up the stairs, and once I reach the top a shot hits the tree next to me. *Shit, he's way too close.* Then a dark growl, Stuart screaming, and another shot going off permeates my brain. Tucker whimpers but continues to growl, the sound of flesh tearing follows. As I turn around, it's a scene out of a horror movie. Tucker, having his jaw tightly clamped around Stuart's throat, tearing and ripping, blood spurting everywhere, Stuart's arms flailing, trying to get Tucker off, gurgling, until his arms flop to his side and stay still. I collapse to the floor, hugging my knees, rocking myself back and forth, while Tucker limps towards me, whining, stubbing his nose against me, dropping himself into my lap. I wrap my arms around Tucker. He is bleeding badly. With no idea how long I sit there with Tucker in my arms, I suddenly hear Slender's voice over my sobbing.

"Ellie! Ellie, where are you?"

Payton Hunter © 2024

"Slender! Oh, thank God, Slender, hurry! It's Tucker!" I scream at the top of my lungs.

"Keep calling, baby, so I can follow your voice!" he shouts, his voice closing in. A few moments later the undergrowth parts, and Slender races into the clearing, followed by Chloe, Raven, Spen, Clusseaud, Ferret, Sparks, Pennywise, and Ratchet. I've never been happier to see such a gathering of Stormy Souls. Slender kneels next to me.

"Tucker is hurt. Help him, please!" I beg him, desperate to get Tucker safe. He saved my life today. I can't lose him. Chloe sits down next to me and, with Slender's help, takes Tucker out of my arms. She applies bandages to his hind leg.

"He'll be okay, Ellie, it's not a severe wound, and it looks like nothing important has been hit." Chloe strokes my hair as she murmurs to me.

"He saved my life," I mutter almost inaudibly.

"Dollface, where are you hurt? Where are you bleeding?" Slender's voice reaches me like through a tunnel.

I glance up at him, sadness almost overwhelming me, but tell him, "I'm okay. It's not my blood." He seems to relax a little.

As though through fog, I hear Raven and Pennywise cussing. Soon after, the guys emerge with the two women and the girl. Chloe moves over to help them. She works on them, assessing, treating, and grabbing bottles of water out of her large bag, passing them out, helping the women drink. I watch as Ferret and Pennywise make their way back down the cells, with Spen following them. Suddenly Spen's wailing and shouting, calling for Debs, drowns out everything else. I don't understand, thought they'd split up a while back, so, where is that coming from? I'm so confused.

Several minutes later, the guys emerge from the hole in the ground, carrying two bodies wrapped in blankets, which they gently place on the floor. When the blanket falls away from one body, I can see her face. In the complete silence in the forest, with not even birds singing, all I can do is scream. Debs, Spen's beautiful wife, is staring up at the sky with empty eyes, which Chloe gently closes. Slender lifts me into his arms and carries me further away before he sits down on the floor with me in his lap, murmuring. I don't take in his words, but his warmth suffuses me, and my screams turn to soul-wracking sobs. I don't register being picked up, barely notice being carried to the parking lot and placed into the van.

Within minutes, the lot is crawling with police, ambulances, and official-looking people. I'm loaded into the ambulance, given an injection, and the darkness closes in.

◊◊◊

The first thing I register when I wake up is, I'm in a hospital bed, in a room with Chloe, Slender, Raven, and, to my surprise, Darcie. Slender is holding my hand, his thumb stroking the back of my fingers.

"Hey, Ellie." He smiles at me. "You've given us quite a fright there," he says, holding my hand gently and staring into my eyes. "How are you feeling?"

"Been better," I reply. "My head is pounding, and my mouth is really dry."

"That would be the sedative wearing off. They gave you one in the ambulance," Chloe explains, coming to the other side of my bed.

"I hope you don't mind, but I called Darcie. I thought she could support you." Chloe tells me.

"Especially since you'll have to give statements to the police," Raven interjects.

That's when it hits me. The events of the last few hours come rushing back to me. My hands shake and tears fill my eyes.

"How are the women?" I gulp between tears.

"The older ones are being treated and checked over. The young girl seems to be faring better. She can go home today," Darcie chimes in.

A knock on the door announces the arrival of the police detectives.

"I'm sorry, Miss Greenwood. We need to ask a few questions. Is now convenient?" the woman entering asks in a kindly voice.

"Yes," I whisper. "But I would like my therapist present. I dissociate, and it's less likely to happen if she stays and supports me."

"Sure, that's no problem," she says, sending meaningful looks in all directions, prompting the others to leave.

"I'll be right back, Dollface," Slender tells me as he kisses my forehead.

◊◊◊

It takes the police a few days to clear everything up. Stuart's office is searched, and they find videos and computer evidence showing how he held and tortured those poor women into submission. It also shows our rescue of the women. The bastard had security night vision cameras running underground. God only knows how. The tapes show exactly what the women went through and apparently it wasn't for the faint of heart. I didn't watch the tapes; I don't think I could handle that. It turns out, a family reported one woman missing, however the other wasn't, and neither was the young girl. Both the woman and the girl choose to stay at the clubhouse for now and are given their own cabin.

Slender has not left my side since the incident. He stayed in the hospital room with me until my discharge, and now we are back in his room in the clubhouse, so I'm not alone. Today, we can pick up Tucker from the vet. He's had an operation to remove the bullet and is doing well. I can't wait to have my hero back with me.

"Ready?" Slender asks from behind me, while I'm standing in front of the mirror, brushing my hair. My eyes are glued to him as he pulls me into his chest, smiling at me in the mirror, and I can't help but smile too. He's been so attentive and gentle around me. Showered me with love at every opportunity. Even though he's not uttered the word, it is obvious he loves me. And I love him too. More than anything. Okay, maybe not as much as Tucker, but that's different.

"Ready," I tell him, turn in his arms, and kiss him thoroughly. I missed his taste, his skin against my skin, the feelings and intensity his touch evoke in me.

"Woman," he groans against my lips. "Kiss me like that and we're not going anywhere." I suspect he's only half threatening. Laughing, I free myself from his grip and walk out of the room, keys jingling in my hand. Before I can even unlock my Explorer, Slender is next to me, grabbing the keys out of my hand, opening the passenger door for me.

"Wow, chauffeur service?" I tease him.

"I know what you're like, Dollface. As soon as you see Tucker, you're gonna want him on your lap instead of in his crate. So, you ain't driving." *Damn, he knows me so well.* I can't wait to see my boy and am tapping my foot the whole way to the vet clinic in eager anticipation.

We enter the clinic and are called into the vet's office. Within two minutes, Tucker comes bounding in, dragging the veterinary nurse behind him. I look at Tucker and can't stop laughing. My boy has been through the wars. He has rainbow-colored bandages around his hind legs, with an area of shaved skin showing. His tongue is lolling, and he smiles big at me, barking in excitement, with his cone of shame around his neck, which looks like an oversized lampshade upside down on him.

"Oh, my poor boy, what did the evil doctor do to you?" I fuss over him. "Did he put a naughty cone on you? My poor baby," I tease Tucker while cuddling him close. Slender and the doctor watching me as though I've lost my mind.

"Baby?" the veterinary nurse asks, laughing her ass off.

"Baby, more like a half-assed sized cow!" the vet agrees, shaking his head at me. *I don't care.* We pay the bill and the vet explains Tucker will have to wear the cone for a week and come back next week to have the bandages and stitches removed. *Again, I don't care.* I've got my Tucker back. That's all that matters to me. And Slender was right. On the way back, I sit in the back seat with Tucker half on my lap. My legs go numb with his weight, but I decidedly don't care. I cling to him for dear life, ecstatic to have him back, and grateful for his heroics. He's more than likely not only saved my life but saved me from a fate equaling those of the women we found.

20 — SLENDER

The past few days have been hectic. Been a long time since the cops have been so far up our asses. Between trying to look after Ellie, Spen, and the girls we rescued, being called in through the ever-revolving doors of the police station for interviews and statements, hardly anything else got done. It's unbelievable that they seriously think we had anything to do with this. We'd never in a million years hurt women, force them to do anything they didn't want, and absolutely no way would we take part in the flesh trade. The people who do are the lowest slimy bottom feeders known to man. We each must have given at least three statements. Even worse for Spen, considering that we found his wife dead. He's inconsolable, blames himself for her death. Despite it not being a rational thought, he tells everyone that if he'd only searched harder for her, she'd still be alive. I understand his reaction. Not that his searching harder would have changed anything. He did his best, but I get why he feels like this.

If I ever lost Ellie, I'd be wrecked, truly wrecked and broken for life. Spen has spent the last couple of days continuously drunk. He sits at the bar in the clubhouse and throws them back until he passes out, trying to self-medicate his pain. Understandable, but I can't sit here and watch him do that to himself for much longer. I don't wanna lose my brother. Seeing Debs like that was horrendous. Naked, bruised, emaciated, her already slim body almost just skin and bone. She looked like someone who'd been through the horror of a concentration camp.

The coroner is still working on the autopsies for both Debs and the Jane Doe. In the meantime, Dougal and Sarah have taken in Jade, the fourteen-year-old girl we found in the cell. Jade was the name she gave, no last name. The police checked all the missing person's records, but no one reported her missing. Sarah spent time with her in hospital, and she slowly confided in Sarah that her mother had *actually* sold her to Stuart, clearing up the mystery of her not being reported missing. Having listened to her plead—begging and sobbing uncontrollably—with Sarah, the woman from Child Protective Services, and the doctors was the most sobering experience.

My heart broke for Jade a hundred times over.

"No, please, you can't send me back there! She'll sell me again; her drugs are more important than I am! Please, I'll do anything, I'll be good, I promise, please don't make me go back!" her desperate voice echoed around the room. That's when Sarah offered for Jade to stay with her until another solution could be found. I left the room as to not explode and punch the nearest thing in my line of sight.

The woman from CPS, thankfully, knew Sarah well through their working relationship at the home for mentally disabled children they both work at. She agreed Jade would stay with Sarah and Dougal.

The other women are having regular therapy sessions with Darcie, Ellie's therapist. We put them in the cabin furthest away from the clubhouse, so the noise and occasional wild party won't affect them. Their trust in the male species is annihilated. Ellie, Ashley, Mom, and Chloe are taking turns to provide them with food and giving them someone to talk to, if they so wish.

Melanie, or Mel for short, is a Hispanic-looking beauty. She was the last of the women caught by the bastard Stuart and his cronies. She's in slightly better shape. After a good long shower with the help of hospital staff, a beautiful woman with long dark wavy hair and chocolate-brown eyes came to the forefront. Difficult to say what she'll be like after a few weeks of good care. She's extremely thin right now.

Amy, however, is a different story. She's not engaging, needs help to eat, almost to the point of feeding her. She's emaciated, weak, has mousy blonde hair with bald patches, where it appears she ripped out her own hair, or someone else did it for her. She's deeply traumatized and does not speak to anyone. Ellie, Ashley, Mom, and Chloe are trying their best, but only time will tell how she'll cope.

Melanie gave a full statement to the cops. The police report, which Ferret obtained a copy of, read like a horror story. Stephen King would have struggled to make it up.

We're boiling with rage and ready to impose our wrath, especially after reading the police report, which spins a terrifying tale of beatings, torture, rapes—even Jade was not spared, deprivation of water and food, and so much more. Just thinking about it turns my stomach. They were supposed to be transported to their new '*owners*' in a few days, or so Stuart told them, before Tucker got hold of him. *Love that dog.* I'll get him the biggest butcher's bone I can find for sure and pay for his treatment.

I made sure Ellie's back with me in my room. It is just not safe for her to be in Superior. No one knows who the scum in the background of Stuart's operation is, or whether he told anyone what was happening. In the meantime, Ellie, and all the other Old Ladies are accompanied by a guard everywhere they go.

Payton Hunter © 2024

I support Ellie the best I can, but understandably, her experience traumatized her beyond belief. Any progress she made, wiped out by what happened. With a deep sigh, I reluctantly navigate the clubhouse and ascend the stairs for an unwanted conversation with her.

I knock on the door before I step in. Ellie's laid on our bed, just staring at the ceiling.

"Ellie, love, can we talk?" I ask quietly, sitting on the side of the bed.

"No need, Slender. I get it, I'll pack my things and move into the cabin with the girls. It's obvious you don't want me anymore." Tears rolling down her cheeks as she replies.

"Ellie, stop!" I growl at her. "Just stop with this bullshit. I love you more than anything. Jesus, I can hardly breathe without you. No way are you moving anywhere. I want you more than I ever wanted anyone ever. How can you even think that I don't want you anymore?" I pull her up to a seated position, grab her hand, and place it against my chest.

"Feel that, Ellie? That's my heart beating for you and only you. It would shatter into smithereens if you ever left me. I'm yours for as long as you want me. Forever, if I have my way." My eyes holding her tear-stained ones, refusing to let her go and keeping hers locked on me, while my hands move to cup her beautiful face and I place my lips over hers, gently kissing her, nibbling on her lips until she opens for me. Deepening the kiss but keeping it gentle, putting all my feelings for her into it, and letting my lips do the talking wordlessly. We are both panting when we come up for air.

"I thought you wanted to break up with me," Ellie hiccups.

"No way, sweetheart, that'll never happen!" I put emphasis on never and hope she gets me.

"Now, sweetheart, will you just listen to me for a minute? I want to ask you something and you probably won't like it. Just think about it, yeah?" I ask her, keeping my eyes locked on hers, trying to impress the importance of this.

"Ellie, what happened put you through hell, yet again. I'm trying to help and support you as much as I can, but I'm running on empty, honey. I love you so much and want to help you more than anything. With you seeing Darcie, I wondered if you'd allow me to come with you. I want to see whether she can help me, to help you. If you don't want me to come, I would still like to see Darcie on my own to get her input into how to best support you. It would mean a lot to me. Just think about it, yeah?"

With a deep inhale, I prepare for her flat-out refusal and nearly fall off the bed when she throws herself at me.

"You'd do that for me, Slender? Why? You don't owe me anything. I love you too, so much, Slender. I just worry that my chaos is gonna drag you down with me. The thought that you'll turn around and decide to walk away because I am too damaged and can't give you what you want or need. It scares the shit out of me. I can't believe you really want to come to therapy with me. Do you mean it? Of course you can come with me!" I try not to laugh as she peppers my face with kisses, her eyes bright, yet still tear-stained and disbelieving, her smile illuminating her face from the inside, making her look like an angel hovering above me. She's straddling me, raining kisses on me, and I can't help but groan as I grow uncomfortably hard. I love her gasp when she sits up a little and unintentionally grinds her heat into my hard cock. Her eyes are enormous when she looks into mine.

"Sorry, baby, that's just the effect you have on me. He can't help himself; he just has to pop up and say hello." I grin at her with an apologetic shoulder shrug.

She takes my breath away when she replies, "Honey, don't apologize, I love that he says hello. Let me tell you, my girlie parts want nothing more than to say hello back and are having a dance right now." She giggles, looking down at me.

"Jesus, Ellie, you are killing me here," I groan, causing her to full-on laugh.

Just then, her cell goes off. She stretches over me to grab and answer it.

"Oh, hey, Chloe" … "Sure, when are we going?" … "Tomorrow is fine. What time?" ... "Cool, I'll be there at six p.m. tomorrow then. See you then!" Her voice sounds upbeat, and she smiles big when she turns back to me.

"That was Chloe. We're having a ladies' night tomorrow. Chloe's picking me up in the parking lot at six, and we're meeting Ally, Caroline, and Ashley. Sarah has the day off from looking after Jade and Leo. Dougal has them both. We want to plan a remembrance night for Debs. Do you think we could have it in the clubhouse?" she asks me.

"I'm sure Chloe would have talked to Raven about it, and I can't see why he would be against it. It should be fine," I answer her.

"Okay, I guess we'll sort out details tomorrow. Oh, Slender, I have an appointment tomorrow at lunchtime to see Darcie. Would you like to join me?" she offers, looking a little unsure.

"Of course, honey, what time exactly and where? I'll make sure I'll be there well in time," I reassure her.

"One p.m. Raven is kind enough to let us use the office for sessions," she replies.

Darn it. I had forgotten that Raven told all the brothers that the office is reserved for Darcie until further notice.

"I'll be back here for twelve, Ellie. We can grab some lunch together before we see Darcie." Winking at her, I watch her bounce up and down on the bed. This is my Ellie. The Ellie I recognize, the funny, quirky girl I fell in love with all those years ago, and hell, it is good to see her shining through.

It gives me hope that she'll not just survive but recover and heal with all our support. I kiss her tenderly as I stand up, pulling her to me and holding her tight.

"Sweetheart, I have to talk to some of the guys and then get back to Ferret, iron out some staffing issues. I won't be too long. When I get back, I'll take you out for dinner."

"Dinner? Like an actual date?" Her flushed cheeks spread into a wide smile.

"Yes, baby, a proper date and a long bike ride, if you'd like that?"

She jumps into my arms, nearly making me lose my balance.

"Thank you, Slender. You are the most amazing man, not to mention the sexiest. I'd love to go on a date and a ride with you. Go do what you need to do. I'll shower and be ready for when you get back. I love you so much, Slender." She squeezes the living daylights out of me before she lets me go and pushes me towards the door.

21 — Ellie

True to his word, Slender gives me plenty of time to get ready before picking me up. I brush my hair until it shines, and a French braid perfects the look. Minimal makeup, tight black jeans—clinging to me like a second skin—paired with biker boots and an emerald-green lacy top; even if I say so myself: *I look hot.*

With my soft leather jacket, helmet and gloves in hand, I follow Slender out to his bike. Before he throws his leg over, he turns and drags me into his arms.

"You look amazing, Ellie, just edible, and you're killing me.

He smiles at me before laying a searing, passionate kiss on me, which has me grabbing hold of his arms to keep my knees from giving out, scorching heat setting my whole body on fire. *Damn, I need to change my panties!*

Once he's settled, I put my foot on the peg, my hand on his shoulder, and swing my leg over, sitting behind him. I shuffle a bit to get comfortable, then tap his thigh to let him know I'm okay and ready. He lets out the clutch and we're rolling towards the gates. The feeling of freedom, peace, and intense need for that sexy biker in front of me is indescribable. If I had to explain it, I couldn't. It runs soul deep, making me throw my head back, my arms in the air, with my thighs clamped to his, and laugh.

Laughing and whooping, I let the pressure of the last few days drain out of me with each exhale. Leaning forward, I wrap my arms tightly around him and shout, "Hell, wind her up, Slender, I need some speed and wind therapy!"

His roaring laughter, and the bike pulling away harder as he increases the speed, frees me like nothing else could. As he leans us through long drawn-out bends and amazing countryside in the evening sun, freedom and peace courses through me for the first time in ages.

As the weight falls off my shoulders, I just enjoy being close to the man I love and the excitement and arousal pumping in my veins. It's been too long since I felt this alive.

After a couple of hours, we head back to town, and Slender parks in front of my favorite Steak House. I scramble off the bike, stow my helmet in the saddlebag, and watch him switch off the engine, kick down the side stand, before he throws his long muscular legs over and stands next to me. Unable to help myself, I wrap my arms around his neck and kiss him silly.

"Wow, what was that for, Dollface? Not that I'm complaining." He smirks at me.

"That was my heart saying I love you, my soul screaming thanks, and my lady parts waving hello." I giggle like an idiot.

He pulls me flush against him, kisses my nose while wriggling his hips, his impressive erection pressing into me.

"Well, he's waving back at your lady parts," he rumbles in my ear, sending shivers down my spine.

The food is fantastic, the company excellent. With no awkward pauses in conversation, we talk about God, the world and everything. Films we've seen, books we've read, people we both knew, climate change, and just about anything that would present a half-interesting topic.

After two glasses of wine with my dinner, Wine Ellie makes an appearance. No idea what it is about wine that affects me so. I can drink tequila, whiskey, anything really, but wine is my nemesis.

It loosens my tongue, and often not in a pretty way.

"Why are you so damn good looking and sexy to boot? You should come with a warning label," I protest with a girlish pout.

Slender just leans back and flashes me a sexy grin.

"And if that bitch over there doesn't stop staring at you, I'll take my earrings out and bitch slap her," I hiss.

My man throws back his head, roaring with laughter.

"Easy, champ. I left the boxing gloves at the gym. Never had you down for being the violent type." He smirks at me.

"I'm not normally, but she's staring at my man, and I can see her drooling from over here."

Before he can react, I'm out of my chair, grabbing my napkin, and walking over to the platinum blonde at the table opposite. I sense Slender standing, following me, trying to grab my hand, but I pull free from his grip.

Standing directly in front of the glorified stripper, I reach out my hand with the napkin, dab her mouth with it, and taunt, "Wipe the drool off your face. No matter how much you'd like to get in his pants, he's all mine. Find yourself someone who's into cheap!" With that I turn and walk towards the door, Slender's laughter ringing behind me.

As I head into the parking lot, I hear familiar voices talking; I stop and turn, only to find Ally and Sparks walking out behind Slender. Sparks standing with his arms crossed, Slender still laughing, and Ally high fiving me.

"Sister, that was hilarious. Please bring Wine Ellie tomorrow!" She hugs me and giggles. I turn to Slender and Sparks, taking an exaggerated bow to Ally's clapping and hooting.

"Come on, tiger, let's get you home," Slender chuckles at me.

Hugging Ally and Sparks while Slender gets on the bike, I grab my helmet, pull it on my head, and sit behind him, waving at Ally when we pull out of the space and filter into the traffic.

◊◊◊

I groan as the sun hits my face. My mouth feels like an old worn-out carpet and a marching band is playing behind my eyes. *Jesus, how could I get hungover from two glasses of wine?* Slowly turning my head to keep the marching band in check, I spot a note next to a large glass of water and Tylenol. Hissing, holding my head, and fighting the need to puke, I grab the Tylenol and take them, drinking almost the whole glass of water.

Then I snatch and read the note.

'Good morning, Dollface, or should I call you tiger? Left you some water and Tylenol. Am in the office with Ferret. Call me if you need me. I'll be with you at twelve, so we can have lunch before seeing Darcie. Love you.'

He makes me smile even when he's absent. I grab my phone from the nightstand and jump out of bed in shock. It's eleven a.m., I slept in, and he'll be here in an hour. *Shit, shit, shit!*

I race into the shower, standing under the hot stream of water until my headache recedes a little, wash and condition my hair, soap, rinse, and grab a towel from the rack, wrapping it around me. Standing at the sink, I vigorously brush my teeth, apply lotion, and pinch my cheeks, as I look like death warmed over. *Damn wine!*

Stepping into the bedroom, I drop the towel and rifle through my clothes, finding a bra and panty set, jeans and a top. As I sling everything on top of the bed, the door opens, and I squeal.

Slender steps in and closes the door swiftly behind him, staring at my naked body, which is currently only covered by my hands and not very well at that. Only so much boob a girl can cover with one hand, while the other covers her bits. A small smile creeps across Slender's lips.

"Am I too early, Dollface?" His rough voice and the need in his eyes scorching me as he stares at my body. Taking a deep breath, unsure where I'm taking the courage from, I drop my hands by my side. The way his eyes devour me makes me feel beautiful, wanted, loved.

Slowly I take a few steps towards Slender, who stands stock still, with his fists clenching by his side with the effort not to touch me. I take his hand and place it on my hip, then the other I hold against my face, pressing my cheek into the palm of his hand.

He pulls me flush against his hard body. I lean back a little, locking my eyes on his, as I move my hands to run them over his wide chest. Feeling my way over his abs, I grab the edge of his T-shirt and run my hands under it. My fingertips touch his hot, soft skin and hard, taut muscle, and trace every outline of every muscle of his abdomen and chest. Slender hisses, swallows hard but keeps still and lets me explore.

When I look up at him, he has his head leaned back and a deep rumble emanates from his chest.

Payton Hunter © 2024

"Dollface, we have to stop this. I'm fighting for control here, wanting to touch you. You drive me crazy. You're so beautiful," he whispers.

"Touch me, Slender, please," I implore as I go on my tiptoe and press my lips to his.

At this moment, all I see is the man I want more than anything in this world. I need his hands on me.

He slowly runs his hands up and down my back and over the globes of my ass, then up my sides, gently caressing the side of my breasts. My nipples are puckered so hard it almost hurts.

When he dips his head and kisses down the side of my jaw, my neck, and then lowers his head to flick his tongue over the first nipple, then the other, I can't help but moan as electricity zings straight to my clit. As he sucks one of my nipples deep into his mouth, I flood, and the wetness between my legs seeps down my thighs.

My hands, roaming free, find his hard cock over his jeans, and I rub him through his clothes.

"Dollface, we need to stop. Otherwise, I'll come in my pants like a horny college boy," Slender grates, clearly struggling to remain in control.

I move my arms around his neck and place a lingering kiss on his lips. The look in his eyes—full of heat and desire—makes me feel loved, cherished, wanted, but safe at the same time. I step back without a word, trying to control my erratic breathing, and step into my clothes, while Slender disappears into the bathroom.

After a few minutes, he returns, pulling me straight back into his arms.

"Oh, baby, you have no idea what you do to me," he whispers in my ear, making me shiver. "Come on, let's get something to eat and then see Darcie." He grabs my hand and leads me out of the room.

◇◇◇

"How's Wine Ellie?" Smirks Ally, driving us to the one and only wine bar in town.

"Shut up," I mutter through her cackling.

She snorts. "Wipe the drool off your face! Man, that was hilarious."

I shrug my shoulders.

"Well, she asked for it, and in my fuzzy head, it sounded witty."

Unable to help myself, I pig snort, trying in vain to stop myself from laughing.

The rest of the girls are already in the parking lot waiting for us as we pull in.

"About time," Caroline grumbles.

"I'm dying of thirst here," Sarah joins in. Chloe merely rolls her eyes, opens the entrance door, and leads us to a table with a 'reserved' sign, sporting her name.

Ashley, escorted by Vegas, joins us only seconds later.

"God damn, I'm pregnant, not infirm. Vegas, do both of us a favor. Fuck off and leave me alone," she hisses like an alley cat, frustration radiating off her in waves.

"Just making sure my boy is safe and sound. Chloe, make sure she behaves."

Chloe stands and salutes. "Yes, sir, of course, sir; she'll be back before curfew, sir, and no alcohol, sir!"

Shaking shoulders betray his amusement as he turns and leaves.

"Gotta love a brother-in-law." Chloe's eyes meet Ashley's. "How are you? Still nauseous?" she asks.

Ashley grins back at her.

"Nah, it's a lot better now. Third trimester and all that. He just annoys the ever-loving hell out of me, trying to wrap me in cotton wool. It's cramping my style. If he carries on like this until the birth, he won't live to see it." She shrugs. "Better than the opposite, I guess."

Chloe smirks. "He's convinced you're having a boy. Imagine his terror if the baby is a girl? We really should do a fake gender reveal just to see his reaction."

As the waitress arrives, we all put in our orders and as we wait, the now suddenly somber mood grips us all.

"How's Jade doing?" I ask Sarah, whose dark-circled eyes show the strain of the last few days.

"I'm not sure," Sarah hesitates, "she doesn't say much really, which I'm sure is normal, but in my opinion, not a good thing. She seems to focus all her attention on Leo. Trying to win his trust. It was a massive change for Leo. First Dougal moving in, and now Jade. He's had a few tantrums, I'm sure the entire neighborhood heard. Miracle, that we haven't had the police on our door for a safety check," she rambles on. Leo, Sarah's autistic son, struggles to deal with any form of change. My admiration for Sarah and Dougal is boundless. Their willingness to open their home to someone else with complex, albeit different needs, makes me feel warm, fuzzy and immensely proud of them.

Chloe looks guilty as she speaks. "Hey, I'm sorry to be a party pooper, but we need to talk about Debs. I still can't believe she's gone. Spen is in no fit state to arrange much for her, so I offered to help with the arrangements. Would you like to lend a hand?" She looks at each of us, and we all nod in agreement.

As the drinks hit the table, I raise my glass.

Payton Hunter © 2024

"To Debs, we love you, friend."

"To Debs!"

Our rather loud toast turns some heads and raises eyebrows, but we don't care. We allow ourselves a few minutes of sorrow, remembering.

Chloe, ever prepared, pulls out a notepad and pen from her bag. Brainstorming ideas, we come up with a plan, dividing responsibilities. All we need now is Spen's approval.

I've been cooking up an idea over the last few days.

"Hey, girls, I need your opinion on something." All eyes are on me now.

"I've been wondering about what to do with the house in Superior. I obviously never want to live there again, but somehow am reluctant to sell it. So, I was wondering, what do you think about turning it into a safe house for women escaping trauma situations? I've even thought of a name: 'Deb's Haven.'"

The silence around the table is deafening, even with all the noisy goings on in the bar.

"Ow!" I screech as Ally hits me right on my arm.

"Shut up, Ellie, you're making me cry," she sobs. A round of teary eyes stare back at me.

Chloe is the one who breaks the silence.

"I love the idea. Spen will too. I'd like to volunteer to help run it and take on medical duties. I have a feeling that Darcie will want in on it, too."

A slow smile creeps over my face.

"Well then, it's a done deal. I'll get in touch with my lawyer tomorrow and have him set up a not for profit and investigate all the regulations."

Sarah throws in: "I'll have a chat at work, see how to get a referral process established and which organizations to make aware."

Wow, it looks as though something good may come out of this tragedy, giving Debs a lasting legacy. For the first time in ages, I feel at peace with myself, knowing I'm doing what's right.

22 — Slender

"Oi! Shut it!" Raven shouts across the table. "This is church, not kindergarten!"

Grudgingly, the guys calm, and order is restored. Tempers are running high after the rescue operation. We're all champing at the bit to get our hands on the bastards responsible for the trafficking, costing Debs her life. Spen is absent and excused today. He is in no fit state.

After a quick update from Dawg, our Secretary, Vegas stands.

"I've spoken to Spen and Ashley. The girls are preparing Debs' wake, and everything else regarding the funeral, including donations instead of flowers for 'Debs' Haven'.

Spen wants a private cremation. Debs' family won't be present. They blame him and the club for her loss. Irrational but understandable from their point of view. He'll let us know when the ashes get returned to him, then we'll handle the memorial and wake." Vegas turns and looks right at me.

"Slender, Ellie is unbelievable. You better nail her down. Pure gold. Only saying that cause Ash is platinum." A few chuckles go around the room.

"The way she's throwing herself into making her house into Deb's legacy is nothing short of amazing."

I swallow hard, trying not to let show how moved I am. All I can do is nod. Raven stands beside Vegas.

"I suggest the club helps with the conversion and covers the costs." His voice rings around the room. Instinctively, everyone raises their hand in agreement.

"I record that as voted and decided." Dawg adds, pen scribbling in his notebook.

Raven motions for Vegas to sit.

"Guys, I know you are all eager to take revenge. I must put it out there, though. The club getting involved with big players here, will bring a lot of heat. If we decide to take them on.

"We worked hard to clean up this club. I need everyone aware of what this could mean for us. That pond-sucking scum will not go quietly because we asked them nicely. This could turn into a war. Are we really prepared to take this on? Think long and hard. The law enforcement agencies will not look away, nor will they be happy that we'll be putting fingers into their pie.

"The repercussions could be huge."

He looks at each one of us, his eyes telling a story of worry and determination.

Pennywise is the first to speak. "I hear ya, Prez, but can we really sit back and let this happen on our patch without acting? I don't think so. In my humble opinion, we ought to continue running our businesses clean. They have nothing to do with us taking out the trash. We cannot have our women and families at risk. This is more than just revenge. I don't wanna sound like a vigilante, but I'm happy to do my bit, leaving this world a little better than I found it."

"I'm in." agrees Moggy, and everyone else around the table follows.

After everyone files out, leaving only the officers, Raven drops into his chair, tiredness radiating off him.

Payton Hunter © 2024

"No matter how hard we try, it seems we always end up knee deep in shit." He sighs. Dawg rubs his neck, his serious face mirroring Raven's.

"What's the plan?" I throw it out there, knowing there *is* no plan.

As Sergeant at Arms, it's my duty to keep my brothers and their families safe. The sooner we get on with it, the better. Ellie had too many close calls for my taste. I want this handled once and for all.

"I'll get on to finding out more details. Have a few favors I can call in. Might get dark net info." Raven nods at Ferret as he turns to leave.

"Slender and I will review all the files we have on Stuart and his crooked-as-fuck firm, see if we can find out more. Also, gonna look at the office CCTV. He must facilitate his contacts somehow."

Pennywise eyes me straight up. Looks like it's the two amigos again. I nod in agreement and push myself out of my seat.

"Come on then, sunshine, time's a wasting." I turn on my heel and head for the door.

"We meet again on Tuesday!" Raven shouts after us. I raise my hand while walking, acknowledging him.

Heading to the bar, I note that the Prospect is absent. In his place is Mel, one of the rescued girls, leaning over the bar towards me.

"What can I get you?"

"Beer please, thanks. Where's Caleb?"

She hands me the beer and says, "He had to use the restroom, so I'm standing in. I used to tend bar before all of this happened. I need to keep busy, or I'll go insane. Plus, it's a way I can repay your club for the place to stay and the board."

Mom appears out of nowhere.

"And she's doing a fabulous job, too. If she now tells me she can cook, I'll adopt her!" Mom winks at me and Pennywise, who followed me out of the office. Mom hands him a bottle of water out of the fridge.

"I'll get Ferret to do a background check. Are you okay with that, Mel? It's keeping you and us safe."

She answers: "Sure, no problem, go ahead. I'll let Ferret have my details. Social security number and all that."

She smiles at whatever is going on behind us, and I sense small warm hands drift under my T-shirt, stroking my back. The smell of Ellie's perfume makes me instantly hard. *Man, it's so tough to keep my hands off her.* I turn around and kiss her smiling lips. The look of love in her eyes almost undoes me. So much trust, so much emotion. I'll go to hell in a handbasket before I neglect to treat her like the Queen she is.

"Hey, Dollface, how's my girl?" I pull her to my side.

"Great actually, I sorted out the appointment with the law firm, and the attorney has set the wheels in motion to register 'Debs' Haven' as a not-for-profit organization. He also started off some grant applications, helping with funding. Slender, he read Rusty's will too. Sorry, forgot to mention that to you!" She's squealing, bouncing up and down in excitement.

"He had five hundred thousand dollars in his bank, plus investments! That will set up Deb's Haven and keep it running for a while. I don't want his dirty money. Signed it all over to the charity." Her eyes shiny with excitement and happiness, make me want to beat my chest like a Neanderthal, club her over the head, and drag her into my cave! Proud is not the word. That woman hits me right in the heart every time. *Mine, all mine!*

Payton Hunter © 2024

I lean over to Penny.

"Can you hold the fort for ten minutes? Gotta take Ellie and show her my surprise."
Penny whistles and gives me a conspiratorial grin.

"Sure, man, I'll make my way to the cabin. Meet me there? I'll set up the laptop and we
can get to work."

"Thanks, brother." I nod at him, grab Ellie's hand, and drag her behind my long strides
out of the clubhouse.

"Hey!" she complains, pulling on my arm. "Slow down, Tarzan, I'm not Jane and my
arm is no vine."

Sparks snickers as he and Ally walk past us.

"Finally gonna show her?" Ally needles me.

"Yup, and don't let your Old Lady spoil it!" I laugh as Sparks puts his hand over Ally's
mouth, who promptly nips him.

"Damn, woman," he complains, "Sometimes you're more trouble than you're worth."

"Care to repeat that, asshole?" Ally's yell sounds over the noisy bar. *Oops, time to leave.*

Ellie, still grinning at me, can't keep her nosey streak under control.

"Where are you taking me, and what surprise? Come on, spill it," she demands, hands on
hips. Instead of replying, I walk towards Raven's house. She follows me, grabbing my hand as
she hurries to keep up. Once at Raven's, I turn down the new access road leading to the building
site we are developing. Raven's house is finished, and it's beautiful.

I pull Ellie in front of me and turn us towards the site opposite. A billboard shows
pictures of our beautiful home as I imagined it. The basement is in and so are the first-floor
foundations.

"Why are you showing me this?" Ellie's surprised voice reaches me, and I have to keep my nerves at bay.

"This is our new house."

She shoots around to face me—"What did you say?"—her eyes as big as saucers.

"Ellie, I love you and want you to be my Old Lady, my life partner, and eventually my wife. I want to share my life with you, grow old with you, have babies with you, watch them play and grow. This is our house, if you want it to be. I know it's a lot and fast, but I want you with me, always."

I swallow hard, preparing to be shot down, but hoping against hope that she wants the same. Ellie takes a few steps back, looking at her feet, and my heart sinks until the moment she laughs and launches herself at me. I catch her, lift her up, and like a monkey, she closes her thighs around my waist. I swing her around, both of us laughing.

"Yes, yes, Slender, of course I want that too. All of it. But the house is a good start, since I'm officially homeless. Can I see the drawings and plans? Oh my God, I'm so excited, I could pee myself!"

"Please don't do that, I don't mind kink, but that's off the menu," I laugh at her, untangling her from me and setting her on her feet.

Dialing Paul's number, I wait for him to pick up.

"Hey, man, can Ellie come to see you? Have you got time to go over the plans with her?" … "Thanks, bro, appreciated. I can't bring her, but I'll get someone to drop her with you, say in an hour? Yes?" … "Thanks, Paul."

Holding Ellie's hand, we walk back towards the clubhouse.

"Dollface, I'm so sorry, something's come up, and I have to work with Pennywise tonight. I'll likely be late," I apologize to my woman.

"That's okay, I'll keep myself occupied, and my mind will be busy anyway with looking at plans and planning the interior of the house." She throws me a blinding smile. *What have I done to deserve her?*

I walk over to Sparks, who's sat at the bar, Ally notably sitting at a table with Sarah, Mom, and Chloe.

"Do you think Ally would mind taking Ellie to Paul's to go over the plans for the house?"

He turns toward me but receives a smack around the head from Ally who sneaked up behind him.

"Don't you dare answer for me, shithead, unless you want to sleep on the couch?" she growls at him. I'd like to say she's kidding, but she's dead serious.

Ally turns towards me, giving me her sweetest smile.

"Of course I will, Slender. I'd love to. Anything to get away from this bogey sucking ogre." Pulling her keys out of her jeans pocket, she dangles them in the air.

"Come on, Ellie, let's go somewhere where monkeys aren't allowed to sit on bar stools. We'll grab a coffee before we hit Paul's."

Ellie is trying her hardest not to laugh. Sparks looks miserable, and I'd be the one staring at Ellie's phenomenal ass walking out the door.

"Bloody women," Sparks' morose grumble makes me smirk.

"You picked her, man, you love her fierceness," I reply, ignoring his gloomy sulk as I saunter toward the clubhouse door.

Time is my enemy today and has me quick marching to Penny's cabin. It's ours really, but I've not slept there in ages. Got a room at the clubhouse as well. Without bothering to knock, I walk straight in and plonk myself on the couch next to Pennywise, who's bent over his laptop, connecting it to his huge-ass TV.

"There's beer and water in the fridge. Help yourself," he offers. My feet travel on their own accord to the mini fridge, grabbing a cold water, although I suspect I'll need something stronger later. For now, my head must stay clear.

We pour through hours of boring security footage. Nothing. Not one measly thing. As much as I love watching Ellie in her business pencil skirt, this is a waste of our time. How do those lowlifes conduct their business, if not through Maxwell's office? His partners come and go all day, but nothing strikes us as out of the norm.

"This is stupid," Pennywise groans, frustration rolling off him in waves. "We have no clue what or who we're looking for. It's like finding a needle in a haystack!"

I must agree. Pennywise grabs his phone and dials.

"Hey, Ferret, any news? We've been trailing through the surveillance, but without knowing who we're looking for, it's pointless." He listens intently.

"Yeah, he's here. Hang on, I'll pass you over." I take the phone from him .

"Yup?"

"Slender, does Ellie still have access to their computer systems? I need to get into those files. There's gotta be a trail somewhere in that damn system."

 "Not sure, man, but call her. She's out with Ally speaking to Paul. She'll pick up for you."

"Thanks, brother."

I stare at the now-silent phone. Ferret doesn't hold with niceties when he's focusing on getting the job done. With a shoulder shrug, I hand the cell back to Penny, and we continue watching the endless hours of mind-numbing nothingness the cameras produced.

Just when we are ready to throw the laptop out of the window, both our cells ding. Penny grabs his.

"It's from Ferret. Picture message," he grumbles. As he opens it up, the face of four smiling surfer boy types stare us right in the face. The one in the middle looks familiar.

Penny brings up the footage on his laptop, rewinds, and sure enough, that guy walks into Maxwell's office. In fact, when we double-checked the videos, he's a regular, twice a week. No way would I have taken him for a trafficker. Blond, tousled, sun-streaked hair, jeans, loud shirt, average height and built. He looks like the guy next door. He can't be older than twenty. Bet he doesn't even shave yet! Anger and disgust roil around inside me. I crack my knuckles since I can't hammer my fist into his innocent looking face.

The door flies open and Ferret storms in.

"Anything?" he growls. I nod and point at the static shot on the screen.

◊◊◊

Raven, Vegas, Dawg, Ferret, Pennywise, and I sit around Raven's desk. We've spent the last couple of hours collating all the information we have. Surfer boy has a name now. James Carpenter, son of William, nephew of Art Carpenter, a very prominent, loaded businessman with political ambitions, who, as far as we can tell, is on the straight and narrow.

Surfer boy and Maxwell have registered an agency business, hiring 'nannies' to well-paying customers. After six weeks, the 'nanny' is sacked and falls off the system. One client used eight 'nannies' in the space of twelve months. In Dubai no less.

We can safely say those buyers are well-connected.

"Man, this ain't gonna be easy," Raven grates out between clenched teeth. All we can do is make plans to take those bastards down with a bang.

"We'll need help with this." Dawg carefully looks from one to the other. We all know he has a point.

Raven sighs and whips out his cell.

"Fury?" … "We have a problem." … "Not discussing this over the phone. I'll ride up and speak to you in person." … "Yes, today. See you soon." He looks at Vegas.

"You're in charge." Vegas nods as Raven strides out of his office.

23 — ELLIE

Today is the big day. Debs' Haven opens its doors. The bustle of panicked last-minute preparations infect all of us. The past three months I've spent organizing, bringing the house up to standard, appointing trustees for the charity, giving interviews, liaising with the hospital, law enforcement agencies, and pulling my hair out in the process. No way could I have done all this without my girl posse.

Ashley waves at me as she waddles past, the other hand cradling her substantial bump. Ally, Sarah, Darcie, and Chloe are flitting around, making sure everything goes to plan. Darcie has her own office on the first floor. She's the trauma counselor for the house. Volunteers have come forward to act as trauma-informed practitioners, helping with intakes and supporting all of us. Mel is putting the last touches onto the improvised outside bar and food tables, talking to a reporter with a beaming smile. She's integrated more and more into our girl gang, and if she's not careful, we'll find her a sexy biker, just so she can join the Old Ladies proper. The thought makes me giggle out loud. Ally shoots me a questioning look, but I wave her off. Best not to put this to her. She'd be on the case in an instant, and I'm not sure Mel is ready for Ally's matchmaking yet.

We, the Old Ladies, are more aware than ever that the boys did not forget Jade, Amy, and Mel's experience.

Debs' memorial was hard on all of us. Spen has not been at the clubhouse since, and no one knows where he is. He took his bike and disappeared. Raven has been away more than home. Slender is strung tight as a bow. All of us ladies had shooting lessons and were put through our conceal and carry permits.

Pennywise is constantly in a rotten mood, and Ferret only grunts at people. The door to church is almost always closed and the Restless Slayers have been in and out of our compound.

They scare me more than any villain ever could, so I stay at home when they are around. Our new house is beautiful, and I spent an obscene amount of money on furnishing and decorating it. It has my dream farmhouse-style kitchen, a den, four bedrooms, four baths, and the most amazing pool and hot tub out back. The yard still needs landscaping, but hey, Rome wasn't built in a day. For the most part, Slender and I are extremely happy, despite his constant club business excuses driving me insane.

I know he means to protect me, but hell, instead he scares me. Something is brewing. We all feel it. Straightening my shoulders, taking a deep, grounding breath, I shake myself out of my thoughts and throw myself into the opening ceremonies.

Amy, one of the women we rescued, is slowly improving, with Darcie's help, and has moved from the clubhouse into Debs' Haven. She helps with admin and the kitchen in return for free therapy, room, and board. Amy remains a work in progress.

Until recently, she's been mostly hiding in the cabin, catatonic, frightened to leave, or go anywhere outside. It's taken time and trauma therapy to progress her to where she is now.

There's something about Amy. She's very private about her past. Other than she's from abroad, we know very little about her.

She's older than Ash, Chloe and me, closer to Raven and Ferret's age, but you wouldn't think it by her looks. She seems a beautiful spirit, and I'm hopeful she'll come out of her shell with Darcie's help and our support. If I have my way, she'll stay forever.

Walking around Debs' Haven, I feel proud and accomplished, not to mention a little smug. Rusty would turn in his grave—if he had one—knowing I spent all his money. It's my way of getting even.

Slender's loving patience and understanding, not freaking out when he's with me and I dissociate has changed my life. He just holds me, hums softly to me until I'm back with him.

Watching him, out of the corner of my eye, interacting with everyone, I realize just how lucky a bitch I truly am. He doesn't need to tell me he loves me. He shows me every single day. Most days now, I just want to climb his muscular, sexy-as-sin body like a demented monkey.

With my bits constantly wet for him, it's getting harder and harder not to ride his juicy dick. Fear stops me, though. I realize I'll have to take the initiative soon, as Slender won't, he handles me like a breakable treasure, but my fragility is slowly giving way to intense, desperate need for him to fill me, stretch me, and fuck me straight out of my mind and into heaven.

I wish like hell I could still give him my virginity, that was taken from me.

Slender will be my first and last. My heart will always be his. As will my mind, body, and soul.

Tanya and Meghan walking toward me, draws my attention. My heart bleeds for Meghan.

"Hey, Ellie," Tanya greets me, Meghan waves with a small smile playing around her lips. She looks better than the last time I saw her.

"Hey, you two, I wasn't expecting you, but hell, it's a pleasant surprise to see you both." I smile at them.

"We came with Dad and the club," Meghan tells me. "We want to support what you do. It's a more than worthy cause. I nagged Dad, and the club is donating from the rally proceeds. It was a bit of a heated discussion, but I won." Meghan winks at me conspiratorially.

"I sold it as raising our profile doing community work." Tanya chips in, shrugging her shoulders.

"That's awesome," I reply, grinning, "but you didn't have to do that."

Tanya scoffs.

"You know what the boys are like. Offer them five minutes in the positive limelight, and they're all over it."

Looks like the Slayers are not *that* much different from the Souls. Tanya stares at something in the distance. My eyes follow her gaze. Slender and Pennywise are standing near the bar tables. Pennywise looks up and toward us, catching sight of Tanya. His smile fades, and lips press together in a firm line. He says something to Slender before walking off in the opposite direction. *What the hell?* I don't waste another thought on this. The local press has arrived, even the local TV station. It scares the living daylights out of me. I hate attention focused on me.

"Girls, please, please, I'm begging you, please, will you stay with me for the interview? I can't do this on my own." My breath is coming choppy and fast. It feels like an elephant is sitting on my chest. I can't breathe! *Yup, I'm having a panic attack.* Suddenly, Tucker's wet, cold nose presses against my hand. He's my constant companion.

"Breathe, girl. Follow my lead. In through the nose, out through the mouth. That's it. You can do it. Breathe." Tanya is looking straight into my eyes, her hands clasping my upper arms. I concentrate on her eyes, voice, and Tucker beside me, pressing into my side, all of which calms me within minutes.

"We'll be with you," Meghan confirms. "I'll speak to Dad, see if he'll let me present the check to you. Would that help?" She smiles.

All I can do is nod, fighting back the tears. These two women, despite being from a different club, seem more like sisters to me. Taking care of me, despite having no reason to, especially after what Rusty did. Yet, they are full of compassion and show me nothing but friendship. It's like there's a kinship connecting us.

Together, we walk up towards the area where the media is congregating. Meghan disappears only to return with Fury and Masher, who walks straight up to Tanya, wrapping her in his arms. Fury waves a check at me.

"Meghan wants to give this to you. You've done good here, girl. I hope you'll accept our contribution. You have no reason to believe me but take it with the respect and honorable intent it's meant."

Struggling to even look him in the eye, I just nod. Dawg walks up to us.

"What ya up to now, Fury, trying to smooth the waves with some green?" He stares at Fury, eyes hard, hands on hips. He's not one to forgive and forget easily, especially where the women are concerned.

I put my hand on his arm.

"Dawg, the Restless Slayers MC has collected money for us. Could you be my hero and grab one of the presentation checks for them? The least we can do is put their goodwill into the paper," I tell him, part serious, part sarcasm.

"No need to put it on that thick, darlin'. Be right back," he answers, walking off, smirking. *Oh well, he has me pegged.* He returns a short time later, with a massive plastic check the size of a flag.

"That big enough for ya?" He grins at Fury, who nods his thanks, and starts filling in the blanks on the spot. I gasp when I see the numbers, slap my hands in front of my mouth, and burst into tears.

"That's too much, Fury, way too much!" I sob.

"No, darlin'," he says, stepping toward me and wrapping me in his arms. "It's way not enough," he whispers in my ear.

"I'm sorry for what we did to you. I lost my mind over Meghan. No excuse, I shouldn't have treated you the way I did." He steps back after kissing my cheek. *Well, I'll be damned.* There *is* a softer side to that hoodlum. I extract myself, just in time to see Slender stomping towards us, not a happy camper. I preempt him, walk toward him, throw myself at him so he has to catch me.

"What the fuck is going on?" he growls.

"Nothing, honey, I'm trying to smoke a peace pipe with Fury, so don't you wreck it, my most loved neanderthal," I tell him softly, clinging to him like a burr.

Slender looks at me, the love in his eyes making me melt.

"Okay, baby, I'll not interfere. Don't like his hands on you, though. So next time, he's in for a thump," he warns me, his kiss taking the sting out of his words. His caveman attitude should concern me, but it doesn't. If anything, I love him more, knowing his possessiveness comes from a place of love.

◊◊◊

"Hi, I'm Rosy Delamore from KBJR." A stunning bleach blonde introduces herself. "Can we start with you, Ellie, then open the questions out to anyone who wants to answer?"

"Yes, that's fine," I answer, holding my hands up to ward off a chick with a powder compact and brush in her hand. They'll have to take me as is.

We shake hands with the media and take our places, Tanya and Meghan flanking me, Darcie, Chloe, Ally, Caroline, and Mel by our sides.

"And three, two, one we're live."

"Good afternoon, everyone. This is Rosy Delamore from KBJR, following up on a story, developing right here, on our doorstep. We are at the opening of Debs' Haven, a safe place for victims of human trafficking and / or sexual assault and trauma to land and start the healing journey. We're all aware the issue of human trafficking and modern slavery is huge, but we never expected to have to deal with it in our hometowns. Let me introduce you to the founder of this special place: Eliza Greenwood, who will kindly answer some questions we have prepared. Give a warm round of applause to Eliza Greenwood!"

I'm scared to death, as I stand, nodding and bowing to the assembled audience, a smile plastered on my face.

"Thank you, Rosy, so kind of you to give our small project some of your valuable time." I say, thinking '*I'll shoot whoever invited them!*' sitting back down.

"Ms. Greenwood—"

"Ellie, please," I interrupt Rosy.

"Okay, Ellie, let me start by asking this: how did you come up with the concept of Debs' Haven?" Rosy asks.

My heart is pounding. I can't possibly tell her the whole truth.

"Well, Rosie, we, as women, are acutely aware of how we're at risk in today's society. Social isolation, Covid, all of those have been factors to reduce social contact for a lot of us.

"When our friend Debs disappeared, we searched high and low. Unfortunately, there was no happy ending. We found her as a victim of a human trafficking ring, in the worst possible circumstances. As you'll have seen in the news a few months ago, other girls were rescued, but extremely traumatized by their experiences.

"Having survived trauma myself, I wanted to set up an organization to provide safety for those victims. The first stepping-stone to recovery. Hence, I converted my home, with the help of the Stormy Souls MC, to make this difference and pay tribute to a close friend," I answer, my eyes swimming with tears, having to swallow hard several times to keep my composure.

"Wow, that's commendable. You sound like an extraordinary person," Rosy continues.

"That she is!" Slender shouts from the sidelines, voice bursting with pride.

Rosy smiles at him, over the top of my head, and I want to claw her eyes out. *Jeez, jealous much?*

"How many people can you house at once?" Rosy questions.

I'm glad when Chloe steps up to answer, taking the heat off me.

"Currently, we have eight rooms available. One of them is in use. Apart from our clients, there is a liaison team for the local hospitals and law enforcement agencies who refer clients to us. We offer in-house trauma-informed therapy by our volunteers, and after that is complete, our in-house counselor Darcie here offers thirty sessions of counseling. I'm available when clients are welcomed, looking after, and assessing their medical needs. We are trying to deliver a holistic service," she finishes.

"Do you have any sponsors?" Rosy asks.

To my surprise, Tanya and Meghan stand. Fury steps forward and hands them the presentation check. *Sly dog.*

"The community has come together and put their support behind this project." Tanya's clear voice rings out.

"Please allow me, though, to officially present Debs' Haven with a sponsorship contribution from the Restless Slayers MC, and all our friends, family, and the biking community. This is such a worthy cause, with the potential to help so many. We are proud to contribute. Also, the Restless Slayers would like to ask if a Debs' Haven could be considered in our hometown. We'd like to support this cause wholeheartedly."

Thanks, Tanya, here I go again with the waterworks.

"Oh my God, thank you so much to the Restless Slayers for the donation of"—I swallow hard—"one-hundred and fifty thousand dollars."

The audience erupts, clapping, hooting, whistling, hollering, leaving me speechless. Can Deb's Haven be the healing balm both clubs desperately need? I step up to Tanya and Meghan and engulf them in a hug, laughing and crying at the same time.

Rosy smiles and continues, "Tell us about the staff, the people who work here?"

Darcie takes this one.

"Hi, I'm Darcie, the counselor at Debs' Haven. Let me introduce you to the rest of the team. Over there we have Sally, Elaine, and Louise, our TIP workers. They are volunteer trauma-informed practice therapists. Chloe, who you spoke to earlier, provides health support, also as a volunteer, and Mel, next to me, provides admin support for everyone and helps in the day-to-day running," she explains.

"It looks like Debs' Haven has a rosy future ahead, with so much community support, as well as support from the official agencies. I spoke to the mayor earlier and he couldn't praise you highly enough," Rosy says.

"Do you want to expand into other towns and cities?" she asks.

"Well," I answer, "with the support from the Restless Slayers MC, it may be something worth looking into, but we have no fixed plans at present. Let's get this project up and running first." I smile at Rosy.

"Thank you for your time and the opportunity to be part of this momentous occasion. Back to the studio," Rosie finishes the interview.

A voice from the front of the audience shouts: "Hey, Mel, you were one of them, weren't you? How were you caught? What should people be on the lookout for, so they aren't caught? Where were you taken to? How did you escape?"

Slender, Raven, Fury, Masher, Vegas, and Pennywise storm up to the unruly reporter, while I keep a close eye on Mel, who's turned very pale and is shaking.

"That's enough!" Vegas, Fury, and Raven growl as one.

"No more questions, leave!" Slender barks at him.

"Get gone!" Masher grates, grabs the reporter's arm, and escorts him to the exit.

Despite the incident, we're all having a surprisingly good time, and when nine p.m. rolls around and festivities draw to a close, everyone leaves, heading to the clubhouse to continue our celebrations there.

◊◊◊

Payton Hunter © 2024

"Hi, Ellie, great to see you. Is Slender with you?" Darcie's friendly, smiling face makes me feel just a little less nervous about my session today.

"Nah, just me today." I shift uncomfortably in my seat.

"What's bothering you? Tell me about it," Darcie asks.

Steeling myself, I take a deep breath. This is all or nothing.

"I wonder how I'll know when I'm ready?" I ask her.

"Ready for?"

"You know, to take my relationship with Slender further. Lately I've been feeling more and more impatient with myself. I want to have sex with him so badly, but I'm frightened that I'm not ready, that I'll phase out when it finally happens." My admissions leave me breathless, just not in a good way.

"Are you maybe putting too much pressure on yourself? Overthinking it? Let's look at it from this perspective. What's the worst thing that could happen?"

"I dissociate and disconnect."

"What would trigger you to do that?"

"If I wasn't in control and felt pressured, got scared or felt uncomfortable. More worried about the ones I don't know yet."

"Okay," Darcie says, taking my hand, "so you know what would trigger you. Slender loves you and is mindful of your needs. Why don't you take the initiative? Do what you are comfortable with? Seduce him if you want to, just do everything on your terms. Tell me your thoughts." She smiles kindly at me.

"I'd have never thought of that." My mouth hangs kinda open. I'm so stunned. It seems so simple when I think about it now. If we do things on my terms, I'm not likely to get triggered.

Payton Hunter © 2024

I beam at Darcie, suddenly feeling a ton lighter, sit back in my seat, now ready for the rest of my session.

Slender won't know what's hit him.

24 — SLENDER

The Restless Slayers are staying at the clubhouse for a few days, so now that Debs' Haven is

open, we can get on with planning to find and deal with the fuckers who tried to grab Ellie and

killed Debs.

"Hey, man, your Old Lady's done a great thing here. Made me think. Wish we had

something like that nearby when Meghan needed it, instead of having to send her to Rapid City.

We'd love to speak to her about expanding her project, if she'll work with us, that is."

Fury has the good grace to look sheepish. He knows it's not up to me, and he's pushing

his luck after what happened only a few months ago.

"You'll have to talk to Ellie, man, and I suggest you grovel," I tell him, only half joking.

"Not beyond that. Know I've made mistakes with her. Gonna man up and apologize, or

else Meg will have my ass for breakfast," he grumbles, kicking his toes in the ground.

Never thought I'd see this hardass looking apologetic. I give him a chin lift and walk up

to our new home. Well, not that new anymore. It's been finished for a month, and Ellie has spent

the last weeks turning our house into a home. Everything but landscaping is done. Had to get

away from Fury before I lose my temper with him. Fucker's in my bad books and will stay there

for the time being.

I step onto our light gray wrap-around porch, unlock the door, and turn off the alarm. We opted for a top-of-the-line alarm system like Vegas'. We recently expanded and installed cameras at the gates, which feed directly into church, Ferret's monitoring system, and the officers' phones. There'll be no further surprises. One shot-up Prospect is one too many.

"Ellie?" I call, hoping against hope that she's back from Superior, where she's had an appointment with Darcie, after handing over to Amy, who is becoming more and more her right-hand woman. I suggested she'd pay Amy and have her as permanent staff. She's come out of her shell a bit since being at Deb's Haven, has bookkeeping experience, and can do most other clerical stuff. It'd free Ellie and Mel up and lower their stress levels.

As I stride into our brand-new quartz countertop shaker-style kitchen, I glance at the stainless-steel industrial-style six-flame cooker, wondering if we'll ever get to use all of them. We're as far away from starting a family as is humanly possible. Some days, my hands are raw from overuse, but I can't help it. As soon as she enters a room, my dick rebels and turns to steel. Never mind our make out sessions. Sighing, I grab steaks out of the freezer, throw together some rabbit food for Ellie. *I don't eat it, yuk!* Rather lick old oil off a sump than eat greens, however, she loves that stuff. I chop some baking potatoes into wedges, coat them in seasoning, and throw them in the oven. I'll grill the steaks out back on the deck when Ellie's back.

As if I'd conjured her up, the car door slams, and the click of her high heels announces her return.

"In the kitchen, Dollface!" I call out. No answer, but her heels click their way toward me. When I turn around to greet her, I cough as my breath whooshes out. In front of me is the picture of a sexy pinup biker chick I'd have tattooed on me anytime! *Instant hard on.* I groan as my dick dances painfully behind my zipper. Her wavy hair bounces around her chin, bright red lipstick, tight tank top with the Stormy Souls MC logo stretching over her tits, a black, soft leather jacket over her shoulder. She smiles at me, turns and my heart stutters. I'm sure there's drool running down my chin. I have to sit; else my legs will give way. Her hot, curvy body in painted-on black jeans and sky-high fuck-me sandals on her feet. She's every man's wet dream come true.

"You like?" she asks, mischief in her eyes.

"Dollface, your gonna kill me. You look stunning! Gorgeous." I have to clear my throat before I croak, like a pubescent high schooler. She takes my breath away.

"Had a bit of time, went to the salon and got some new clothes. Chloe gave me the tank top, though."

I swallow hard.

"Ellie, you're killing me, baby. Right now, I want to rip your clothes off and worship every damn inch of you." I'm certain my tongue is hanging out.

"Would you now? Interesting." She winks at me. "What's for dinner?" she asks, opens the fridge, grabs two beers, and walks towards the large patio doors, leading out towards the deck.

"You!" I shout after her, loving the girly giggle leaving her mouth in reply.

I grab the salad, plates, cutlery and carry it outside.

"Wedges are nearly done, baby. Just gonna fire up the grill and cook our steaks. That alright?"

"Sure, honey; thanks for cooking. Didn't expect that," she answers, while her eyes roam my body. I can feel the fiery trail her eyes are blazing. Something is different with her today.

"How did it go with Darcie?"

"Great actually, we talked about lots of stuff. My triggers, and that I don't know them all. Darcie had some keen insights. I felt validated and came away having learned something new about myself."

"Oh? What's that? Wanna share?" I ask her, curious about what goes on in my woman's head.

"Later," she answers, grinning at me. Can't be bad then. She looks relaxed and calm.

"I offered Amy the job as my personal assistant and deputy manager today," she says. I wait for her to continue.

"She accepted. Under the proviso, she doesn't have to have anything to do with the club. As in attend clubhouse parties etc. She's not up for that. Did you realize she's forty-three?" My stunned look must have answered her question for me.

"I didn't either, thought she was mid-thirties, but no. She has a grown-up son and daughter who live in the UK," she continues.

"I gathered she wasn't from here. Her accent is pretty obvious. But damn, she doesn't look old enough to have grown up kids." I'm dumbstruck.

"Has she told them about what happened?" I ask, my interest piqued. If I was her son, I'd want to know.

"No, honey, she hasn't. Said she will though, when she's better, feels more able to explain." My girl takes a deep breath.

"I can't imagine what she went through. How she's smiling again and even starts joking about it, I'll never know. I've got so much respect and love for her." The sadness in her voice kills me.

We continue chatting, eating our steaks, finishing a second round of beers, before we carry everything inside and tidy the kitchen together.

Hand in hand, we make our way upstairs in peaceful silence.

"Shower with me?"

I groan. As if she has to ask. Might get my dick a bit of release. I swear, if she even looks at me the wrong way, I'll explode.

My eyes follow her as she turns towards me, turns the shower on to warm it, and takes her sandals off. Slowly, she peels off her jeans. Jeez, watching her drives me insane. Sexy smile beaming at me, she pulls her tank off and throws it at me. I catch it, sniffing, inhaling her scent. I'll never get enough of her. This is torture. Watching her standing in front of me, unclipping her sky-blue lacy bra, letting it drop off her shoulders, onto the floor, followed by her matching boy-shorts. If I didn't know better, I'd think she's putting on a show for me.

"Unless you want to shower in your clothes, you better get undressed," she giggles at me.

Well, looking the idiot is not something I can help, especially when it comes to my pixie. I hurriedly throw off my clothes, step towards her, and draw her into my arms, kissing her deeply. Heat explodes between us like a firecracker.

Somehow, we drag each other into the shower, under the warm water. She picks up my body wash and a sponge. Running the soapy sponge all over me, she's driving me insane. Her sensual light touch is almost more than I can bear. My entire skin breaks out in goose bumps. Not a word is spoken between us. I groan as her gentle soapy hand grips me around the root and moves gently up and down my shaft, which is hard as steel and pulsing under her ministrations.

I turn her toward me, grab the sponge, and run it all over her delectable body. Her nipples—beaded and puckered—get extra attention. She moans and her head falls back in pleasure, her eyes closed. My fingers find their way to her tight heat. She's slick, not from the shower either.

We rinse off; I wrap a towel around my waist and wrap her in a big bath sheet.

"Slender," she whispers, eyes a dark emerald now with need. Watching her, I wait.

"I want you so much. I need you inside me," she implores.

It hits me as though I've been thrown out of a plane without a parachute.

"Please, honey, I need this. Let me." Her pleading eyes staring at me. I get it. She thinks she's ready.

"Are you sure, baby? We don't have to. I'll wait until the end of time if I have to."

"No, baby, I'm sure. I need you. I love you so much. I need to feel you inside of me. Need you to complete me."

"Oh, baby," I groan, my lips crashing down on hers. "We go at your speed, Dollface. You're in control. I'll catch you."

Aware she knows what I'm talking about. I'll do everything in my power to keep her in the present.

She shyly smiles at me, takes my hand, and leads us to our bed, where she urges me down to sit on the edge. My heart somersaults as she lowers herself to her knees, pushes me back onto the bed, and her hot mouth closes around me.

"Fuck!" I hiss. "So good, baby, you feel so good around me," I tell her while her tongue drives me insane, flicking the tip of my cock, dancing lightly over it.

When she leans down and takes most of me into her mouth, to the back of her throat and swallows around me, a shout leaves me, and I can't stop my hips from coming off the bed. *Mind. Blown.* When she hums around my super sensitive, straining cock, I almost lose it.

Payton Hunter © 2024

"Baby, gotta stop. Won't last much longer," I croak.

In answer she hums again, takes me deeper and swallows again, before she lifts up and slowly lowers down again, humming, taking me all the way, swallowing deep in her throat.

That's all it takes. I have no warning. My balls pull tight, and I come down her throat on a long groan. Lights exploding behind my eyes, eyes rolling back into my head. It's the closest I've ever come to passing out with an orgasm. She swallows all I give her, every last drop of me, licks me clean, and smiles like a cat that got the cream. Pun intended. My panting breath the only noise in the room.

She crawls up to me, guides me up to the headboard, and snuggles into me. *Oh no, miss, not the time for snuggles.*

"Your turn," I tell her, hardly recognizing my own voice it's so rough with my need for her.

Leaning in, I kiss her senseless, our tongues dueling for domination. I can taste myself on her and that has my dick perking up again. My lips run down the side of her neck, kissing the hollow by her throat, watching her whole body erupt in goose bumps. Her hard nipples are begging for my attention. I suck one into my mouth and she arches her back, groaning. My girl loves her nipples played with. I change sides and lavish the other nipple with attention while my fingers keep playing with the first one, kneading her luscious tits. Trailing kisses down her abdomen, I can smell her arousal, and damn if it doesn't make me hard as stone.

"Slender," she groans, my head shooting up, making sure she's okay.

"Don't stop, honey; more, I need more," she whimpers. She doesn't have to ask me twice. My lips find her mound, kissing and licking, my fingers delve deeper between her slick folds. Her heat scorching me. My girl is hot for me. As my tongue hits her sensitive clit, her hips come off the bed, pushing herself into my mouth. I love it. I lick and suck, tease her folds, nip them carefully, until she's thrashing around on the bed, her fingers buried in my hair, pulling me closer to her. If I die of pussy suffocation, I'll die a happy man. Pushing two fingers deep inside her searing heat, I fuck her with my fingers. Slow and deep, curling my fingers, so I hit that sensitive spot inside her every time, feeling her flutter around me.

"Oh God, I'm coming!" she wails, her pussy tightening around my fingers and clenching me, as her cum gushes over my fingers; I lap it up greedily.

"Stop, stop," she moans, moving away from my mouth. She leans up on her elbow, pulls me up with the other hand, crushing her lips to mine, ravaging my mouth. *Wow, my girl is horny as hell.* She pushes me onto my back and straddles me. I take a deep, calming breath.

"Dollface, are you sure? I don't want you to do anything you're not ready for."

"Slender, shut up. I need you inside me now. I swear if I don't impale myself on you, I'll go stir crazy." Doing as I'm told, I smirk and shut up. My dollface. Love her so much. Especially when she's bossy and sassy.

I observe her face, my eyes locked on hers.

"Eyes on me," I instruct.

Nodding, she lifts, and her hand grabs my pulsing dick, guiding it to her entrance.

With her eyes locked on mine she slowly lowers herself down my cock until I'm fully seated inside her. My eyes roll back, and I struggle to keep them on hers, as much as I struggle not to fuck up into her, hard.

"Okay?" I ask her. Her only reply is a blinding smile and her raising and lowering.

When she sings 'Save a horse, ride a cowboy' and winks at me, I can't help the laughter bubbling up.

"Yee haw!" I blurt out and raise my hips to hers, fucking up into her for the first time, while we're both giggling like naughty preschoolers.

"Help me," she moans. I grab her hips with both hands and guide her up and down my shaft.

"Dollface, you're so tight, your pussy is strangling my dick. So hot," I groan between thrusts.

"You fill me up so good," she moans. "I love how you feel inside me. Love you, Slender, all of you. Need you closer, honey."

I take her cue and roll us over, with her now under me.

"Close enough?" I whisper, my forehead on hers, our lips so close they're almost touching, our breath mingling. Our eyes locked and unfocused. I fuck her deep, bumping against her cervix every time, eliciting little moans and whimpers. *God, my girl is so damn sexy.* It drives me insane. I want to savor finally being inside her, but her hot, wet, tight pussy is strangling my cock. I let her set a slow, deep sensual rhythm that has me panting within two seconds flat.

"Yes, just like that. Oh God, baby, I'm nearly there," she whispers, her eyes still locked on mine, and I know for certain she's here, with me, in the present. My heart is ready to burst with happiness and pride in my amazing woman.

I feel her fluttering against me, and my balls drawing up tight, the bottom of my spine erupting into fireworks. A long loud wail escapes my baby, then her walls clench me tight. On the second clench, I groan and explode deep inside the love of my life. This was not fucking; this was making love. Something special, like a tight band snapping between us anchoring us together. I know it sounds stupid and soft. My brothers would kick my ass for being so sentimental, but it's the only way I can describe it.

I look into her eyes and see my feelings mirrored in her freshly fucked green ones.

"Wow, honey, that was something else," she gasps as our breaths are calming. "Never thought anything could be so intense, so all-consuming."

I roll to my side, don't wanna crush her, wrap her in my arms, and pull her tight into me.

"Me neither, Ellie. I've loved you for so long. Never thought I'd be lucky enough to have a shot with you. Making love to you—with you, is the most special experience I've ever had," I reply, kissing her hair.

"When can we do it again?" she asks, and laughter bursts out of me.

"Dear God, I've created a sex monster."

She slaps my pecs quite hard, making my nipple sting in the best way.

"Feeling violent now, huh?" I smirk at her, rolling over her and settling between her legs, closing her laughing mouth with mine.

25 — ELLIE

Ever since I had my way with Slender, I carry a constant grin plastered across my face. Happiness lighting me up from the inside out. Against all my fears, I had no flashbacks, no dissociations. I stayed present the whole time. Slender made me feel things I never believed possible. Just thinking about his mouth on my clit makes me shiver. Admittedly, I'm quite sore and I think my hu-ha needs a break, before Slender destroys it completely.

Mel and I decide to spend the afternoon shopping. Ally, Sarah and Caroline join us in town.

"Hey, girlfriends!" Sarah shouts across the parking lot.

"Hi to you too," I reply, dragging Mel behind me and toward the girls.

"Coffee first," Ally decrees. "I can't deal with this lot without caffeine," she grumbles, giving Sarah and Caroline the stink eye.

"Stop bitching. You love us really, Ally-pally." Caroline smirks at her. Ally's brows draw together.

"Bitch, don't call me that, or I'll sing 'Sweet Caroline' see how you like it."

"So good, so good!" shouts Sarah.

Mel looks from one to the other as though they've grown two heads.

"Nutters, the lot of you," she says, shaking her head in disbelief.

I try to ignore the bickering behind me and walk to the nearest cafe in the mall. After we're all squeezed tight around a table in a booth, we give our orders to the server and wait.

"Ellie, you look different," Ally says. "If I didn't know better, I'd say you and Slender have been bumping uglies." She smirks at me.

I just look at my hands and smile.

"You so have, spill it, sister!" Caroline screeches, sure the whole place heard her.

"Sweeet Caroline!" I sing.

"Dum dum da…" Ally, Sarah and Mel join in.

"Shut it, bitches," Caroline grumbles.

"So good, so good, so good!" we all chorus. Well, apart from Caroline, who's shooting dagger eyes at us, while we struggle not to laugh while singing.

The bickering goes on, and I continue to refuse giving details about my newfound sex-life with Slender.

An hour later, tired and shopped out, Ally drags us into a beauty outlet store, where she stocks up on all sorts of wild hair colors. Mel and I browse the make-up counter while Sarah tries any bright red lipstick she can find.

"I'd like to get me some new perfume," Mel tells me. "Been years since I had anything new. I know I shouldn't waste my advance like this, but—"

"Stop right there," I interrupt. "You need this stuff, and it sure ain't wasting money. Now then, Missy, let's get you some perfume," I insist, dragging her out of the shop and next door to the perfume outlet. As we enter, Mel freezes on the spot and panic-stricken pulls me back, running into the beauty outlet, dragging me behind. I nearly stumble. She's that fast.

"What's wrong?" Ally races towards us, taking in Mel's state.

"It's him, it's him, it's him," Mel repeats to herself in an endless loop. I'm stumped and shocked. Can't figure out what on earth is going on?

"It's who, Mel?" Ally gently asks her.

"Th… e… G… g… uy… who nabbed me!" Mel stutters, becoming more and more hysterical.

"Where? Mel, where?" Ally holds Mel's face in both her hands, trying to get her to focus.

"Perfume counter…" Mel whispers.

"Stay with her," Ally orders. "Phone Raven."

Caroline is on the phone, and I'm holding Mel close while Sarah and Ally go next door to the perfume counter.

I can't help myself, push Mel towards Caroline, and follow Ally and Sarah.

They both stand at the counter, asking for various testers. There are three guys at the other end of the counter, talking amongst themselves while waiting for their purchases to be rung up. Ally spots me, gestures to me to take pictures. What the hell is she up to?

"Hey, guys, you look as though you have taste." She beams at them, walking straight up to them, while Sarah is left standing, with her mouth gaping open.

"This one? Or that one?" She lifts her wrist up to the guys, who step closer, sniffing her wrist. I take photos on my cell while she distracts them.

"This one," a deep, caramel smooth voice says. *Where have I heard that voice before?* I wrack my brain. Then the guy removes his sunglasses, smiling at Ally, and it hits me. That's

James Carpenter. He was a regular in the office and Stuart's client. *Oh shit!* He's related to the Carpenter empire! Some of the richest folks in the state. If he recognizes me, I'm done! He knows I've been working in Stuart's office. Panic-stricken, I turn on my heel and race back into the beauty shop, where Caroline is rocking Mel, and behind them, a furious Raven, followed by Vegas, Slender, and Fury are stomping up towards us, Dawg close on their heels.

"Where?" Not sure who growls at us, but I wouldn't want to cross them.

I tip my head towards the shop next door, but before they can march over there, Ally and Sarah return.

"Did you get the pictures?" Ally asks.

"Sure did," Sarah answers.

"I know the guy you spoke to," I croak.

"Which one? The blonde surfer dude? Or the Hispanic?" she queries.

"Both," I answer. "The blonde one is James Carpenter, and the Hispanic looking one— his name's Benito Lacasa. He was another of Stuart's clients. He runs a van delivery service out of Superior. Didn't know the third guy."

"Ben, I know that guy. He's the one who killed your friend after they took a turn on her. They took turns on all of us!" Mel sobs.

We miss the guys running next door. Only Dawg remains, his arm clutched tightly around Caroline.

Mel sobs uncontrollably.

"I'm sorry, I'm so sorry."

"What are you apologizing for, sweetie?" Ally softly asks Mel. "You have nothing to be sorry for, darlin', let's go get you home."

Payton Hunter © 2024

She places her arm around Mel, and we take her between us. The furious brothers, meanwhile, return.

"Fuck!" Raven shouts, drawing the sales assistant's attention.

"Please, sir, leave before I call security," her snobbish voice reaches us.

"Don't worry, we're leaving," Vegas throws at her. "In the future, we will take our business elsewhere," he adds. Not that it impressed the clerk any.

We grab our bags, and the men escort us to our vehicles, get on their bikes, and insist we follow them to the clubhouse. Nauseated, I think about Mel, Debs, and Amy. The horrors they went through, thanking my lucky stars that Amy wasn't with us today.

Back at the clubhouse, we are escorted straight into Raven's office.

We're met by Fury and Raven, who's pacing a hole in the floor; Slender takes me in his arms, checking me over, making sure I'm okay. I nod at him reassuringly.

Vegas returns from the bar with two glasses of double shots of whiskey. One for Mel, one for me. We pick them up and throw them down in one, the burn down my throat fortifying me.

The door flies open, and Ferret storms in. The guys are all talking over each other, anger getting the best of them.

"Calm the fuck down!" Ferret shouts into the room. "We need to go at this orderly. Losing our shit isn't helping anyone!"

He looks around with a wild look in his eye.

"Are the women alright?" He looks us all over, and with a nod from each of us, he relaxes a bit. He drops the laptop he'd been carrying under his arm on Raven's desk and sits down. Raven and Fury take a seat behind the desk and the rest of us just sit on the few remaining chairs. Slender pulls me up, sits, and drags me down into his lap. His warm and hard body infusing me with strength I didn't know I had. Dawg has Caroline on his lap, Pennywise, who joined us, leans against the wall. Fury's leg is restlessly bouncing. He struggles most with keeping his temper in check.

"Now then," Ferret says. "Start from the beginning.

Ally starts and tells Ferret what she knows.

Raven is furious.

"You did what?" he grates at her.

"Damn, woman, did you not think how dangerous that was? They could have taken you and Sarah!" he hollers at her.

"Keep your hair on, Raven, it's unlikely. They didn't know me, nor Sarah from Adam, we were perfectly safe, just two chicks testing perfumes," she hollers right back.

"Not to mention I got a good look at them, and Sarah took some photos," she finishes.

"No thanks needed either, Mr. '*my ass is on fire*'." Her sarcasm cuts as sharp as a knife, and I don't miss Raven flinch.

"She's got a point, man," Fury agrees with Ally.

"Hand me your phone?" Ferret demands. Sarah pulls it out of her pocket and drops it into his outstretched hand.

Within a minute, the pictures Sarah took are on his laptop screen.

"Fuck," he cusses.

"What is it?" Raven asks.

"This, my friend," he says, pointing at the Hispanic guy, "is Benito Lacasa."

"Should we know him?" Fury asks with a raised eyebrow.

Payton Hunter © 2024

"Yes, Fury, you should. Especially since he's related to the Cabal Cartel. Old man Orlando Cabal's grandson," Ferret explains.

"Holy fucking shit, you're fucking with me, right?" Fury jumps out of his chair, now pacing again.

"Nope." Ferret pops his p for good measure.

Fury takes his cell out and makes a call.

"Get your ass in here now!" he barks.

The mood in the room has changed drastically. I'm waiting for the icy wind and tumbleweed to run across the floor. It is that tense.

The door opens, and Masher strides in, waiting for Fury to put him in the picture. Raven holds up his hand.

"Ladies, since you are safe, there is no reason for you to stay. Mel, could you get with Ferret tomorrow and fill in any gaps in the story you already told us?"

"I can do that," she whispers, still shaking.

"Go home, ladies, no need for you to stay," Raven says, clearly wanting us out of their hair, so they can talk club business. *Man, I'm sick of hearing about club business.*

"Come on, Dollface, I'll walk you home." Slender puts me on my feet and leads me out of the office. Those are the first words he directly spoke to me since he arrived at the mall, and it pisses me off.

"I'm fine, thank you. Thanks for asking, by the way. I'm quite capable of making my own way home," I gripe at him. Yes, I know I sound like a petulant child.

He pulls on my arm and brings me to a screeching halt, catapulting me against his hard chest.

"Woman, don't start with this shit," he barks at me. "You scared the shit out of me when Raven ordered us to ride. I thought you were dead in a ditch somewhere, the worst scenarios running through my head. Mel recognized the guys, and what did you do? You watched Sarah taking pictures? Are you serious right now?"

I've never seen Slender this angry before. He's dragging me along behind him to the house, lets us in, drags me into the hall, slams me against the wall, and cages me. When his mouth crashes onto mine, it's pure fury radiating from him. And I'll be damned if it doesn't turn me the hell on. *What is wrong with me?*

"We talk later, when I can guarantee not to put you across my knee and spank your ass!" He growls as he lets me go, both of us panting hard.

"Asshole!" I can't help myself. It just slips out.

"Don't fucking push me, Ellie, not the time," he grates, turns on his heel, walks out, and slams the door. Hard. Tears are burning in the back of my throat and the whole stress of the situation crashes over me. I'm shaking and crying when I walk into the bathroom, turn on the faucet, and run a bath. I don't know how long I sit in there sobbing, but by the time I've calmed, the water has gone cold, and I have to run more hot water to wash the day off me. When I get out, utterly exhausted, I drag myself into the bedroom, climb into bed and fall asleep.

◊◊◊

Sunbeams dancing on my face tickle me awake. I turn to face Slender, only to find the space next to me empty and cold. It's six a.m., meaning he hasn't come to bed at all.

Throwing on a robe, I pad down the stairs, into the kitchen, starting a pot of coffee, before I walk into the living room, where on one of our oversized, overstuffed couches, Slender lays with his arm covering his eyes, gently snoring. I bend down and gently place a kiss on his chin. He grumbles and his arm falls away from his face. Placing a gentle kiss on his lips, his hand snakes around my neck, pulling me down to him.

"Morning, gorgeous," his sleep roughened voice murmurs into my ear.

"Whatcha doing on the couch?" I ask.

"Didn't wanna wake you, only got back in a couple of hours ago." He sighs, pulling me on top of him, my body covering his completely. I snuggle against him, sighing happily, feeling as though I've come home.

"Wanna talk about it, baby?" I ask, knowing full well that I'll get "*Club business, baby!*" To my surprise, he shuffles us upright, me sitting in his lap.

"Rode out last night, trying to find those cunts. Spend literally all night riding, searching high and low. Couldn't find them." Exhausted and bleary-eyed, he leans his head against the back of the couch. I can only imagine the frustration running through my man. As the club's SAA, he prides himself on keeping everyone safe, but this time, he feels he failed. Debs, me, Mel, and Amy, and the club as a whole. Knowing this, I lean into him, gathering his face in my hands, looking deep into his eyes.

"Baby, you know this doesn't reflect on you, right? Those men, they are criminals, hiding in plain sight. They've done this for some time. This is not on you, honey. You're doing the best you can, and you'll find them. Of that I'm certain." My reassuring words doing nothing for him. He lifts me off him and stands.

"That coffee?" he says, his head turning towards the kitchen, following the rich aroma emanating from there.

"No, actually, it's my new body wash, like it?" I wink at him.

Payton Hunter © 2024

"Minx." He smirks, walks past me, swatting my ass. Well, got a smile out of him, so I take that as a win. He walks straight to the coffeepot, grabs two cups and fixes them, while I open the fridge and getting breakfast ready. As I finish the pancakes, the front door opens.

Vegas, Raven, Chloe, and Ashley walk into the kitchen. Followed shortly after by Pennywise, who looks a lot worse for wear.

"You alright, Pen?" I throw at him.

"Fine, Ellie, just didn't get much sleep." He grins, stretching his arm over his head, baring his midriff.

"Phew," Ashleys says, fanning her face while staring at Penny's six pack.

Vegas elbows him in the ribs.

"What the fuck, man? Indecent exposure to pregnant ladies now?" he says as he holds his hand over Ashley's eyes, who laughs and slaps his hand away.

"Is that lipstick on your neck, Penny?" Chloe teases. Penny instantly raises his hand, rubbing his neck.

"Better fucking not be," he grumbles, to everyone's laughter.

"You carry on like that, ya little manwhore, it'll fall off," Raven winds him up.

"At least I'm not getting wived up, like you lot, not wearing my balls in a purse," Pennywise bats back.

"It'll happen one day, and I'll be there to watch the mighty fall," Vegas wisecracks.

"And anyway, my balls are way too big for Ashley's purse, so speak for yourself, teeny - weeny."

I shake my head at this unruly lot. Good job I made plenty of pancakes. Ashley slaps a tray of bacon on the counter, and Chloe brought eggs.

Payton Hunter © 2024

"Thought we'd contribute to breakfast," Chloe states while rooting through cupboards to find a bowl to scramble eggs in.

"Pregnant woman, out of my way," Ashley declares, shoves Penny off his bar stool, and takes a seat. "Heathen," she exclaims, while Pennywise struggles to regain his balance and not fall on his ass.

Breakfast is a banter-filled fun affair. I look around me and see so much love, laughter, commitment. It fills my heart to the brim. This is what family is supposed to look like.

The love, respect and loyalty displayed right in front of me makes me realize how lucky I am to call this bunch of misfits my friends—my family.

26 — SLENDER

I'm still fucked off to hell with Ellie. How could she be so stupid? Going into that shop, watching Sarah taking pictures? Now Ally, I expect this kinda stuff from, but Ellie? After what she experienced? Shit, if anyone had recognized her, she could be directly in their line of fire now. I know chances are slim, since Tucker took care of Maxwell, and he was the only one there in the woods, but there is no telling whether he got a message to his compadres while down in the cells. We can't be certain of anything at this point. The thought of anything happening to Ellie makes my skin crawl. It'd destroy me.

Bad enough I couldn't protect Debs. I'll never forgive myself for not having insisted to Spen that the club needed to look for her. I'm the SAA; I'm supposed to keep everyone safe. My family suffered because of my decision, and within the space of a few months, we had to attend not one, but two funerals for our family members.

When I found out she took pictures, I wanted to throw her over my shoulder and spank her ass raw. It took everything I had not to flip on the spot.

We mounted a hunting party last night. All members rode out to search Duluth, Superior, and surrounding areas for these guys, joined by the Restless Slayers contingent, who seem to have made their home here now, which grates on me no end. Wherever I turn I stumble across one of them, not to mention they brought Tanya and Meghan, which as far as I can tell are in as much danger as our girls, if only by association. I didn't believe either Masher or Fury to be so goddamn stupid, but here we are.

Pennywise keeps butting heads with Tanya, which isn't helping matters, neither is the way Masher is constantly glowering at him. The whole situation sets my teeth on edge. The tension is palpable. I'd much rather we'd handle this ourselves, but finding out that Benito Lacasa is involved, threw not just a spanner but a whole workshop in the works. The Cabal Cartel is way too big for us to tackle. Even on the off chance that Benito has gone out on his own, his connections make it necessary for the Slayers to be involved. They have relationships, however tentative, to the Cabal Cartel. We need them if we don't want this to turn into an all-out war.

And that pisses me the fuck off.

We spent an age last night in church trying to work out a plan on how to get them. Ferret is doing his darndest, working with Ghost, his restless Slayers' counterpart. Don't think either of them have slept much since Ghost arrived.

We've got guys riding out every night, making connections, squeezing our informants, asking questions, letting it be known Slayers are interested in the skin trade. That's our plan so far, couldn't think of anything better.

The girls are clueless, thank fuck. Ellie would put a contract for my castration out to Tanya without a second thought. The sick shit is, Tanya would do it. That woman is scary fierce.

Planning on keeping the girls as far away from this shit as possible.

◊◊◊

Payton Hunter © 2024

Every seat in church is taken with the officers of both clubs. Fury, Masher, Ghoul, and Ghost are joining Raven, Vegas, Pennywise, Dawg, Ferret, Clusseaud, and myself around the table. We've kept it to 'officers only' meetings and those are difficult enough to keep on track.

Everyone is eager to get their hands on those sick bastards.

"I spoke to old man Cabal," Fury opens the discussion today.

"Orlando had no clue about what shit his blood was pulling. He agrees. This can't be happening. For him, it draws attention to his businesses, and he's pissed. He guaranteed no blow back for Slayers or Souls. He wants this handled."

"Cabal deals in coke and weapons, not flesh. Flesh trade they see as extremely unsavory," Ghoul adds.

"His lieutenant is getting back to us with a location for Benito." Fury looks around the table. "They can't be seen to be involved, since it's family. They have to keep their asses lily-white on this. So, putting a stop to this is up to us."

Ghoul's phone rings. He holds up his hand and answers.

"Yup?" … "Aha" … "Yeah, got it, hang on." He grabs Dawgs pad and pen and starts scribbling.

"Sure" … "Will do, Tone, catch ya later. And Tone?" … "Thanks, man, we owe you one."

He looks around the table, clicking the pen, shoving it over the table towards Dawg. Then a face splitting grin appears on his face before he yells, "Gotcha!"

Whoops and whistles break out around the table, a lot of table slaps and everyone talking makes it impossible to hear anything specific. Raven bangs the gavel several times.

"Settle down, Let Ghoul speak," he orders and everyone calms.

Payton Hunter © 2024

"According to Tone, there's four of them: Stuart Maxwell, James Carpenter, Benito Lacasa, and Ernest Digby," he says.

"You're shitting me," Dawg groans. "Digby? As in Ernest Digby Haulage? Fuck! I worked for the cunt for a few weeks! He has his fingers in many pies. Container shipping, long-haul freight, short haul, you name it, he does it. Even runs his own parcel service. That guy is loaded, and his reach is far and wide. If he's involved, it'll be like finding a needle in a haystack."

"Good job Tone has a guy digging then," Ghoul replies and turns to Fury. "Orlando is seriously pissed. He wants this stopped but can't be seen to do it himself. He sanctioned Tone to get some guys on a fact-finding mission and relay the info straight to us. No marker either." He nods at Fury.

Ghost and Ferret throw pictures onto the screen behind Raven, Vegas, Fury, and Ghoul. I groan as I see photos of a huge haulage yard next to a container port, next to other Digby businesses. Underneath, photos of Maxwell, Digby, Lacasa, and a mugshot of Carpenter fill the screen.

"Carpenter has a record as long as my arm," Ghost adds and replaces the mugshot with a rap sheet.

"Sexual assault, taking a minor across state lines, indecent exposure, attack on an officer, and a boatload of misdemeanors." He whistles through his teeth.

"Lookie here, he's done ten years for transporting a minor across state lines in 'Big Sandy' Pen, Kentucky. Ladies, I think we have the head of our fucker brigade right here on a platter."

"Not yet, but it soon will be," Raven grates, looks at his cell, then bangs his gavel. "Meeting adjourned until three p.m. this afternoon. Get lunch and have a think about how we'll best catch those motherfuckers."

◊◊◊

By the time we had the bare roots of a plan, midnight had come and gone. Dog tired and in a rotten mood, we all made our way to our beds. Ellie is fast asleep, Tucker laying at her feet in the bed.

"Tucker, off the bed! Get down!" I hiss at him, to which he growls at me, yawns, and continues to snore. *Alright then, no action for me tonight.* I throw my cut over the chair by my side of the bed, kick off my boots, and move my ass into the bathroom, where I lose the rest of my clothes and take a quick shower. In my mind, I go back over the plan. This thing is too big for us alone. Even with the Restless Slayers at our back. That much we came to realize tonight. We need an in with Rigby. That's gonna be the most troublesome part. Word on the street is that quiet reigns. No more missing girls, at least for now. We also need to get eyes on Carpenter and Lacasa.

Raven and Fury are following up that lead with Neil, our bar manager and ex-military. Dawg could pass as a driver for Rigby haulage, but we need to get someone into the office there. That'll be the toughest part of the plan. Never mind the sickening fact that we need to find someone to act as a buyer.

Bile burns in the back of my throat just thinking about it. If we pose as buyers, we're potentially putting more women at risk, as it'll likely force their hand to abduct more. My mind runs in circles, and I can't find a second's peace. Taking my pacing downstairs, not to disturb

Ellie, I walk to the fridge, pop a beer, and grab a bottle of Bourbon out the cupboard, filling a glass.

I throw half of it back in one go, relishing the burn, flop onto the living room couch, beer in one hand, whiskey on the table, and run a frustrated hand through my long hair, still knotted from toweling. I lean forward, grab my tumbler, and take a deep drag. My feet hit the table as I lean my head back and close my eyes. I can't keep my thoughts in line. They're racing from one corner of my mind to the other. A cold nose lands on my chest and makes me jump.

Tucker, good boy, knows Daddy is out of sorts. He snuggles closer, his huge body crushing my legs as he plonks himself onto my lap.

"Oof, you're getting heavy, boy, gotta stop feeding you Prospects." Tucker looks at me with a smile. Folks think dogs don't smile; I beg to differ. Tucker is clearly laughing at me. He got the Prospect joke.

Two small, warm hands grip my shoulders from behind. I inhale and can smell her sweet scent.

"Hey, honey, it's late. Can't you sleep?" she whispers in my ear.

"Nah, Dollface, my mind is running a marathon in circles. Can't get it to shut off."

"Long meeting, honey, can I help?"

"Dollface, just be yourself. That's all I need," I tell her, tilting my head back. She lowers her head and traces her soft lips across mine.

"Lay on your front," she instructs, and I oblige. A huge breath sighs out of me when her hands knead my neck and shoulders, which are solid and knotted. She tenderly works my strained muscles, and for the first time today, I'm able to relax a little.

Payton Hunter © 2024

"Love you, Dollface, your hands are magic," I half groan half mumble with my head buried in the couch cushion.

"Love you too, big man. Glad I can help." I can hear her smile and know her eyes are crinkled in amusement, even though I can't see it.

"Ah, yes, just there, baby, a little lower," I direct her towards my lower back. She pulls the towel I'd slung around my waist out of the way, leaning down, blowing a warm breath over my taut buttocks. *Holy hell, that is hot.* Even without touching me, she gets me hard in two seconds flat. I groan at her heavenly ministrations, just about ready to either hump the couch, or throw her under me and love the hell out of her. Until Tucker's nose dives between my cheeks and takes a sniff. Never moved so quick in my life.

"Tucker, you dirty bastard!" I shout, watching Ellie laying on her back on the floor, laughing and thumping her fists, rolling around, howling, coughing.

"Good boy, Tucker," she gasps between laughing and coughing, tears running down her face, and Tucker? He sits in front of me, staring at me with his big smile, tongue hanging out and tail wagging. *Fuck my life.* All I can do is watch Ellie and Tucker and let the pressure inside of me out in roaring laughter.

◊◊◊

"What crawled up your ass?" I ask Pennywise, who's sitting at the bar next to me. He's been in a filthy mood for weeks now.

"None of your fucking business."

"Woh, man, chill the fuck out," I tell him. His snarky reply really getting up my nose.

"What the fuck is wrong with you lately? Need to get laid, man?" I ask.

"Sorry, bro, got problems, man. Nothing I want to talk about, so just leave it, yeah?" he replies. His face looking like a smacked ass.

"Seriously, man, you need to get laid or lighten up. The brothers are all traipsing around you, avoiding you, and the women are much the same. Ellie asked me what's going on with you. Everyone's noticed."

"Slender, telling you, leave it be, man. Don't need you to do your '*Dr. Phil*' routine. Bad enough, Mom is riding my ass. Don't need your input, either," he growls at me. *Seriously? He did not just growl at me.*

"Talk to me like that again, Pen, and I'll see you in the ring. Might be the best way to get whatever it is out of your system."

"Don't fucking push me, brother, or you'll find yourself on your ass in a hot second!"

Vegas appears outta nowhere, putting his hand on Pennywise's shoulder.

"I suggest you get your ass out into the fresh air and calm the fuck down. Sick of your PMS. Get a grip, we have enough shit on our plate, don't need you running your mouth." Vegas stands his ground, looking Pen straight in the eyes, eyes narrowed to slits.

"Fuck you!" Pen spits at him, standing toe to toe. Vegas draws himself up to his full height until Pennywise's shoulders slump. He turns on his heel and stomps out of the building.

"Shit, what's up with him?" I ask Vegas, who shrugs his shoulders.

"If I didn't know better, I'd say bitch trouble."

I smirk.

"Didn't know he had a bitch to be troubled about."

"Only thing I can think of, man. Gotta shoot. On a carrot cake run, for her indoors."

"Man, you're so pussy whipped." I laugh at him.

Payton Hunter © 2024

"You wait until Ellie's pregnant, hormonal, and horny as hell." He smirks. "See if you don't happily go on craving runs, man. I'll be the one laughing at you, then."

Ellie? Pregnant? I'm surprised I'm not running out the clubhouse screaming. Instead, I visualize Ellie growing my child in her. A little girl with red hair and green eyes. My heart melts. Gonna have to talk to her about this; wanna put my baby in her soon, build a family with Ellie.

Lost in thoughts, I don't notice Dawg approaching.

"Hey, man, just wanting to let you know I won't be available for security in the next few months. You pay me shit, hence I had to take a job as a container driver at Digby Haulage. Starting on Monday," he says.

"That easy? That quick?" I ask him.

"Yup." He pops the p. "Easy as that. No in-depth background check or nothing. Accepted my references without even checking them out, since I've driven for him before."

"Now we just gotta get someone to get into the office," I reply.

"That'll be easy. His office wench told me she's only part-time. Amazing what a bit of flirting and taking her out for a coffee can do." He winks at me.

"For fuck's sake, don't let Caroline hear you. You'll be the dickless wonder," I warn him, only half joking.

"Nah, not that stupid. Told her I took one for the team. She's not happy but understands it's for club business. Will cost me an expensive holiday though." He shrugs.

"It'll cost you your dick, old man, if I find out you did anything else but take that bitch to coffee. You got off lightly with that holiday, which I will book, and you will pay for." None of us noticed Caroline sneaking up behind Dawg. It's only when she slaps him round the back of the head and cackles like the wicked witch from the East that we notice her. Damn, we must be more careful with all the women hanging around the clubhouse.

Dawg just laughs at her, throws his arm across her shoulder, and plants a seriously X-rated kiss on her.

I turn and walk towards Raven, gesturing to join me in his office. He nods at me in understanding.

"Dawg is in," I tell him, as the door closes behind Raven.

"Good, that's one thing off the list," he answers. "Now we just need to work out who to plant in his office and how."

"Dawg mentioned the office bitch is only part-time, so getting someone in shouldn't be difficult, just a question of who?" I muse. "I don't know anyone we could ask, fitting the bill."

"Who do we know with office experience? Can't plant anyone green, that would scream suspicious. How about Ellie? She's experienced?" Raven asks.

"No, no fucking way! Over my dead body!" I yell at him. If he thinks I'll let Ellie anywhere near this, he's got another thing coming. My fist into his face. President or not, I don't give a fuck.

"Calm down, asshole. I didn't mean for her to go in. I meant asking her if she knows anyone trustworthy. Settle down, dickweed," he growls at me.

"Our women have no business being involved in this, in any way, shape or form," I growl back at him, pissed beyond belief.

"I agree, Slender, but what other options have we got? Other than ask either Ally, see if someone in the Wild Pixies would be suitable, or Ellie if she knows anyone. It's the most difficult part of the plan," Raven replies, rubbing his hands over his tired face.

Much as I hate it, he has a point. With a sigh, I get out my cell and shoot a text to Ally and Ellie. We need help with this. None of the brothers can be spared, nor would pass as an office wench. Let's hope either Ally or Ellie come through.

27 — ELLIE

Ever since we discovered those dirtbags in town two weeks ago, I, or rather we, have had a shadow assigned to us, whenever we're not on club property. The brothers are totally overreacting. I feel sorry for Caleb, the cute Prospect, as he pushes my cart in the grocery store.

"Sorry, Caleb, you must be bored out of your mind by now," I apologize.

"No, ma'am, it's fine. I don't mind. Gotta keep everyone safe."

"Caleb, please, don't call me ma'am, I'm not *that* old. Call me Ellie."

"No, ma'am, no can do. My grandmother would turn in her grave."

Oh my God, he's adorable! Caleb's been prospecting for a few weeks now, but hasn't lost his yes, sir, no, sir, yes, ma'am, no, ma'am manners, which is refreshing to say the least. He holds open doors, lets us women walk through ahead of him, never swears when we're around— he's almost too good to be true. I want to shake his mama's hand for bringing up such a superb specimen of a man. Him being around is no chore, and it helps that he's easy on the eye too. I'm so lost in my thoughts, I don't notice the other cart come screeching around the end of the aisle.

"Oof." The impact knocks the wind out of me.

"Oops, Ellie, sorry, I thought you saw me," a very guilty looking Ally tells me. "Sorry, hon. Didn't mean to attack you."

"Hey, Ally, I was miles away. No need for apologies." I wave it off.

"Ellie, was gonna ring you later, but now that I've got you here, do you fancy a girls' night soon? I know we can't go out, but we could have our girls' night at the clubhouse. Dancing, jukebox, and lots of tequila! The drink variety, not the club bunny." Ally smirks.

"Sounds like a great idea. We could all do with letting off some steam. Who else is coming?"

Ally thinks for a moment. "I've asked Ashley, Chloe, Sarah,"—she points her finger at me—"you, Caroline, Jules, and was thinking about asking Tanya? Since she's here so often."

"Sounds like a great line-up. Count me in. Who's Jules though, never heard of her?" I ask.

"Oh, she's one of my girls. She needs to meet with Raven, and I thought we'd kill two birds with one stone. She can meet him and then join us for a few drinks."

"Great, just let me know when," I reply, wave at Ally and push the cart on.

Ally winks at me, pointing at Caleb, fanning herself. Yes, Caleb is hot. Scorching hot.

◊◊◊

"Tucker, sit!" I command. No way is he going to jump up on Tanya. He's a big boy, he would throw her over.

"Oh, you great big cutie pie!" Tanya squats down next to Tucker. "Who's my good boy? Who's my good boy?"

Why do people do that? I roll my eyes. *Baby language? Really?* In response, Tucker wags his tail and licks Tanya's face.

"Oohh, lovely kisses, yes, good boy, lovely kisses," she encourages him, while Tucker slobbers all over her, treating Tanya like a long-lost friend. I can't help it. my heart swells a little watching Tucker with Tanya.

"Hey, Tanya, come in," I invite her, opening the door wider, letting her walk past me into the entrance hall.

"Wow, Ellie, this place is gorgeous!" Tanya exclaims, looking around our kitchen. She pulls up a stool by the island and hops on.

"Coffee?" I gesture to the pot.

"Yes, please, need a pick me up." Despite her grin, the dark circles under her eyes tell their own story.

Over the past few weeks, Tanya and Masher have spent a lot of time here with the club. Not sure why, but Tanya seems to be always around. She's become more or less part of the girls' clique. Which in itself is weird, considering she's from a different club. A one percenter club no less, wearing their diamonds with pride. Somehow, she just fits in though, and despite our differences, we're becoming friends. Unlikely friends, but friends, nevertheless.

"What's up, chick? You look like you've been hit by a bus?" I ask her.

"Wow, thanks, friend, I think. Nothing's up as such, just not sleeping well."

"Anything you want to talk about?" I look at her expectantly.

"Nah, Ellie, nothing you can do, nothing anyone can do. Just gotta sort my life out. Dad wants me to think about taking an old man, but I'm just not up for it. I want to run my own life, choose my own friends and certainly my own man, not be *'guided'* by my father… I'm my own person, you know?" she finally tells me.

I get it. I wouldn't want anyone to make my choices for me. Rusty tried and failed, but nearly broke me in the process. However, Masher isn't Rusty. It's clear he loves Tanya and wants what he believes is best for her. Unfortunately, his opinion and Tanya's seem to be miles apart.

"I don't know what to say, Tanya," I commiserate. "Must be difficult. Is he pushing you?"

"No, not really, he drops hints now and then, but pressuring me? No, can't say that he is."

"Maybe you're overthinking this?" I suggest.

"Maybe, but I don't believe so. Thing is, Ellie, I want to live, have fun, experiment, experience life to the full. I'm only twenty-two. I want to enjoy the best years of my life before I settle down. Life is for living, you know?"

"How's Meghan?" I ask, making a deliberate decision to change the subject.

"She's doing well. A bit stifled by Fury keeping such close tabs on her. She literally can't turn around without someone on her ass. If it's not Fury himself, it's a Prospect or a member. She has no life other than when I drag her with me over here. Fury will let her go with me; he trusts me to keep her safe. Which can be awkward, because I sometimes feel like her safety enforcer, rather than her best friend."

Sounds like Tanya has a lot on her plate.

"I'm so glad she is doing well but I can't help feeling guilty every time I see Meghan," I admit quietly.

"Don't you dare do this, Ellie, don't you dare." Tanya looks me straight in the eye. "It wasn't you; it was Rusty. You had nothing to do with all that, weren't even in the same county, never mind anything else. You're not responsible for any of it."

I know she's right, but I can't help the way I feel. The guilt sits deep and nags on me. Darcie calls it survivor's guilt, and we're working on it, but it's a work in progress—*I'm a work in progress.*

"Okay, so let's talk about Ashley's baby shower. What's the plan?"

"Erm, I don't think there is one," I tell Tanya.

"Well, that's just shocking. We need to sort it, girlfriend. She's not got long left. I bet Vegas is crapping himself." Tanya giggles. "Do they know what they're having?"

"Nope, they want it to be a surprise, but we have a pool going. Dawg started it. I predicted a six-pound girl." I wink at Tanya.

"Wow, must find Dawg later and chip in."

"We can discuss a baby shower tonight, maybe?" I suggest. Tanya nods in agreement.

I nearly drop my coffee cup when the doorbell gives me the fright of a lifetime. Tanya falls about laughing as I place my shaking hand on my heart, then my almost-spilled coffee onto the island, and walk to the door. A pissed-looking Pennywise stares at me.

"She here?" he grunts. I punch my hand on my hip, cock it, and don't even try to keep the sarcasm out of my voice.

"Oh, hello to you too, Pennywise. What a lovely day. Can I help you at all?" Beaming a saccharine sweet smile at him.

He has the good grace to look embarrassed.

"Is Tanya here? Masher is looking for her. I don't have time to play errand boy," he gripes. Tanya appears behind me in the doorway.

"What's up" she asks. Man, her tone is colder than Elsa's castle.

My head is ping ponging from one to the other, watching their exchange.

"Get in touch with your dad. Let him know where you are," he rebukes her.

"What the fuck?" Tanya hisses at him.

"I ain't his messenger. Got more important shit to do," he growls back at her.

"You better take your tiny little ass away from here then, before I kick it for you," Tanya snarks.

"Huh, you and whose army? Grow up, for fuck's sake," he volleys back, turns on his heel, and marches back down the path towards the clubhouse. *What in the hell just happened?*

"Asshole!" Tanya shouts after him, before she rips the door out of my hand and slams it shut, leaving me outside, on my own porch, feeling bewildered.

◊◊◊

The clubhouse is rammed as usual on a Saturday evening. Tanya, Caroline, Sarah, Ashley, Chloe, and I are already there, at our usual table, starting the evening with a round of shots. Well, all apart from Ashley, who is nursing an orange juice.

"So"—I look at Ashley—"let's talk baby shower."

"No, please," she groans. "No baby shower for me. The mere thought of having to play games, everyone drinking when I can't, and waddling around all day makes me want to vomit. Not to mention that I maxed Vegas' credit card out, doing baby shopping last weekend." She winks at us. "He'll have a shit fit when he gets the statement." She laughs.

"Shit fit about what, princess?" Vegas sneaks up on Ashley, wrapping his arms around her from behind.

"Nothing, dear." She smiles serenely at him.

"Not long until your daughter is here," Sarah teases him.

"No way, it's a strapping boy, playing football in there on the regular." Vegas's protest is instant.

"Well, I guess we'll all soon see. Four weeks is not long to go," Chloe adds.

"Sure," I agree, downing another tequila shot. It warms me from the inside out and I feel great, laughing and chatting away with the girls.

"Welcome, lovely ladies!" Caroline calls over to Ally and Jules, who are both making their way towards our table. Ally does the introductions. Jules plonks down next to Ally, who places a tray of orange juice and a vodka bottle down on the table.

"Jeez, this is torture," groans Ashley. "At least you could have brought me some carrot cake to keep me entertained, while you're all getting sloshed."

"Ta-da!" shouts Caroline and pulls half a carrot cake out from underneath the table. "Never say I don't look after you, friend." She smirks at Ash.

Vegas snorts, rolls his eyes, and walks back to the bar.

"God, his ass is hot!" I hear myself say. *Oops, looks like Wine Ellie is making an appearance.* Ashley looks at me and bursts out laughing.

"It is, isn't it? I get to see and grab it every night! Not just his ass, though. That man has skills." You could have heard a pin drop at the table. Everyone staring at Ashley.

"What?" she asks. "He knocked me up within twenty seconds flat. That man has super sperm! None of this pump, dump and roll stuff for us. No, sir!" she exclaims. By which time, we're all roaring with laughter. Tanya, so much so she has tears rolling down her face.

"Oh, G… God… can't breathe," she stutters, choking with laughter.

Jules elbows me and points at Caleb behind the bar.

"Who's that tall glass of chocolate buttons? Wouldn't mind being in his pole position."

"Sister, he's a Prospect, unlikely he knows what to do with his pole," Ally jokes.

"Never too young to learn. With him, I might take pole dance classes." She smirks.

I burst out laughing. "Look at that big dude at the bar, to the left of Fury. Tell me he doesn't look like Hagrid," I whisper shout.

"That's Bear, one grumpy-ass fucker. He's a member of our club," Tanya informs me. "He's evil and tough as hell," she carries on.

I get up, swaying slightly on my feet. One of the four shots I've had, must have been off.

"No way," I tell Tanya.

"What are you up to?" She furrows her eyebrows.

Not listening to her at all, I run through the clubhouse, storming towards the gigantic monster of a guy who turns round, watching me approach, a puzzled look on his face. I trip over my own feet, throw my arms out inadvertently, fall onto the big guy, hug him, and shout: "HAGRID!"

He looks at me as if I crawled out from under a stone, laughs, hugs me back, spins me around, turns me towards our table, and gives me a gentle shove to set me on my way. Maybe time to lay off the shots, at least for a while. I can't stop the giggles, despite slapping a hand in front of my mouth.

Ally stands and shouts: "Attention, Wine Ellie is in da house!"

"Shots!" Caroline yells.

"My turn," Sarah insists, and sways to the bar with the tray.

"That's my song!" I shout, humming happily.

Jules leans towards Ally. "Does she know there's no music?"

"Beats me." Ally shrugs her shoulders.

Payton Hunter © 2024

Sarah returns with another tray of shots. She looks around the table and asks, "What's the difference between a Harley and a vacuum cleaner?"

"No idea," Tanya answers.

"The position of the dirt bag." Sarah winks. Chloe cackles.

"I got one." I smirk. "What's the most dangerous part of a motorcycle?"

"The nut that connects the seat to the handlebar…" Caroline answers. "That's an old one."

"You getting into mischief, Dollface?" Slender's voice in my ear makes me shiver. That man is just so hot.

"Hey, you sexy beast." I smile at him. "Take me home, stud, your pole needs to meet my ho—" Suddenly I'm upside down.

"Don't finish that sentence!" Slender growls at me. I push myself up as he walks us out of the door and wave at the old ladies' table—smirk on my face—to their hollering and whistling.

28 — SLENDER

It's seven p.m. and yet another church meeting. Can't be helped, I know that, but, man, I spend more time in church than anywhere else lately. I left Ellie sleeping this morning. My Wine Ellie was lit last night, and I reaped the benefits. Still getting the shivers remembering. My woman is a wildcat in bed when drunk. The scratches sting on my back, but hell, it was worth it. Good job we made it home and into our bedroom, else the brothers would have lodged noise complaints.

Still smirking, I rip open Pennywise's door. The fucker needs to get his ass into church. Everyone's waiting. The noises greeting me, make porn look tame.

"Oi, shithead, drop the patch whore and get your ass into church," I shout as I step into his bedroom. *That'll piss him off.*

"What the fuck, man!" he yells, throwing a boot at me. I close the door, laughing. *Hang on, was that?* No, no way. He wouldn't be *that* stupid.

The door flies open.

"Patch whore? Are you fucking kidding me? Patch whore?" A furious Tanya, whole body vibrating, stares me right in the eye while screaming and jabbing a finger in my face. I shrink back, valuing my balls. Knowing only too well just what she's capable of.

Pennywise appears behind her.

"Calm down, woman. Gotta get to church, don't need your drama. Time for you to go."

His growl makes me stiffen. Does he have a death wish? He must have, since he's obviously been fucking not just Restless Slayers MC property, but their SAA's daughter. The SAA sitting in church at this very moment.

"I gotta ask, brother? Are you nuts? Want to end up in a shallow grave? What the fuck?" I tell him, shaking my head in disbelief.

"None of your fucking business," he snaps back at me. "You gonna rat?" He moves, standing nose to nose with me.

"Brother, your business, not mine to yak about. Your funeral." With a shrug of my shoulders and a smirk, I turn and walk back down towards the clubhouse, hearing my brother behind me, taking deep breaths.

◊◊◊

"'Bout fucking time," Fury growls as we walk in and take our places. "Need a babysitter? Or think you can honor us with your presence." Fury's dark, pissed-as-fuck eyes shooting daggers at Pennywise, whose hands rise trying to placate the Restless Slayers' Prez.

"Fucking playschool, you got going on here," Fury gripes at Raven.

"Right, brothers and sisters." His sarcastic tone could strip the paint off the walls. It's only then that I notice Ally and Jules having joined us at the table. Fury's not a happy camper, needing the help of the Wild Pixies WMC.

"Can leave, brother?" Ally's equally caustic voice replies with a raised eyebrow.

"How about you put your shovels and spades away and stop the *kindergarten* games? No hair pulling or shin kicking needed in this room," I boom at them, thoroughly fed up with their antics.

"Let's get this over with. Got an Old Lady at home and better things to do." Right now, I don't give a fuck. Just want this over and done with, so I can spend some time watching Ellie's lush lips closing around my dick.

Raven slams the gavel down, and the room calms, with the official meeting start. Everyone is on edge. We need to find those motherfuckers, not fight amongst ourselves. Priorities.

"Okay, so here's an update," Raven says. "Dawg is in with Digby Haulage, driving container freight. He's been playing nice with their office chick. She told him they're looking for a full-time office assistant, since Digby has been expanding."

"Fucker!" "Bastard" sound from the table.

"Ally suggested we send Jules, since no one wants an Old Lady in that position." Raven's declaration is met with stunned silence. Ally and Jules nod at him.

"I used to be a transport office manager," Jules adds. "My cousin went missing years ago. She was only twelve. I can't help her, but I want those motherfuckers found and dealt with. Anything I can do, I will."

"We won't be able to babysit or protect you when you're at Digby's," Masher says.

"No need. I can look after myself." Jules nods at Masher. That's when I notice her Sergeant at Arms tape. Didn't even realize Wild Pixies had one.

"Gonna throw fake nails at them?" Fury scoffs.

"I can shoot your ass from a mile away, dickhead. Oo-rah!" Her outburst shuts up Fury, and everyone else murmuring around the table.

"Marine Corps?" Raven asks.

"Yup, sniper," Jules answers, shrugging her shoulders.

"I think I'm in love." Ratchet smirks.

"Shut up!" Dawg hollers

"Got your shit together, Jules?" Dawg asks her.

"Yup, all my documents, references, portfolio, all ready to go. Even got an interview Monday morning," she replies.

"Right"—Fury stands—"old man Cabal has come through with info. He's had Tone digging. The way they operate is, they snatch women to order, then wait until they have enough orders to make a container worthwhile. They use fold-up cots, army rations, and bottled water, making sure the cargo arrives wherever it's going alive."

I shudder at his words, bitter bile rising in the back of my throat, remembering the underground cells and their stench.

"I found them on the dark web," Ferret spits.

"We must be in control. Question is how?" Ghoul asks.

"Only way is to pose as a buyer and place an order." Fury shrugs.

All heads turn towards him. Mumbling rises around the table. Unease so thick you could cut it with a blunt knife.

"You sure?" Ghost checks, laptop open in front of him.

"See no other way, but if the brothers have a better idea, bring them forward." Fury runs his hands through his hair, visibly uncomfortable. You could have heard a pin drop. Silence reigns supreme in the room.

"Do it," he commands.

The only noise in the room is the clacking of keys on Ghost's laptop.

"Just put in an order for a slim blonde, a redhead, and a brunette. Late twenties-early thirties. Delivery to Dubai, time scale: four weeks," Ghost confirms. "Have to consider shipping times if we want to make it believable. Found one of their former customers," he continues. "Used him for a fake reference."

He smirks at Ferret. "Clever hacking, brother."

"I hate having to put more women at risk, lets pray we don't have blood on our hands. That won't sit right. The whole thing doesn't sit right," Pennywise says.

"I hear you, brother," Masher agrees, "but what other choice is there? None. I can promise, other than those motherfuckers *will* die. We will deal with it since we have the 'Grandpa' connection. Orlando has expectations and we can't have this impact on our business."

"Suits us," Raven says. "We'll help. Want our shot at the bastards, though. For Debs." Nods all around the room.

Raven slams his gavel and the meeting closes. Everyone files out and into the bar.

"Hold up." I grab Pennywise's arm as he squeezes past me.

If looks could kill, I'd be a shriveled heap of ash on the floor. I grab two beers from behind the bar and Penny's arm, dragging him outside. We walk around the back of the building and sit on top of a picnic table.

"What's going on?" I ask him. He groans and shoves his hand through his hair, pulling it.

"Fuck!" he shouts. "I got myself into a right fucking mess. Been fucking Tanya on and off since the rally. One and done, but on a frequent basis." He scoffs, looking at his boots.

"Don't want no Old Lady, don't want complications. It was a stupid drunk thing that got out of hand. Now I'm struggling to get out of it. She must have a magic pussy," he jibes, more at himself than me.

Payton Hunter © 2024

"Masher is gonna gut me. Fucking idiot me, had to be *his* daughter, didn't it? I dicked her at the rally, but the way she dealt with Rusty? Man, that made me hot under the collar for all the wrong reasons. Now I can't stop."

"You gotta stop, man. If Masher finds out, you're dead. Right now, I'd say dead man walking. Does she see it as one and done on repeat?" I question.

"Fucking hope so."

"Hope ain't gonna cut it, Pen. You need to know for sure."

"Wish it was as easy as that."

My head swivels to him so fast, my eyes have trouble catching up with my head.

"What d'ya mean?" I ask, smelling trouble.

Pennywise's lips press into a thin line. He stands, kicking gravel.

"Never mind, got me in this mess, will get out of it, one way or the other." He pats my shoulder, turns, and leaves.

What in the hell is he playing at? Pennywise's been my best friend since childhood. I hate him feeling he can't trust me. Equally, I hate having to keep his secret. Feeling like I'm disrespecting not only Masher, but my club, rubs me the wrong way. As SAA, it's my job to keep the club safe, and I can see a rough ride ahead with the Restless Slayers being die-hard one percenter, and us desperately trying, mostly, to stay on the right side of the law, despite not willingly involving the law in our business. Relations are strained as it is. It will only take a tiny spark to guarantee a major explosion of this half-full gas tank called a bond between our two clubs. We all must tread carefully. Fucking the Restless Slayers SAA's daughter isn't that.

Payton Hunter © 2024

In autopilot mode, I start walking, ending up at my own front door. Ellie's Explorer isn't in the driveway, and Tucker greets me with a wagging tail. After letting him out to do his business, I walk into the kitchen, where Ellie's note sits on the counter.

'Out with the girls, having a girls' night. Don't wait up. Love you, Ellie xoxoxo.'

Smiling, I grab the note, walk into the bedroom, shed off my clothes, and step into the inviting heat of the shower. Steam envelops me, melting away the day's tension, and I let the scalding water cascade over my skin. My mind drifts to Ellie, wondering what she and her friends are up to on their girls' night out.

After the shower, I emerge from the bathroom, less tense. My cut, neatly folded, hangs in its usual place over the bedroom chair. It's a testament to the life I chose. A brotherhood that runs deeper than blood.

With a cold brew in hand, I plop down on the couch in front of the TV, trying to push thoughts of Penny away. The game blares from the screen, and I let myself get lost in the familiar cadence of football. The adrenaline, the strategy, the camaraderie of the players—it all serves as a temporary distraction from the complicated world we live in.

Ellie's gentle kiss on my head wakes me from my football-induced sleep. I glance up, and there she stands, a vision of beauty with her tousled hair and a smile that could melt the Antarctic.

"Hey, babe, sorry, didn't mean to wake you. You looked so peaceful, I couldn't resist," she says, her eyes sparkling with affection as she leans down to kiss me. I sit up and pull her onto my lap, relishing the softness and heat of her embrace. The scent of her perfume, the softness of her skin—it all feels like home.

"No need to apologize," I murmur, savoring the taste of her lips on mine. "I missed you."

She chuckles softly, running her fingers through my hair.

"I missed you too, handsome. Now, tell me, how was your night?"

As I recount the game and the thoughts that had been swirling in my mind, leaving Penny and the church well out of it, Ellie listens attentively, her presence calming and grounding. It's moments like these, when it's just the two of us, I cherish the most in my unpredictable world.

In the dimly lit room, we find peace in each other, knowing that no matter what challenges, we'll face them together.

◊◊◊

My cock is throbbing as I rise through a dream state to consciousness. *Damn!* I can still feel her lush lips wrapped around me, taking me deep. Imagined vibrations make my hips lift off the bed. That's when I realize that this is reality, not a dream, nor wishful thinking. I lean up on my arms, looking at Ellie's naughty eyes smiling up at me, her lips wrapped tightly around my dick, and her hand encircling my root. With a groan, my head falls back onto my pillow, my arm covering my eyes. *Man, what a way to wake up. Little minx.* I open my eyes and watch her hollow her cheeks and suck me in deep.

"Fuck me," I groan.

"That's the plan," Ellie sasses before going straight back down on my throbbing dick. I can feel my balls boiling, shivers running down my spine. Her hand goes to my balls, squeezing and pulling my sack, rolling my balls in her hands. No gentleness, but to the point of just below pain. They draw up. When one of her fingers tracks down to the sensitive area below, I hiss. My head is ready to explode from all the need she evokes in me. Every time she comes up, her tongue plays with my sensitive eye, lapping and circling, teasing me to within an inch of my sanity.

"Oh yeah, just like that." My rough voice encourages her. On the next turn, she takes me deeper, I can feel the back of her throat tightening as she swallows around me, no gag reflex at all while she deepthroats me. I can't take any more. She needs to stop, or I'll only last about another two seconds.

"Dollface, stop," I demand, sending her giggling around my cock, the vibration nearly shoving me over the edge. I grind my molars, trying to stave off the need to shoot down her throat.

"Ellie, stop, baby." She looks up, her eyes dark with her own arousal. Her hand squeezes my root harder, her eyes locked onto mine. She traces a finger further down, circling the puckered ring she finds, and I'm damned if it doesn't make my entire body jerk and my need ramp a thousand-fold. My hard-on throbs painfully in her mouth. She repeats her ministration, and I can't stop the inevitable.

"Fuuuuck. Jesus," I groan while my universe implodes, flashes behind my eyes. I'm struggling for breath and my balls empty inside her gorgeous throat.

As my breathing slows, I look down to Ellie, who smiles as she gently laps me until I soften. *God, she was so worth the wait.*

29 — Ellie

Guilt overwhelms me when Slender asks me at breakfast what I'll do today. I want to tell him but can't. The sisterhood decided, the old ladies voted, and old ladies' business is not for the men to get involved in. Good for the gander, good for the goose.

Last night, we all met up at Ally's. Tanya, very pale and very pissed, put us in the picture. Never mind the gasps from all of us when she fessed up to having been bonking Pennywise for weeks now, along with Sarah's inappropriate questions about Pennywise's dick size. She also told us how Slender caught them. She made tracks, but sat under the window outside church, to listen in to the brothers' meeting.

All discussions about Penny's manhood faded into shocked silence when she recounted the plan, and that the guys put in an order for women. The anger rushed through the girls like a hurricane.

"Fucking bastards! What in the fuck do they think they're doing, putting innocents at risk! I'm gonna go there now and shoot the lot of them in the balls. One by one," Ally screamed. Not shouted, screamed at the top of her voice, her face a furious grimace. She even put the fear of God into Caroline, who doesn't scare easy.

"Well, Ally, you and Jules were there, remember?"

"Yes, we were, but I vehemently disagree with putting innocents in the line of fire!" Ally yells. "We have to do something!"

A plan evolved. We're gonna shit on their party piece and deal with the fallout later.

No way in hell will we let innocent girls be harmed. No fucking way in hell. The mere thought makes me cuss and my insides broil. As far as we're concerned, no one else goes through hell. We're strong women, we can take it. Although admittedly, it scares me senseless. The risk to us is very real, and we know that the shit will hit the fan big time with the brothers once they've worked out what we're doing. We don't plan on cluing them in. All I hope is that Slender will forgive me.

Ally informed the Wild Pixies of our little *adventure,* putting Jules, her SAA and Enforcer on alert, as well as Hazel, her VP. They'll get the dirty job of informing the men. I don't envy them. They'll blow not only one, but a whole set of gaskets. At least we have Jules in the know. We're waiting for a call from her, letting us know whether or not she got the job, or if she'll be joining us in town. Stuart kept bragging at the office that he and his rich friends hang out and pull at the Spirit Room in Superior, a posh cocktail bar. So that's where we're heading, since it's Saturday. Probably our best shot. If not, we'll just trail through all the upmarket bars. See if we can engage them, trail them, and prevent any unsuspecting girls from being taken,

◊◊◊

"Wow," breathes Caroline. "This place is quite something." She's right. In all my years of living in Superior, I've never been here before. Too pricey for me. The bar is packed with the upper echelon of Superior society. Thanks to Tanya's sneaking, we know who we're looking for and, surprise, surprise, find them, stood at the bar, in deep conversation. Can it be that easy? Surely not?

Sarah, Caroline, Ally, and Chloe march up to the recently vacated table near the bar, while Tanya and I stand in line at the bar, getting our drinks in. We order a cocktail pitcher, which has the assholes turning, grinning at us.

"Sex on the beach is just what I need." Tanya smirks in their direction. *Jesus, hold your horses, woman.* I need at least a couple of drinks for Dutch courage before we get stuck in.

We carry our trays with glasses and our pitcher to our table. My skin crawls with eyes burning holes into my back.

"The surfer boy, what's his name?" Ally asks.

"James Carpenter," Tanya offers.

"Yeah, him, Ellie, he's staring at you. As though he knows you?" Ally asks.

"Hm, he's been in the office a few times, so he might recognize me from there, but I've never spoken to him," I explain.

"We'll find out in a second. He's walking over here," Sarah hisses, turns to Caroline, laughing at nothing, but Caroline leans in, pretending to be in on the joke, giggling, nerves obvious.

"Hey, do I know you from somewhere?" a deep, smooth voice says behind me, when a hand on my shoulder encourages me to turn around.

"Oh, hi, I'm not sure, but yes, you look familiar." I take a deep breath, holding my hand out to him. "I'm Eliza, pleased to meet you."

"Eliza? What a pretty name. I'm Jim. Pleased to meet you. Hang on, did you work at Maxwell and Partners? Your name is not very common," he asks, his blue eyes gazing at me. His smile not quite reaching his eyes.

"Yes, I did until a little while ago, when I moved to Arnold," I reply.

"Fancy that." He laughs. "Small world, isn't it? What brings you to Superior tonight?"

"Heard about this place from Stuart, so thought it would be an ideal place for me and my friends to have a girls' night," I explain, smiling at him with fake friendliness, my stomach churning, nausea rolling through my stomach.

"These are my friends. Tanya, Ally, Caroline, Chloe, and Sarah." I introduce the girls.

"Pleased to meet you, ladies. If you'd like to join us for a drink, you are very welcome." He points at the bar where his mates are waiting, watching us.

"I need to dance," exclaims Sarah, dragging Ally and Caroline to the dance floor.

"We might take you up on the offer," Tanya tells Jim. "Or you could just bring your friends over here, since we have a table, and you don't." She winks at Jim, throwing her long, newly blonde hair over her shoulder, flirting. She's going all out. I'm scared out of my mind, and her determination to pursue her single-minded goal does nothing to reassure me. *Oh well, in for an inch, in for a mile.* It's gone too far to back out now, so I'll have to pull my big girl panties all the way up and push the gnawing fear aside. At least for now.

We party, laugh, dance, drink, the whole time bile burns at the back of my throat, my constant reminder that this is no joke. Not a fun night out. We're well aware of the risks we're taking.

"Excuse us, need to visit the facilities." Tanya giggles. I know she's not as drunk as she's making out. She grabs my hand and drags me off toward the ladies.

"Looks like they're on the hook. Line and sinker," she tells me after checking the bathroom is empty. I'm tipsy, but not drunk. I've been nursing a second cocktail for ages.

"Are you sure there's no other way? We could call the brothers and get them here while we keep them entertained?" I ask her.

"No, we can't call them yet. What proof do we have? None. We'll string them along a while longer. Are you armed?" Tanya's eyes search my face. Instead of replying, I pull my Baby Browning out of my purse. Tanya nods.

"You better stick that somewhere else on your body," she suggests, pointing at my high leather boots. She's got a point, so I double check the safety and shove it deep down into my right boot.

"What about you?" I ask Tanya. She smirks and instead of replying, she pulls her sexy leather jacket to the side and turns, revealing a handgun in the back of her jeans, turns again, pulling a switchblade out of her bra. *Jesus, this woman means business.* Just what is she getting us into? This is too big for us. I lean over, hands on my knees, trying to stave off my impending panic attack.

The door flies open and Ally steps through it.

"You better get back. They are getting nervous, and Sarah is getting bitchy," she warns us, stepping up to the sinks and washing her hands. Tanya looks at me and nods towards the door. I inhale deeply through my nose, letting my breath out slowly through my mouth, open the door and walk out, back to our table, Tanya hot on my heels.

"I wanna go home, Sarah whines.

"Yeah, I'm ready for bed," Caroline agrees.

Before I can stop her, Tanya opens her mouth.

"Chloe, it's okay if you want to take the rest of the girls home. I'm sure these gentlemen won't mind giving us a lift back." She winks at the guys, who nod eagerly.

"Are you sure?" Ally asks from behind us.

Tanya nods, and Jim adds, "Sure, no problem. Benny is our designated driver. We'll make sure they get home safe."

Ally shoots us a hard look, my eyes pleading for her not to leave us with this scum. When she nods and turns, grabbing her jacket, as the others are, giving me a hug, she whispers in my ear.

"Don't worry, I'm right outside in the parking lot, keeping an eye on you. Just text 911 and I'll be riding in with the cavalry."

My breathing rate has picked up, Ally's reassurance falling on deaf ears. I nearly run after her when she turns and walks out the door with the others. I want to back out, call Slender, fess up, and get him and the boys to come and get us, before things go too far.

Tanya shoves my glass at me.

"Drink up. Jim is eager to buy us tequila." She grins at Jim. "Mine's a Patron Extra, double please."

Jim coughs. Is she crazy? That's three hundred dollars plus a bottle, and I dread to think what it'll cost here.

Ben laughs.

"The lady has excellent taste. This one's on me. Why don't we go double or nothing?" He winks at Tanya.

"Challenge accepted." She smirks at him.

Ben goes to the bar and, a short while later, returns with a tray of four shots. My laughter sounds fake, even to my ears. The tray hits the table and I'm on it. Salt on my hand, I lick, bite the lime, and slam the shot back. Instead of a harsh burn, smooth liquid fire runs through my throat, warming me from the inside. Now I appreciate why the stuff is so damn expensive.

We hit the dance floor with the guys and dance our asses off to the thumping club rhythms droning through the speaker. I'm sweating by the time we return to our table. Tanya takes her seat.

"Hmm, think I had enough, am feeling the booze and am getting tired. Would you mind if we left, and you took us home?" Her slurred words surprise me. She's not drunk that much. But I agree. Sudden tiredness rises over me like a cresting wave, forcing me to yawn. Slapping my hand in front of my mouth, eyes wide, I giggle.

"No problem," Jim says. "Come on, Ben, let's take these ladies home. Where to?" Panic-stricken, I blurt out Debs's Haven address. Amy is there and we'll be safe.

I get up off my stool and stumble. Jim catches me. Something isn't right. Dizziness sets in. My heart is pounding in my chest like a double-time kick drum. My vision blurs, and I'm gonna be sick. Looking over my shoulder, I watch Ben help Tanya, who struggles to walk at all. He more carries her than Tanya moving under her own steam.

The light bulb moment hits me. *Fuck, they roofied us!* My mind spinning, I just make it outside before I empty my stomach contents onto the sidewalk. Jim, rubbing my back, holding my hair, tries to reassure me.

"It's okay, Eliza, you had too much to drink. Let's get you home." I nod, knowing my time is running out. As I turn, I watch Benito carry Tanya towards a minivan, before my world goes black.

30—ALLY

For what feels like the seven hundred and fiftieth time, I press the side button on my screen, lighting up the display, showing me I only checked the time about two minutes ago. This is taking too long. I find it hard to contain my antsy nerves and guilty conscience. As part of the officers' group leading the charge on the trafficking scum, I should have talked those crazies out of their stupid undertaking. I understand the not wanting to put innocents at risk. At the same time, I'm angry at Ellie and Tanya for putting me into this situation. Though I should be furious with myself. It was me who agreed, and me who's now trying to be the safety net, I'm certain Ellie and Tanya will need.

"Oh fuck, here we go," I mutter to myself between clenched teeth, watching a dark minivan drive up towards the front of the building. The bar doors open at the same time as the van doors. The two assholes are supporting Ellie and Tanya. Halfway to the van, both the girls get picked up, as their legs give way, and are placed in the van.

Oh shit, they've been roofied! I grab my phone, dial Raven, throw it on the passenger seat as it connects to the car stereo, and follow the van, keeping my distance. If they make me, the girls are in serious trouble. Not that they aren't already.

"Wassup?" Raven answers the phone.

"Shut up and listen. We have a 9-1-1 situation. No time to explain everything, just get the guys ready to ride. Carpenter and his fucking mates have taken Tanya and Ellie!" I holler at him, my heart beating in my throat like a drum.

"What the hell are you talking about? The girls are back here. I just spoke to Chloe and Sarah," he answers, bemused.

"Listen to what I'm telling you!" I hiss at him. "Ash, Chloe, Sarah, and Caroline went home. Tanya and Ellie stayed. They tried to catch Carpenter's attention and succeeded. I've just watched, both of them unconscious and being carried into a minivan I'm following." I rattle off the license plate.

Commotion breaks out as Raven relays what I'm telling him. Masher's roar in the background near deafens me. With a silent hiss, I draw my shoulders up to my ears. He has every right to his anger and desolation. My guilt ramps up a hundred-fold. I push it all to one side and concentrate on not losing the van. We're heading out of the city, and through the suburbs, then quiet country roads, making it more and more difficult to stay undetected.

For the next ten minutes, I keep up my running commentary, and know Ferret and Ghost are pinging my phone, so they have a general direction.

"Stay the fuck on the line!" Raven's cutting voice sounds through the speaker. In the background, I hear bikes starting up.

"We're riding out. Ghost is tracking your phone. You should have stopped them!" he screams at me. "If anything happens, it's on you, stupid bitch!"

His fury makes me wince. He's right, I should have tried, but if I'd refused, Ellie and Tanya would have gone ahead with this shit anyway, without a safety net at all. So, Raven can take it and shove it where the sun doesn't shine. Pointing fingers is not important now. Keeping the girls safe is.

The pitch black of the night makes following them unseen a challenge. I stay back so I can just see their rear lights and keep my headlights off. Every time they turn, I speed up, wait at the turn for a few beats, and follow on. How I've not ended up in a ditch, I do not know. This shit is hard.

At the next turn, I switch my headlights on for a second, as they round a corner ahead of me. Superior Municipal Forest, the signpost in front of me illuminates for a mere second.

"Shit!" I cuss.

"What?" Raven bellows through the speakers.

"We're heading to Superior Municipal," I answer.

"Fuck!" he yells. "I know where they're taking them. Bet it's that underground shithole Ellie found. Shit, should have ripped the damn place down."

"At least we know where they are taking them. How far are you behind?" I ask.

"'Bout fifteen minutes, I reckon," Raven confirms. They must have broken every speed limit to catch up that quick.

"They'll likely stop in the lower parking lot. Wait there for us. Are you packing?" he checks.

"Sure am, not promising to wait for you, though. Want to keep an eye on them close up," I grate.

"You fucking wait," he hisses. "If they see you, you'll all likely end up dead."

A hundred yards in front of me, the minivan turns to the right into what looks like might be a parking lot. Shit, I can't do anything right now. I pull up, turn off the engine and wind down my window, hoping that the night carries their voices. There's only a thin line of trees between me and them. Turning the stereo off, I take my cell off speaker, pressing it to my ear.

"We've stopped; they're in a parking lot, I'm at the side of the road," I whisper to Raven.

"ETA ten minutes. Don't move!" he grates.

In the still night air, I'm able to hear the bastards' voices clearly. Not as though they're trying to be quiet, either. How they didn't see me is beyond me. Just goes to show how stupid they are.

"Man, this one's heavier than she looks," grunts Ben. "Just goes to show, muscle is heavier than fat."

Is he seriously not aware of his stupidity? Unable to believe what I'm hearing, I want to shoot him in the nuts. A clattering sound grabs my attention.

"The bitch is armed! What the fuck, look at this!" Benito calls to the others. Shit, they found either the gun, or the knife, or both.

"Nice!" James says. "Shame she won't need that blade or the gun anymore where she's going. I'll take that."

The sound of his evil laughter carries through the relative stillness of the night, sending shivers up my spine.

A hand shoves over my mouth through the open window. *Fuck, I'm done!* The air leaves my lungs and I'm not able to take a breath deep enough to scream.

"Shhhhh, open the passenger door."

My breath rushes from my lungs in relief as Jules' voice hisses into my ear. Up to now, I wasn't aware of how scared I am. Thank God; I was on the phone with her, putting her into the picture, when the minivan drove up to the bar doors. Behind me is her whisper-quiet Tesla. She must have had the lights off as she got closer.

"Got your location from Ferret, who's doing his nut by the way, oh super intelligent boss of mine. How damn stupid can y'all get? I was all set to start on Monday! This little shitshow? Doesn't just put the girls at risk, but the entire operation!" Jules whisper shouts, anger rolling off her in thick waves. Gone is the soft, laughing, always fun-loving Jules, and my SAA has taken her place, just like a personality transplant. I love her for it.

"Shut up, Jules," I whisper back, keeping my eyes peeled on the guys now standing at the sliding door of the minivan. "I made a decision and stand by it. We cannot see any innocent bystander harmed. We already lost Debs, and I saw what this shit did to Amy. Tanya and Ellie are strong and intelligent enough to pull this off.

"Anyway, what are they gonna do? Shoot me? Not likely," I scoff, meaning the enraged brothers on their way to us.

"You are up shit creek without a paddle, girl." Jules leaves no doubt about how pissed she is with me.

"Look, they're moving. Who's the third guy?"

I shrug. No clue, didn't pay attention, didn't care enough to see who the driver was. Only care about keeping my girls safe. We watch as the three men carry our girls off into the woods, flashlights lighting their way. I open my door, tiptoe out of the car, and silently close the door. Jules mirrors me, the only noise we hear being their voices fading in the distance. I reach into the open window, grab an infrared flashlight, my gun, and a bottle of water. We can't free the girls, not if we want to bust the entire crew, but we can make sure they're as okay as possible, and perhaps shoot the fuckers on the spot.

Payton Hunter © 2024

Footsteps creep up, and a furious Masher appears in front of me, followed by a Raven; in my panic I had forgotten all about them. The cold bastard, eyes hard as steel, face a mask, giving away little emotions at all. His look spears me like a dagger, right through the heart. Maybe I shouldn't have joked about them shooting me. Raven, right now, looks capable and willing. I take a deep breath and start to explain, when his raised hands and ice-cold killer eyes stop me dead in my tracks. *Hang on a fucking second.* I'm an MC President, just like he is, and am due respect.

"If you think you can steamroller me here, pal, I have news for you. Not happening. Go fuck yourself." I stand there, toe-to-toe with him, staring him straight in the eye. No way will I cower. Just no way. "We can discuss this later once we make sure Ellie and Tanya are alright. Then we have all the time to argue the toss out of this. Not now."

Masher grabs my arm, fingers like a vise. *That'll leave bruises.*

"I'll hold you responsible, bitch. Anything happens to my daughter, I'll fucking shoot you," he hisses and lets go of my arm as I nod at him.

We start up into the woods. Raven and Masher taking point, Jules and me behind them, followed by Sparks and Slender. Neither of them will even look at me. Think it might be my turn to sleep on the couch tonight. I love Sparks to death and get why he's pissed. This is not gonna go away anytime soon. All I can hope for is that he eventually understands.

We're about ten minutes into our trek when we notice voices coming toward us. We scatter, hiding in the undergrowth. I duck down, flatten out on the floor as the three walk not three feet past me.

"Might have to come back tomorrow and play with the brunette," an older guy's voice sneers.

"No!" Benito cuts him off. "The order states no damaged goods. We can't afford another fuck up; we'll lose the contract. James, you'll go out tomorrow, empty the buckets, leave food and more water. Transport is set for the day after tomorrow."

"Yup," agrees the older guy. "Got an office bitch starting tomorrow. Leaves me time to sort out the container, stock it, and make sure of ventilation. Wouldn't want corpses to hit the other end now, would we?" he scoffs.

Shit, that must be Ernest Digby.

We wait for them to pass, pray they don't recognize the two cars by the roadside, and get back on the path as they're out of sight. No stopping Slender now. He's overtaking Raven and racing towards a point only he knows for sure, leaving us struggling to keep up.

I may have taken this too far this time, however, I'll worry about the fallout later. For now, my only priority is the safety of my friends.

31 — SLENDER

Panting hard, my breath saws in and out like a rusty chainsaw as I run towards the clearing. I don't notice the twigs snapping, battering my face, leaving deep gashes in the skin of my arms and face. My entire body is flooded with adrenaline, fear, and anger like I never felt before. Like a roaring beast, my demon rises to the surface, screaming for blood in the dark of night. If anything happens to Ellie, I won't be held responsible for what I do. My head is seconds away from exploding.

Bursting into the clearing, I don't even stop to catch my breath. I can see where the leaves and dirt have been disturbed over the trap door I know is there.

The thought of Ellie being in there, broken and bleeding, makes me physically sick. I turn and vomit, the taste of bile coating my throat, feeding the beast inside of me. Wiping my mouth on my arm, I kick the leaves to the side and grab the ring on the wood door with all my might, pulling it up, nearly ripping it from its hinges!

"Ellie!" I can hear a hoarse voice shouting, realizing it's my own.

"Ellie, sweetheart, Tanya! Where are you?!" It's pitch black inside the underground cavern. Behind me, feet drum staccato down the narrow stairs. Raven's hand lands on my back.

"Keep it together, man," Raven growls in my ear as, with a click, a bright flashlight blinds me for a second. Masher shines it through the cavernous space, lined on both walls with small cells. Two of which hold the prone figures of Ellie and Tanya. Raven picks the locks and in seconds, both doors are open. I race into Ellie's cell, picking her limp body off the floor, sinking to the floor, holding her tight in my arms. Her breathing is even and strong. She's been drugged but seems otherwise okay. No signs of beatings or interference with her clothing.

Raven is on his phone, bellowing at whoever is on the other end. Ally, stands quietly leaning against the cell bars, unable to meet my eyes. How could she have let the girls get into something so dangerous, so insane? My anger flares to an all-time high.

"Happy?" I roar at her.

"Sorry, Slender, I tri—"

"Shut up, you stupid bitch, I don't wanna hear your shit! Look at her! Drugged to the eyeballs, only a sniff away from being sold to the highest bidder! Fuck you, Ally, fuck you!" If I never see her traitorous face again, it'll be too soon.

"You better leave before I shoot you!" Masher growls at her.

With that, Ally turns on her heel and walks away from us. Unable to say how long I've been sitting on the cold dirty floor, rocking Ellie back and forth in my arms, the sudden touch of a small warm hand on my cheek brings me out of my thoughts. Chloe is crouching in front of me, her mouth moving. Slowly, her words filter through.

"Slender, sweetie, I brought Doc. Please, Slender, let him have a look at her. He brought the most common antidotes and will try his hardest to bring them around. I brought water and warm blankets too. Please, honey, we're trying to help." Her calm voice penetrates my cold, hard soul, calming the beast inside. She spreads warm blankets on the ground, and I gently place Ellie on them. Sitting against the cell wall, my head on my knees, taking deep, grounding breaths, I will my anger and hatred at the world under control, my eyes following the movements of a man I've never seen before. He watches me, his movements slow, his hands shaking, bleeding out his nerves. He quietly confers with Chloe. I don't take in what they are talking about. It's just a blur of word soup wafting right over my head.

Chloe turns to me.

"Slender, I'll give Ellie a shot. Hopefully, this will bring her round. If not, we have a second and a third option to try." Her gentle tone soothes my fractured mind. *Please let Ellie be okay.* Life without her is inconceivable. I won't survive being parted from her again. My subconscious vaguely registers Pennywise, roaring with frustration and rage, but my eyes stay glued to Chloe, watching with desperation as she injects Ellie, praying for the shot's effectiveness.

Within moments, Ellie moves. Her eyes flutter and a small groan leaves her as she tries to open her eyes and move her limbs. *Thank fuck!* I sit back on the floor and lift Ellie back into my lap. I can't handle being physically apart from her.

"Shh, honey, I've got you." My voice a mere whisper in her ear, as some of the tension drains from her body.

"Slender, my head hurts." Tears are trailing down her beautiful face.

"Here, honey, drink this," I encourage her, holding a bottle of water to her lips. "It'll make you feel better." Ignoring the commotion all around us, I take care of my woman. It rips me to shreds to see her in so much pain and discomfort.

After an hour, the initial commotion dies down, and the girls gradually become more cognizant. The anger-loaded atmosphere seems to crackle all around us.

"What the fuck were you idiots thinking?" Raven bellows at the girls. Ellie sits up ramrod straight, militance running off her in palpable waves.

"Shut the hell up, Raven! How dare you speak to us like that? You may be the Stormy Souls' President, but that does not give you the right to treat us like imbeciles! We had a plan, a very well-thought-through plan, may I add, and the fact that you are all here just goes to show that our safety precautions worked. So, pipe down, hold your temper, and let us explain," she hisses at Raven. Ellie has jumped to a stand, fists balled on her hips, confronting Raven. My little kitten turns into a roaring wildcat. It shouldn't make me smile, but it does. I'm so proud, her strength becoming obvious to everyone around us.

"You go, girl," Tanya encourages her, snickering quietly, before making her way to Ellie's side.

"Where is Ally?" she asks, glaring at Masher and Raven.

"Don't talk to me about THAT," Masher hisses. "My trigger finger twitches just thinking about that bitch."

"Shut up, Dad, you can stop right now. I'm a grown woman, not a five-year-old, making my own decisions, whether they fit into your tidy little game plan or not. You leave Ally the fuck alone. Same goes for you other cavemen! We have a plan, a good plan at that. It will take these assholes out of circulation. We knew you'd throw a fit; hence we implemented phase one without you knowing, but certain that we'd have backup. And, Dad, just for your information, I'm leaving. I'm done with the Slayers MC and won't be returning to the clubhouse. I'm my own person, not club property!" Tanya pants with her outburst. Her face is a whiter shade of pale, her fury unmistakable.

"Think carefully, before you say anything else, father of mine. Ally invited me to patch into the Wild Pixies WMC as a full member, and I have accepted. I expect to be treated accordingly." *Jeez!* Tanya's tone makes an Alaskan glacier feel like a hot tub.

"Now, get Ally!"

Masher, shocked and speechless, was not what I ever expected to see. Neither is Pennywise, sitting in the corner, not knowing whether to smile or pull his hair out.

Could this damn day get any more fucked up?

◊◊◊

Everything inside me screams not to allow Ellie to go through with their plan. Admittedly, it is a good and relatively safe one, which clicks right into our own, but what if?

What if those scumbags find Tanya and Ellie's weapons? Yes, we left them with a way to defend themselves after Tanya's armory fell to the enemy. Not only that, but Ferret brought up some trackers, which we concealed on their bodies.

It's been two days since they were taken. Forty-eight hours seem like a lifetime right now.

Jules is firmly installed in Digby Haulage, as is Dawg. Everything seems under control, but I can't help feeling like I'm dancing on a high wire and one wrong step will cause catastrophe. It takes everything I have to stay calm, projecting fake composure to the outside world. Not to mention that Pennywise is acting like a complete dick with everyone around him, and Masher walks around the clubhouse, aggression barely in check. I feel for Chloe, who has to put up most with his rude, angry ass, as he's staying at Raven's.

My intuition is scratching the inside of my brain raw. Something stinks to high heaven, but I can't put my finger on what it is exactly. We have Caleb in the woods, close to the site, keeping an eye, checking on the girls as soon as their captors come and go. It's the only way we can ensure they are okay.

Both of them are so strong. I want to sink to my knees and thank God for their resilience, strength, and ability to work in an impossible situation. I'll allow nothing to touch my dollface ever again, I swear on my life. She's the woman I want to spend the rest of my life with, see her belly grow with my children, protect my family, and make her so happy she's floating on a cloud. Every minute apart from her feels like I can't breathe fully. I'm so lost in my thoughts that I almost miss the church door. Shaking myself, I try to get it together as I walk into the packed room.

"Just heard from Caleb, man"—Ferret looks at me—"we are a go. They've just moved them from the cells." He turns the laptop, and I can see two small blinking dots moving across a map.

"Everyone is in place." Raven's strained voice reaches my ears.

"Something's wrong." Concern bleeding out of Ferret as he speaks and looks at us.

"The trackers aren't moving!"

"Fuck!" Raven yells. "Caleb, what the fuck is going on?" he barks into his phone, which is on speaker.

"Get the fuck here, now!" Caleb shouts back while gunshots ring through our ears.

Within seconds we're out the door and on the road, following Ferret, who has the tracker open, leading the way.

The scene opening before us as we race around the last bend is carnage.

A station wagon with all four doors open, bodies in the road, Caleb kneeling next to Tanya. No idea how I got off my bike, but I run full pelt towards the scene.

"Ellie!" *Where is she?* I can't see her anywhere. The relief when she walks out from behind the vehicle is instant.

Tears running down her pretty face as she throws herself at me, clinging like a monkey in a thunderstorm. Not giving a shit about what's going on around us, I sink to the floor with her in my arms, peppering her face with kisses.

"Are you okay, Dollface? Are you hurt?" I ask her, scared of the answer.

"No"—she snuffles and hiccups into my neck—"just shaken up, but Tanya—"

"Shhh," I shush her, stroking her head and back, rocking us both. "Everything will be okay, Dollface. Tanya will be okay."

Behind us, Masher roars, cussing. I draw Ellie up, wrap her tight into my side, and guide her back to the others. Raven is on the phone, ordering clean up, Caleb and Striker are placing Tanya on the back seat of the club SUV, a half-assed bandage on her thigh. Masher is kicking the shit out of the dead body lying in the road, while Pennywise tries to pull him away.

"I'll take Ellie back," I tell Raven, who simply nods.

Leading her to my bike, I climb on, encouraging her to follow my example and hold tight. Her arms around my midriff nearly shear me in half she has them wrapped so tight. I hit the starter and pull back into the road the way we came, feeling her head on my back, her shoulders shaking. I know she's crying and needs me to be strong for her, but I need to get her out of here before I can give her my undivided attention.

32 — Ellie

Two Days Earlier

My head swims and the banging inside it feels like my brain is attempting to break through the top of my skull. I dimly register being held and Slender's voice filtering through the thick brain fog surrounding me.

"Shh, honey, I've got you." His voice a bare whisper, but it unravels a tight knot deep in my soul. *I am safe.*

"Slender, my head hurts," I whisper, unable to stop the tears from falling. The pain is unimaginable.

"Here, honey, drink this." His tender, encouraging voice blends out everything around us. He holds a bottle of water to my lips. "It'll make you feel better."

I take slow sips of sweet-tasting cold water, blocking the commotion around us out, concentrating on his hands running up and down my back and the soothing rocking motion while he holds me. When I look into Slender's eyes, the pain I see reflected back hits me like a ton of bricks. *I did that. I put that pain there.* Overwhelming guilt courses through me, and I can honestly say that I've never felt as guilty as I do right now.

"I'm so sorry. I didn't mean to scare you. We had a plan. I'm so sorry." Hot tears of guilt and regret run down my face.

"Dollface, you scared me and the guys to death. What were you thinking?" His voice is tender but has a hint of steely admonishment, increasing the sensation of guilt running through me.

Closing my eyes, I lean back into him, trying to let his presence soothe me, breathing through the waves of nausea and headache rolling over me, dozing on and off in the safety of his arms. None of us speak, not wanting to upset the other more than we already have.

◊◊◊

"What the fuck were you idiots thinking?" Raven bellows at us.

What the ever-loving hell?

I pull out of Slender's arms, jump to my feet in front of Raven, not caring one bit that he's the mighty Prez.

"Shut the hell up, Raven! How dare you speak to us like that? You may be the Stormy Souls' President, but that does not give you the right to treat us like imbeciles! We had a plan, a very well-thought-through plan, may I add, and the fact that you are all here just goes to show that our safety precautions worked. So, pipe down, hold your temper, and let us explain," I hiss, my voice shaking. I'm so damn mad.

"You go, girl." Tanya snickers quietly. She walks up and stands beside me.

"Where is Ally?" She glares at Masher and Raven

"Don't talk to me about THAT," Masher hisses. "My trigger finger twitches just thinking about that bitch."

"Shut up, Dad, you can stop right now. I'm a grown woman, not a five-year-old making my own decisions, whether they fit into your tidy little game plan or not. You leave Ally the fuck alone. Same goes for you other cavemen! We have a plan, a good plan at that. It will take these assholes out of circulation. We knew you'd throw a fit; hence we implemented phase one without you knowing, but certain that we'd have backup.

"And, Dad, just for your information, I'm leaving. I'm done with the Slayers MC, and I won't be returning to the clubhouse. I'm my own person, not club property!" Tanya pants with her outburst. Her face white with fury.

"Think carefully, before you say anything else, father of mine. Ally invited me to patch into the Wild Pixies WMC as a full member, and I have accepted. I expect to be treated accordingly." Tanya's icy voice shocks Masher into silence.

"Now, get Ally!" she commands.

After a few minutes of frosty, stunned silence, Caleb and Striker lead a silent, shaking Ally in.

"Oh, fuck," Sparks whispers. Her head shoots round to glare at him.

"Brother, I think your nuts have just been frozen off," Pennywise quips at him. Ally's eyes shoot to Pennywise.

"You, dickhead. better shut up before I shoot your nuts clean off!" Ally growls at him. *Wow, she is pissed.* She turns to face Raven and Masher. "Just to make one thing crystal clear to you buffoons once and for all. I am Rainbow. Friends call me Ally, but I am Rainbow, President of the Wild Pixies WMC. You will treat me with the respect due. I am your equal, not your Prospect or club member. Let me introduce you to my officers." I hadn't noticed Jules and Greta, Caroline and another lady I never met following her in.

"This is Hazel, my VP, Jules my Sergeant at Arms, Tanya, my newly joined Enforcer, Greta our Road Captain, and Caroline our Scribe. Yes, Masher, gasp all you like, Tanya is my new Enforcer, and I've arranged for her to stay at Debs' Haven until she can find her own place to live." Ally stands tall, not intimidated by all that testosterone around us when she turns to Sparks.

"You don't like it? Move into the clubhouse. I am your Old Lady, but I am also Prez of my club. You can't deal with that? Leave." Her glare shrinks Sparks into himself.

I can't help but feel empowered by her strength and ability to stand up to those men. I walk up next to Ally. Time to be counted.

Masher and Raven's mouths gape open. This is a side of us ladies they've never seen before. Despite not being a member of the Wild Pixies, and I never would consider becoming one, their strength and pride suffuse me, making me stand taller, head held high.

"Let's get out of this shithole and talk," Ally commands, turns and, to my surprise, everyone follows her outside. Slender supports me up the steep narrow steps, and I draw the clean, woodsy air deep into my lungs, enjoying feeling safe. Ally turns to look at me and winks.

"Okay, ladies"—she pointedly looks at Masher and Raven—"here's our plan." She motions for me to explain, and I love her for the trust and support she is literally heaping on me right now.

"Okay…" I clear my throat and take a deep breath. "You decreed that Jules and Dawg infiltrate the trucking company. But you forgot it could take ages for anything to happen. So, we sped things along, to make sure no other innocents are hurt.

"We kept tabs on those assholes, waiting for an opportunity, which presented itself last night. Ally and the Pixies formed our safety net. They were always close, monitoring us." I nod to Tanya, who takes over now.

"I heard through the grapevine that you lot put in an order." She grins at Masher. "Some of you boys are a little loose lipped. Didn't take much to get the info I needed."

"And," she continues, "our plan worked like a charm. We knew we'd likely be drugged and expected that. Ally was always gonna follow and call you if needed. Had we discussed this with you beforehand, you'd have dismissed us. Not a chance we were going to take.

"I'm armed, and so is Ellie. They think they found all our weapons, but more fool them for not searching us properly…" She pulls the cover of her cross necklace, revealing a sharp, three-inch blade. I step forward, pulling the blade hidden in my belt buckle, the gun from my boot, and activate the spring out mini knives on my rings.

"Not much, but enough to cause damage to slow them down enough until the cavalry arrives. Since you are all here, it obviously worked. Now calm your tits."

Jules scoffs. "Thought you'd put me in a cushy office, and I'd be a good little girl? Here's how this plan goes. Either with or without you." She turns to Ferret. "Ferret, do you have trackers?" she asks, watching Ferret nod.

"Get them and put them on Ellie and Tanya. That way, we'll know exactly where they are, all the time. Now that we're all here, Tanya, catch." She throws a Glock 42 at her, which Tanya catches with practiced ease, and shoves it her boot holster. "Make it count, sister."

She grins at Tanya, who sports a slightly maniacal grin before answering, "Yes, ma'am!".

"We leave Tanya and Ellie here, check on them every day, make sure they're unharmed. When they transport them to Digby's, we have the trackers to make sure everything goes according to plan. Once they are on the premises and stowed in the truck, Dawg and I are in place with you all sorting out their take down. If we take Tanya and Ellie now, those bastards will work out we're onto them.

"It's more of a plan than we had," Masher admits begrudgingly.

"Are you fucking insane?" Slender shouts at Masher. "That's your daughter and my Old Lady you're putting at risk! Over my dead body!"

I take a step toward him. Wrap my arms around his neck, pulling him down so he has to look straight into my eyes.

"Baby, I'm fine. I want to do this. This scum needs to be taken off our streets now, not next week or next year. Think of all the girls they have put through hell. Remember Debs, who died at their hands. Think of the other girls you rescued. How many more women must go through this hell? I'm stronger than I look. I can and must do this. I couldn't live with myself if another woman disappeared and I hadn't tried everything in my power to prevent it."

Watching the fight leave Slender's body is the toughest thing. I swallow back tears that threaten to break free. This man is so used to protecting me, being strong for me, it's ingrained deep in his soul. I physically feel the pain and doubt rushing through his veins.

The discussion lasts another hour or so. In the end, everyone agrees it's the best plan we have. To walk back down into our *prison* for however long this will take, fills me with dread, anxiety lashing my body and brain.

With reluctance I watch as Raven locks us back into our cells, looks back at us, and pleads, "Be careful!" before he climbs the steps and lowers the door back into its place. Listening to the scratching and noises above the trapdoor, panic threatens to overwhelm me.

Payton Hunter © 2024

"Ellie, deep breath, in through your nose, out through your mouth. Breathe with me." Tanya's voice cuts through my fog. I follow her instructions, and slowly, the panic recedes.

"We are safe for the moment, Ellie. Let's try to get some sleep while we can. We need to keep a clear head. The clubs have us."

I sigh and try to get comfortable on the cold, hard floor. Not realizing how tired I am, and the side effects of the drugs they gave us are still in my system, I drift off to sleep within minutes.

◊◊◊

My fuzzy brain alerts me to noises coming from somewhere in the darkness. I do not know how long I slept. I've lost all perception of time.

"Up! Lazy bitch!" a voice growls at me. I don't recognize the figure bent over me. With the ski mask he wears, it makes him impossible to recognize in the dark, even with the beam of a flashlight shining into my cell. He drags me up by my hands, which he cuffs in front of me. He pulls me to the cell bars and forces me against it with the weight of his body. His erection pressing into me, makes me physically sick. As I start dry heaving, he jumps away from me.

"Stupid bitch! Don't throw up on me if you know what's good for you!" In my mind, he transforms into Rusty, his sneering face scaring me witless.

"Hey, fucker, leave her alone. Why don't you come and pick on someone your own size?"

Tanya's yell breaks through my vision.

"Just wait your turn, whore. I'll be with you in a minute." He cackles at her, evil leeching into his voice, scaring me for Tanya. I pray to God to let us get out of this in one piece.

He works around the cell, throwing a blanket on the floor, emptying my bucket, and throwing two bottles of water and a small bag, which I believe contains food, onto the blanket, before he grabs my breasts and squeezes them painfully.

With a scary laugh he tells me: "Well, bitch, I'll be back soon. Don't get too comfortable." Turns on his heel and leaves, slamming the cage door behind him, turning toward Tanya.

"Well, well, well, what have we here? Little Miss Big Mouth, too big for her britches. You need to be taught respect." With that, he opens her cell, steps inside and I watch in horror as he punches Tanya in the face, lifting her clear off the floor, catapulting her into the cell wall. I hear the click of handcuffs, him moving around, the bucket scraping, and things being thrown onto the floor. Making myself as small as possible, I curl myself into a ball on my blanket, trying to be invisible. A short while later, his stomping feet move up the stairs and the trapdoor slams shut again.

"Tanya, are you alright?"

"Yes, Ellie, I'll be fine. Bastard caught my eye," comes the answering groan.

"Shit, he got me good. Don't worry about me, chick, I'll be fine. Thank fuck he cuffed my hands in front of me. At least I can eat and drink. Are you okay, sweet?"

"I'm fine. He didn't hurt me, just… touched me." Only then do I notice the tears streaming down my face in an endless river. Wracked with guilt and shame, I open a bottle of water, chug half of it, reach in the bag for what feels like a sandwich, unwrap it and take a big bite, not tasting what I swallow, just feeding my body.

With a click, a small light illuminates our dire circumstances.

"Ferret gave it to me last night. It's only small, so won't last long. We must ration it," Tanya explains. I look across and literally watch as bruises form around her eyes.

"We have to be more careful." She hisses in pain, carefully touching around her eye. "We need to stay quiet and small, let them think they have us under control. We can't afford them drugging us again, nor cuffing us at the back."

I nod at her. She's right. If we want to get out of this misery alive, we have to comply, completely, as much as that scares the living daylights out of me. After finishing our food, we decide to pass the time, playing *Never have I ever*, until the darkness lulls me to sleep again.

Next, I'm woken by Caleb, who kneels by my side, gently shaking me.

"Wake up, Ellie, time to go outside." I shake off the drowsiness and get to my feet. Caleb unlocks my cuffs and I rub my wrists where the cuffs cut into them.

"Holy crap!" he groans when he finds Tanya. "Masher is gonna lose his shit when he sees you." Tanya nods at him while he unlocks her cuffs.

◊◊◊

Two long days we've spent in this hellhole now, the guys barely keeping it together. Masher predictably flipped when he spotted Tanya's black eye, and it took everything we had to persuade him to let us get on with our mission. We learned from our experience and keep quiet whenever our prison guards made an appearance, not getting drawn into exchanges, simply cowering in the cell corner.

Today looks to be the day. Paralyzed by fear, I follow Tanya up the stairs.

"Move!" commands one of our capturers, who I've never seen before, shoving me so hard I fall to my knees on the rickety stairs. His voice is unfamiliar. Ski masks obscure our view of the men, who so obviously enjoy their harsh treatment of us, pushing, shoving, and touching us wherever and whenever they like. Bile rises into my throat, and it takes everything I have not to vomit. Bright sunlight blinds my eyes. Before I can even react, someone blindfolds me, forcefully tightening it, almost pushing my eyes inside my skull.

We're led down a path, stumbling over tree roots. The second time I hit the ground, I see stars as pain explodes in my knee from hitting a sharp stone.

Soon the ground underfoot changes to even tarmac. The beep of a central-locking system piercing through the silence surrounding us.

"Get in," the faceless evil instructs, while the other guy shoves us without ceremony into what feels like a car's trunk. The lid comes down, but unexpectedly, we can move.

"Station wagon," Tanya whisper hisses at me.

Four doors slamming have me jumping. I'd only counted two men. I try to count turns as the car moves, concentrating instead of losing my mind to the fear pulsing through my veins. Tanya's movements beside me gives me hope. She is so strong, much stronger than me. Her calm seeps through my dread. Loud dance music blares through the speakers, covering any noise of our attempts to free ourselves.

"I've got the key," she whispers in my ear. Silently she fiddles with my handcuffs, which give way with a click. Holding my breath, I wait for our attackers to notice, stop the car, and kill us, but nothing happens. I free my hands out of the cuffs with slow, careful movements. Anything to not attract their attention. Ripping my blindfold off, Tanya's merciless stare meets mine. Just her look has ice running through my veins, leaving me in no doubt that by my side lays a woman ready to kill. Phenomenal darkness radiates from her as she hands me the keys and I unlock her cuffs.

Payton Hunter © 2024

"Please stop the car. I need to use the toilet!" Her ice-cold eyes, in stark contrast to her pleading voice, Tanya gets our captors' attention.

"Not stopping bitch!" the driver replies, his voice unfamiliar.

"Okay, I'll just piss in the boot and bleed in it, too. Nice DNA evidence," Tanya sounds back, calm and collected.

"For fuck's sake, can't wait to be rid of ya!" the driver yells. The force of the car stopping throws us against the trunk lid.

All of them get out. We exchange a look, nod at each other, and get ready. *Them or us.* The trunk opens and instinctively I click my ring blades out and grab my belt blade tighter. They've spotted our blindfolds are off. "Fuck this. Next time I duct tape you bitches." His voice dripping with disgust as he grabs my hair and drags me out of the trunk. I dig my knife in his side, feeling his warm blood gushing over my hand. "Shit!" he yells.

The sound of shots ringing out, bodies dropping, the screeching of tires, and the pounding of feet as two guys run for the woods assaults my ears. When I glance around me, Tanya lays in the road, next to two bodies, one still moving.

"Watch out!" I scream. The bastard is lifting his gun. More shots ring out until finally the body falls back. I grab my gun, pointing it in the direction the shots rang out from.

"Ellie, it's okay, it's me, Caleb, the guys are on the way!"

With a loud sob, I drop the gun and crawl behind the station wagon, leaning against it, surrendering to my tears.

More bikes arrive.

"Ellie!" Slender's shout reaches through my misery. Still sobbing, I get up and walk out from behind the car, my legs running to him on their own accord. I throw myself at him, clutching and clinging to him. *I'll never let him go again, ever.* He grabs me and lowers us to the ground, peppering my face with kisses.

"Are you okay, Dollface? Are you hurt?" he asks.

"No." I can't stop snuffling and hiccup into his neck. "Just shaken up, but Tanya—"

"Shhh," he shushes me, stroking my hair, rocking us both, "Everything will be okay, Dollface. Tanya will be okay."

I don't know why, but I believe him.

Behind us, Masher roars, cussing. Slender drags me up, pulls me tight to his side and guides me back to the others.

"I'll take Ellie back," he tells Raven, who merely nods. Leading me to his bike, he climbs on, encouraging me to follow suit. I cling to him for dear life, holding on way too tight, but can't help myself. He is my savior, my light in the dark, and I'll never let go again.

33 — SLENDER

It's been five days since our attempts to trap the trafficking gang went wrong. Ghost and Ferret are working nonstop, trying to get information on their identities. We thought we knew, but obviously didn't.

Tanya shot Benito, old man Cabal's grandson. An enormous bunch of flowers appeared in Tanya's hospital room, with a card attached.

'Thank you, my dear. I owe you a favor. OC x'

So, we're pretty sure there will be no blowback from their side.

The clubhouse has been manic, Restless Slayers coming and going as though it's their right, which pisses the officers off, but we keep our feet still. Masher is walking around, silent but deadly. Not speaking to anyone other than Ghost and Raven. And that's only if he can't help it.

Ally keeps a low profile and stays well out of his way, with a face like a slapped ass. The mood is dire, and we need something to bring our spirits up. I'm grateful for Chloe, Caroline, and Ashley. Their diplomacy and patience keeps us all from exploding.

The mission wasn't a complete failure. We, or rather Tanya, got a bunch of flowers for taking out Benito, and Caleb proved his mettle when he took out the other trafficker, who we now know was one of Ernest Digby's minions. Through Jules and Dawg, we know he continues as though nothing happened. The grapevine has been busy, we heard that two more girls are missing, and as those bastards destroyed their base in the woods, we now don't know where they are keeping them.

Church is so explosively charged that the smallest spark will be enough to get everyone to blow.

"Settle down!" Raven bellows through the noise.

Once silence descends, Raven starts the meeting officially. He sits at the head of the table, with Vegas and Ferret to his left, me and Pennywise to his right, Dawg and Clusseaud next to Ferret, with Pennywise opposite Dawg. Anyone else just parks their asses where there's a free chair.

"Update!" Raven thunders.

"Club is secure, all threats are being investigated. Despite everything, Leather and Lace is up and running, Dawg will report further. Chris, the new guy at Lightning Security, has checked out solid and signed his contract. Matters of our ongoing investigations will be dealt with separately, so this is all from me for now," I finish.

Dawg follows with financial updates, scribbling while he talks.

Payton Hunter © 2024

"Business is good, the opening of Leather and Lace was a success, the rooms are fully booked, and Neil reports the girls and bar staff are happy and everything is going tickety-boo."

Zippy is next with an update to the new tattoo shop.

"Sparks, have you asked Ally about this new artist yet? I can't keep up."

"Sorry, man, forgot all about it, been carrying her details in my pocket for weeks now," Sparks replies and shoves a piece of paper towards Zippy.

"Thanks, man, I'll make contact."

"Right, that's the official bit over. Pennywise, go grab Masher and Ghost."

As Pennywise leaves the room, it is clear for anyone to see how tightly strung he is.

For weeks now he's been off, his moods unpredictable. I tried talking to him several times, but he blows me off. The slamming door pulls me out of my thoughts.

"How's Tanya?" Raven asks Masher, who has taken a seat next to him at the head of the table.

"Better. Doc says she can go home this week," Masher replies. "They're keeping her for some more tests. I tried to persuade her to come home with me, but she's stubborn. "

"Wonder where she's got that from?" Dawg mutters under his breath.

"Shut your mouth, before I shut it for you!" Masher grates at him.

"That's enough! Keep your childish attitudes out of my church, before I kick the shit out of the both of you," Raven seethes. "You can hate each other all you like. In here, you will be civil, or I'll set up a match in the ring for ya."

Animosity crackles between Masher and Dawg.

"Now then," Raven continues, "Ferret, Ghost, any news?"

"They've gone underground. Can't find any trace of them or work out who else they're working with. It's as though they've disappeared from the face of the earth," Ghost reports.

"We'll keep trying, and we'll find them. They can't hide forever," Ferret adds.

"Masher and I are gonna leave after this meeting and shake some trees at home. Got a lead to follow. Nothing concrete though," Ghost says. "I'll keep in touch with Ferret, and we'll coordinate virtually."

"You better look after my girl, Raven. Anything else happens to her and I won't be held responsible for my actions," Masher threatens.

Raven stands, leaning forward on his hands. "Looks like we'll best coordinate virtually too, since I won't be threatened in my own clubhouse, not even by you! I think it's time the Slayers left," he grates and nods at me. I stand and hold the door open for Masher and Ghost, encouraging them to leave.

"Any other business?"

I stand and look around the brothers.

"I'm claiming Ellie."

"Finally. What took you so long, dumbass?" Dawg smirks at me.

"Anybody got any objections?" Dawg looks around the table. "I'll order her cut then."

"Anything else?" Raven asks. The silence is deafening.

"Congratulations, Slender, church closed." He bangs his gavel, and we all traipse into the bar, where my brothers congratulate and back slap me until my shoulders are sore. Not even that can wipe the smug grin off my face, though. Finally. Ellie is mine. Forever.

◊◊◊

"Honey, I'm home!" I holler into my room, Ellie's giggles making me stand taller.

Payton Hunter © 2024

"Hello, stranger," she purrs, fluttering her eyelashes at me with a grin a mile wide. I throw myself onto the bed next to her, making her bounce off the mattress, pulling her into my arms as I stretch out with her.

"How's my Dollface?" I whisper in her ear.

"I love you, Slender, so much it hurts," she murmurs as she nuzzles my neck.

"Love you too, Ellie. Always and forever, you're it for me." I discreetly adjust myself in my jeans. My woman just turns me the hell on.

"Let's go home, Dollface. I need to show you how much I love you." Grinning, I waggle my eyebrows at her. It takes my mind off the nagging itch in my brain. There's something coming for us. Something big. My gut is screaming at me, which is difficult to ignore. I wish I knew what it was. Makes me feel damn useless as SAA. It's my job to protect my club, my brothers, my family, and the community. It's a tall order.

◊◊◊

We've spent the last few days recovering from the ordeal Ellie and Tanya went through and, during that time, almost christened every room in the house.

Standing in the bedroom, looking out the floor-to-ceiling window into our now beautifully landscaped garden.

"We should have breakfast outside. We've not christened the back deck yet." I smile, winking at her.

Her giggle breaks the tension. My dick twitches every time she laughs. Her silky hair slides through my fingers as I run them through it. Her breath catches as I lower my lips to her soft ones. I revel in the moan that escapes her. She opens for me, as my tongue teases the seam of her lips, and her tongue strokes against mine, while the blood is pounding in my ears. Her soft little hands find their way under my T-shirt, her nails gently scratching my sensitized skin, has me shivering. Deepening the kiss, our need ramps up.

"Off," she mutters, pulling on my T-shirt, trying to get it over my head. I sit on my haunches, making short work of stripping off my tee, throwing it behind me. She has her top and bra off before I can even blink. My dollface needs me. I smile down at her.

"Are you in a hurry?"

"Stop talking, Slender, get naked," she instructs me. I stand, unlace my boots, throw them off my feet. My cock is hard as nails for her. I smile down at her as I draw down my zipper, pulling my jeans, boxers, and socks off in one go, my throbbing cock slapping against my stomach.

"Like what you see?" I tease her. Instead of answering, she lifts her arms to me, waving her hands in an unspoken invitation. Her eyes are dark, burning with need, and I know they reflect mine. Leaning over her, my lips seal hers again, in a deep, passionate duel of tongues. I kneel between her legs, leaning forward, taking one hard pebbled nipple in my mouth, sucking. She bows off the bed when my hand rolls her other nipple between my fingers and my teeth gently graze her.

"Slender, more, please," she moans, her hands restlessly moving up and down my stomach, touching and stroking anywhere she can reach. Her hands reach for her jeans' button, but I move them away.

"Let me," I whisper, releasing the buttons, tugging her jeans down her legs, throwing them behind me. She lays in front of me in nothing but her birthday suit.

"Oh, baby, you are so wet for me. I love being able to smell you like this," I rasp, watching her as she tries to pull her thighs together, squirming, to get more friction to her clit.

I spread her out before me, inhaling her intoxicating scent. I'd love to feast on her soaking pussy, but need her to come on my cock more. It takes all I have not to lose control and ram straight into her tight channel. Instead, I lean down kissing her deeply, releasing her lips, breathing her in as she breathes me in. I swear my dick is gonna explode any second, and another piece of my soul connects with hers on such a deep level, it's overwhelming.

"Please, baby, I need you inside me," she implores, moving restlessly against me, our lips almost touching. My blood sizzles, thundering in my ears. Her breasts are heaving and the pulse at the base of her neck is racing when I run my tongue down the column of her neck.

Her small hand closes around my length and guides it to her drenched entrance. I can't hold off any longer and sink balls deep into her wet heat until I fill her completely.

"So good!" she moans, her eyes slamming shut. Her legs lock behind my ass, and she raises her hips towards me, provoking me to move. Slowly I draw out until my tip is kissing her entrance, before pushing back inside her more forcefully. Her walls tightening around me as her soft moans fill the space around us.

"Harder," she groans. "I need you harder. You won't break me."

Drawing my hips back, I power back into her, feeling the wall of her cervix on the tip of my cock, driving me wild. Every time I hit it; she gasps in pleasure. My dollface has a wild side.

Grabbing her legs, pushing them forward changes the angle so I sink even deeper into her tight, dripping heat. Her frantic breathing and scratching nails on my scalp spurring me on.

Her little gasps, moans and sighs set off a tingle deep at the bottom of my spine, and my balls tighten. I can't hold on much longer.

"Come on my cock, baby, come for me," I urge her, sitting back a fraction, wetting my finger in her arousal, watching my dick disappear into her, my thumb finds her engorged, hard clit and pushes down, rubbing tight circles.

Her pussy tightening like a vise around me leads me to the point of no return. My balls fizz and her clenching heat draws my own orgasm from me, my vision growing spotty for a moment, through the monumental release as I fill her full of my seed, our mixed release gushing all over my cock. I collapse on top of her, holding my weight in my arms, waiting for my choppy breathing to calm.

"Wow"—Ellie looks at me with a dreamy smile—"that was amazing."

Rolling to the side, I playfully swat her butt.

"Okay, living room next." I pretend to pull her up. She laughs and slaps my hand away.

"Feed me, big man. I'll fade to dust if you don't. If you want me in the living room, you need to keep my energy levels up." Still giggling, she rolls off the mattress, grabs one of my old T-shirts, drowning her tiny stature, and walks ahead of me down the stairs. I quickly pull on a pair of boxers and follow her down.

I watch as she grabs her cell and orders pizza, shrugging, silently mouthing, "Can't be bothered," to me, and I don't blame her. The recent past has been extremely fraught and took it out on everyone. Now, I'll enjoy having my dollface all to myself, loving the shit out of her, promising myself that nothing bad will ever touch her again. I'll protect her with my life from now until forever.

Epilogue

One Year Later — Ellie

"Mom, seriously, I hate you!" Sitting on our porch, cradling my bump, I cackle as I watch Jade slam Sarah and Dougal's door and stomp off their porch, getting onto her dirt bike.

"Helmet!" I shout across at her, earning me a searing teenage anger / hate look, that would make many burst into flames and burn to ashes. As Jade starts the bike and roars off toward the dirt bike track, Sarah comes out and joins me on our porch.

"Wow, I thought Leo was difficult with his autism. Someone should have warned me before the adoption went through what bitches teenage girls can be." She sighs as she drops into the chair next to mine. "I try to excuse her behavior. She's had a hard life until last year, but my patience is running thin."

I get it, and hope to God that our little one will be a boy, with his father's great looks.

Watching Jade growing up has kinda scared me off girls. Not to mention that any daughter of Slender's would be wrapped in cotton wool, and I'm sure a shotgun to keep the boys away would be added to our gun safe.

Huffing and puffing, Ashley joins us, carrying Alex, her and Vegas' chunky little boy, who's ten months old, and into anything and everything he can reach. He lights up everyone's world and is spoiled rotten. As we speak, the brothers are setting up a play area behind the clubhouse, with swings, slides, trampoline, and anything else a kid's heart could desire. There is a palpable shift from the violence of the past to the developing family loving care. Not that the brothers haven't always cared, they have, and they love their old ladies fiercely. But the appearance of Jade, Leo, and Alex on the compound seems to have mellowed them.

"Look, look!" Ashley's shout draws me out of my thoughts, and I watch as Alex stands free, on his own for the first time.

"No hands! What a good boy… come on, come to Mommy," she encourages him. Alex smiles big at his mom and takes one faltering tottering step forwards, making cute baby noises before he topples and falls on his well-padded butt.

"Did you see that? He took a step!" Ashley is bouncing up and down on my porch, clapping, behaving like a mom lunatic. Sarah smiles at her best friend.

"Yup, girl, and soon you'll be too busy to run after him to have hot meals or coffee. His revenge for you torturing us with carrot cake and chamomile tea," she cackles. "If he turns into a fussy eater, it's payback for your weird pregnancy cravings. Poor kid didn't stand a chance to begin with."

I shudder at the memory of Ashley's pregnancy, well, there was something. Luckily, weird cravings passed me by, as had morning sickness.

"Coffee?" I ask the girls, struggling to push myself up out of my seat.

"I'll get it. You sit and put your feet up," Sarah orders, walks into the house, and comes back with ready-fixed coffees for all of us. We sit and chat the Sunday morning away, knowing our men are busy playing behind the clubhouse after their church meeting.

◊◊◊

Payton Hunter © 2024

Slender

"It's gonna end in tears," Raven prophesizes, standing next to me, arms crossed over his chest. The mountain of a man looking on as the Prospects and brothers try out the freshly concreted in seesaw. An old-fashioned style log one, to give character to our new playground.

More and more kids are popping up and old ladies seem to fall pregnant just by looking at the brothers.

Right about now, there are twelve brothers trying to sit sidesaddle on the log, attempting to cram as many of them on as possible. In slow motion we watch as the whole thing tilts to one side, topples over, spilling the brothers on the ground. Amidst lots of groaning and ribbing, they all get to their feet, looking guiltily in our direction.

"Well, what are you waiting for, boys? Put it right! My nephew needs this shit to be safe! Get digging and fixing!" he thunders at them.

"But, boss, I have plans," Moggy whines.

"See if I give a fuck," Raven growls at him.

Moggy has not been our favorite brother since the Rusty fiasco, and the longer we look on, the weirder he gets. He sees a girl in town now, and is more off the compound than on, shirking his responsibilities, pissing off the brothers who have to pick up for him. It's becoming more and more obvious that there will have to be a discussion.

Pushing those thoughts to the side, I ask Raven: "Do you still need me?"

"Nah," he answers, "go take care of Ellie. Not long now, is it?" He smiles at me.

"Four weeks." I grin back at him. "Can't wait. Nursery is all set up, and we have everything ready, thanks to the ladies' baby shower."

Payton Hunter © 2024

"Ugh… don't remind me," Raven replies, flinching at the reminder of the party at Leather and Lace, complete with male dancers. You'd have thought it'd been a bachelorette party! Ellie wears my cut and my ink on her, but doesn't want to get married, not yet anyway. Eventually, yes, but not yet. For now, what we have is enough.

It took a while for Ellie to stop looking over her shoulder all the time, but it's becoming easier. A life full of love, laughter, surrounded by the people we love and respect, growing our family is all we need right now, and we enjoy living it with each other. The last year was tough, and trouble always seems to find us, despite us not looking for it. But amidst all the chaos, I am secure in my love for my Old Lady, my unborn child, and my club.

Let the future run in. With everyone by my side, I am invincible. Bring it on!

THE END